"What I want is for you to want me like I want you!"

I clamp a hand to my mouth. Regret slaps me in the face.

Javier pulls my hand away. His stare takes in all of me. My eyes. My lips. I'm embarrassed by what I said. I'm embarrassed by my ridiculous heart, which thumps loudly, echoing his every touch.

"You want me, *mami?*"

Yes. In the deepest parts of my bones, yes.

Silence.

"Answer me." His voice is demanding.

"No," I say, stubborn.

A grin crawls across his face.

"I owe you an apology," he says. "I couldn't talk to you earlier. Wanted to. But I couldn't. You understand?"

"Not at all."

Javier's warmth reminds me of the water. Of wanting to jump in. I'd do anything to cool off.

"If I explain it to you, will you remember in the morning?"

"Probably not," I answer honestly. "But then again, you're hard to forget."

ALSO BY AMBER HART

Before You

after us

AMBER HART

KENSINGTON BOOKS
Kensington Publishing Corp.
www.kensingtonbooks.com

KENSINGTON BOOKS are published by

Kensington Publishing Corp.
119 West 40th Street
New York, NY 10018

All Kensington titles, imprints, and distributed lines are available at special quantity discounts for bulk purchases for sales promotions, premiums, fund-raising, educational, or institutional use.

Special book excerpts or customized printings can also be created to fit specific needs. For details, write or phone the office of the Kensington special sales manager: Kensington Publishing Corp., 119 West 40th Street, New York, NY 10018, attn: Special Sales Department; phone 1-800-221-2647.

KENSINGTON and the K logo are Reg. U.S. Pat. & TM Off.

First trade paperback printing: January 2015

10 9 8 7 6 5 4 3 2 1

ISBN-13: 978-1-61773-118-1
ISBN-10: 1-61773-118-1

First electronic edition: January 2015

ISBN-13: 978-1-61773-119-8
ISBN-10: 1-61773-119-6

To the girls who wear their scars proudly,
quietly or loudly.

ACKNOWLEDGMENTS

The thing about writing this book—and any other book for that matter—is that it never would have happened if not for many childhood trips to the library. That is where my love of reading began, and reading spawned my love of writing.

Dad, thanks for letting me get lost in endless novels, and for never telling me what kind of books to read but always letting me love what I loved. And Justin, thanks for being the kind of brother who hid with me in the dark dusty corners of bookshelf aisles. Remember how we used to open our Goosebumps books and pretend we were living in an enchanted magical world? Truth is, between pages, we kind of were.

Because books were always available to me as a child, I found a forever love that led to this moment. Thanks to the people who made *After Us* possible. Beth Miller, for being a dream agent, for giving me a chance, and for telling me that the wait might be long but that it will be worth it. Writers House, I've said it before and I'll say it again, you are the best home an author can ask for. Thanks to my editor, Alicia Condon, for wanting more stories like *Before You*, and to my publisher, Kensington, for your support and for such a beautiful cover.

Sophie Jordan, K.A. Tucker, and Lucy Connors, thank you for blurbing the Before and After series. Sophie, thanks for all the encouraging texts. And K.A., you've been uplifting from the start. I will never forget the first message you sent after reading *Before You*. I'm sorry I made you cry. Well, kind of.

My friends Jenn Sy and Genevieve Gagne-Hawes, I am so grateful for you both. Jenn, you told me to go for it, so I did. And Genevieve, I saved all those e-mails where you not so subtly hinted that Melissa and Javier deserved their own story.

To my family, you know how much I adore you. You pull me out of my writing cave when I'm too deeply submerged. You hold my head up through the rough times, and you celebrate with me during the good times. You are my team, my foundation, my heart. I love you.

R, thanks for teaching me Spanish. And thanks for being my best friend through it all.

Mom, I miss you. You can't read this, but it makes me feel better to write it. I'll meet you where the angels sing.

And readers, each of us has scars. I hope Melissa and Javier's story helps you recognize your own scars and wear them proudly. If nothing else, remember that there is always this:

Hope.

melissa[1]

The beach is a moving canvas of people.

Cabanas and waves and bathing suits and sand castles all blend together to create a serene picture of life on the coast. The sky is on fire with blues and yellows and oranges. Tiny puffs of clouds like wisps of cream. Sunscreen lotion saturates the air, smelling like SPF and sweat. I squint through the blaring sun and walk toward a crowd of girls lying on their bellies with the strings to their tops undone. Bare backs naked of tan lines.

"Frozen margarita, extra salt," I say, giving the drink to a girl with blond hair a shade darker than mine.

I balance the tray on one palm. Hand off drinks with another. Like a machine dispensing snacks.

"Piña colada." Next girl. "Sex on the beach." Next. "Vodka and tonic." Last. "Rum and Coke."

I smile. Compliment one of the girls on her leg tattoo. Girls love compliments. Eat them up like sugar. Delicious sugar that serves to fatten my wallet.

I don't know these girls. I don't know most of the people splayed out on the beach like a deck of cards. Ordering alcohol like water, trying any reprieve to cool themselves down from rays that bake them to burnt crisps.

It's too hot to be alive today. The air is breathing fire all over me. The sun is pressing so hard into my skin that it's turning red. If I close my eyes, I can imagine my skin melting off like wax. I'm dripping sweat. Body glistening as though I've jumped in the water. I haven't.

"Thanks," the girl with the leg tattoo says.

One of the girls ties her top and flips over, insistent on showing me her hip tattoos. Two pink bows wrapping up the package of a perfect body.

I remember what it was like to have a perfect body.

"Love it," I say. And I do.

I can never get a tattoo there.

I don't wear bikinis anymore. My swimwear is a collection of one-pieces. Covering certain fragments of me that I'm not willing to show. Holding me together. Though admittedly still racy, especially the one I've got on today, which hugs me like a glove, fitting my every muscle and curve. It's white with wavy ruffles like sea foam over the material around my breasts, plumping them up. A simple tie in the back to support the front. A runway of fabric lining my stomach. Nothing but tiny pieces coming together, exposing skin.

My tray is still stacked full of drinks for another group of people. They look like towers. Like a whole miniature city of skyscrapers and small circular buildings crammed together. Drowning in liquid.

I wait for cash.

A quick glance tells me that the five girls have tipped me something close to fifteen bucks. Not bad.

"Enjoy the heat," I tell them by way of good-bye.

On to the next customer.

All around me, sun tints skin a soft brown, sometimes

red. Corners of beach towels flutter in the slight breeze like stingray wings. It hurts to look at the ocean, glittery and reflecting light, a million liquid jewels on display.

I've already checked IDs for the five guys waiting for drinks. They're tall and muscular—with the sort of deliciously ripped bodies that belong in a place like this—each ordering Corona bottlenecks. I hand out beers and accept their cash. Flirt a little. Makes for better tips.

"What are you guys doing out here today?" I ask. Grin.

"*Nada, mami*," one says in a Latino accent, taking a seat on a lounge chair. The others follow suit. "Just enjoying this weather. Wanna enjoy it with me?"

He pats his lap. Like I'd actually sit on it.

"Can't," I say. Wink at him. "Have to work."

The guy leans forward. Checks me out. I check him out right back. Shaved head, nice lips.

The others check me out, too. Except for the one that walks up behind me, joining the group. He sits with his body angled toward the water, dark sunglasses on, hair falling in his face.

"I'll have one, too," he says, still not looking my way.

What is so interesting that you can't look a person in the eye?

I check the water. Nothing out of the ordinary.

"ID, please," I say. Nothing personal—can't serve underage. Even though I'm eighteen and understand. It isn't worth losing a prime job at the busiest hotel on the beach. A job that pays really well, with customers that tip even better.

He hands it to me, still not looking up. I glance at it. I don't need to see his full face to know that it's not him. Looks more like the guy sitting next to him than the guy handing it to me.

"Gonna have to do better than that," I say.

I need the money that this job provides. With three sisters away at college and Mom working double nursing shifts to support them, I need whatever I can get. Everything we have is already stretched thin. A bubble about to pop.

His rough sigh says he's not happy with my response. He turns to me. I can see his full face now.

Tick, tick, tock.

Boom.

Time breaks into a million shards. Tiny slivers of moments. Trapping me. My breath catches. Nerves are a fishhook reeling in any response I could've had.

He sees me then. Moves his sunglasses to the top of his head to get a better look. He's watching, watching, watching . . . me. Eyes narrow. Unbelieving.

I can't find enough seconds to understand what's happening here. I heard he moved away. I'm searching desperately for a breath of fresh air, but I can't find one.

Wavy brown hair that's almost black. Thick lips that I've kissed once before.

I'm staring at tattoos that wrap around his shoulders, hugging him. A hundred different images, all black and white. Photographic. I'm looking at a sun over his left collarbone, the only bit of light shining into the chest piece. Clouds ripple under his neck like waves. His shirt is off and I'm staring too hard, I realize, because his friends start laughing.

It's a memorial. The piece is to remember someone he lost.

"Melissa?"

There's a timbre in his voice that makes my insides gooey. I'm melting ice cream on this hideously hot day. He says my name like it's painful for him, looking at me with those incredulous eyes. Willing me to say something, anything, but I can't. I can't.

I run away instead. My feet propel me forward, fast, churning sand beneath my heels. I don't care when a shell cuts the underside of my foot. Or when tiny grains of sea bottom become a natural Band-Aid.

I need to breathe.

I hate that he is here right now.

I love that I've been given another chance to see his face.

"Wait," he calls from behind me.

I won't stop.

Fast, fast, faster.

He won't stop.

Just go, just go, just go.

I'm not quick enough.

"Wait," he says again, grabbing my arm lightly.

Five fingers that burn memories into my skin.

I turn to the sound of his voice.

"Javier," I say, choking on his name. Choking on the memories.

Me and Faith, my best friend. At this same beach. Months ago.

Javier and his cousin Diego, in the water. Faith needed to get Diego's attention. Faith needed Diego in so many ways. I needed to know what Javier's mouth tasted like. I told myself that it'd be fun.

Love was Faith's style. Fun was mine.

I try to shut out the memory, doors closing on my past. Can't.

Javier's lips were every bit as amazing as I'd thought. Plump and gentle and rough and perfect.

We never did more than that. Never talked about the fun day at the beach. Never pursued what we left behind.

I never told him that I've wanted him ever since.

"What are you doing here?" Words are talons clawing their way through my throat.

"I'm with *mi familia*," he replies, greedily drinking in my features. "My brothers and a couple *amigos*."

I wonder if he notices that my hair's grown longer, silken fingers tickling my waist. How my eyes have grown heavy with the burden of worry. Javier's face is too much. His face reminds me that I don't have Faith anymore because loving Diego broke her. Faith's in another country now, building schools for underprivileged children, because she doesn't want to live near all the memories. And I'm a memory. Javier's face reminds me that Diego is gone. Both realities are excruciating.

"I thought you left," I say.

"Melissa, cabana five needs their drinks," a coworker says, passing Javier and me in the sand.

I barely hear his voice. I'm too lost in Javier. My coworker, Brock, stops. Sees Javier. Backs up.

"Everything okay?" Throws a defensive arm around me.

Brock is protective like that. He looks out for the girls that work here. It's necessary with all the alcohol we serve. Every now and again, a guy thinks he has the right to a piece of our skin.

"I'm good," I tell him, shrugging his arm off.

Javier looks at Brock, an empty stare.

"Holler if you need me," Brock says.

At more than six feet, Brock is built strong and tall enough to intimidate. He's half Latino, all dark eyes and hair. But Javier has the advantage by a short inch.

"Will do," I say, and Brock leaves.

"I made a trip up the coast for a couple weeks, if that's what you mean." Javier picks up where we left off.

I want to ask more. *What's up the coast? When did you get tattoos?*

Why do you look so much like Diego now?

Not so much in his features, though they were cousins, so there's a family resemblance, but more in the air about him. His hair is longer, brushing the back of his neck, mixing with his eyelashes in the front. Ink marks him. He's still Javier, but roughened. I guess that's what grief does to a person. When the pain is too much to bear.

"Okay," is all I say.

"You work here," he says.

His eyes steal a glance at the water. I wonder if he's remembering our time together. I am. His lips on mine. My body so close to his. Two people, a tangle of limbs. The water licking our nearly bare skin. A prickling up my back as his fingers braved the peaks of my spine. A place and time when Diego and Faith were here.

He tears his eyes away.

"I should go," I say.

I don't want to go. I don't want to stay.

"Yeah," he says. "Me, too."

I want to ask if he's okay. A glance tells me he's not. His eyes give him away. Their look betrays his pain. Diego was Javier's cousin, but they were best friends, too. I know the void of losing someone you love. I miss my best friend so bad that it hurts, that it actually nips at my heart to remind me daily. But at least I know she's still there. That maybe one day I can visit her.

Diego isn't anywhere.

Javier slips his sunglasses back on, a cover to shield his soul. I'm telling my feet to move because I need to get out of this spot. But all I can think about is how I can't see Javier's eyes anymore. I need to see them. Even with shades on, I *feel* his stare.

"Melissa," he says, like he needs to tell me something. Like maybe I don't need to leave just yet.

"Yes?"

One look.

Then.

"Take care."

And he's gone.

2
javier

I'm walking away from Melissa, but every step I take is painful.

Slicing me up, these memories.

I hadn't planned on seeing her.

I hadn't planned on remembering the day we spent together. That was a time when things were good.

"Javier, man!"

My brother Eduardo is on my trail.

"Espérate."

He wants me to wait for him, but I need to be alone. Alone, alone, alone. My thoughts are alone in their misery. I don't dare share them. I lock them in separate files within my mind and never for one minute let anyone see the full scope of what I have planned. Of the anger I wish I could unleash on the ones who took my cousin from me.

To them, Diego was a pawn, at their disposal.

He wasn't a heartbeat that they had the right to end.

Diego became another name in their book of murders; another forgotten cause; a face that they blink at and instantly the memory is gone. Job done. On to the next one.

They stole a member of *mi familia,* my blood. My best friend. There are so many, many memories.

Us playing soccer as kids. ¡Golllllll! *Diego would yell every time one of us scored. Competitive by nature. Brothers by heart.*

Us eating mi mamá's *home-cooked food, mostly grown in her kitchen garden, slim as the portions may have been. She could make something out of nothing, that woman.*

Us as children barely tall enough to reach the counter, grabbing a piece of candy from the local store whenever they gave it away for free on holidays. Because we couldn't afford much. No, that's a lie. We couldn't afford anything. But we were together, always together.

I walk to the parking lot, carrying my sandals in my hand. I welcome the burn of scorching hot pavement on the pads of my feet. Welcome the pain because it's all that I know now.

My brother follows. I hop in my truck. Close my eyes.

"Give me a sec," I say through the open window. Though I know there's no way that'll happen.

"What's with that girl?" Eduardo hops in the truck with me.

"*Chica* I used to know."

A *chica* I didn't bother to date since *mi mamá* has never been okay with her boys dating girls who aren't Latina. Family bonds and all. She's old school. Thinking that I need someone who knows the culture and food and ways of our people.

I close my eyes and recall the night that reminded us all.

"¿Quién es ella?" mi mamá *asks in Spanish, wondering about the girl Pedro's brought home for dinner.*

I watch the girl, brown hair and the lightest shade of gray eyes. She's pretty, I find myself thinking. But white. Mi mamá's rules are clear when it comes to white girls.

"My girlfriend, Teresa," Pedro answers.

"¿Tu novia?" she asks. "No. Imposible."

"It's not impossible, Mamá," Pedro replies.

Mi mamá's eyes narrow. I know this look. We all do. Her temper is hotter than the spices she's setting on the table.

"You," she says, looking at Teresa, "get out of my house."

She's not yelling. Her voice is frighteningly calm. A harsh breeze laced with the coldest chill of winter.

"You have no place here," she tells Teresa. "And you"— she points to Pedro—"know better."

Teresa looks scared. Pedro stands his ground.

"Now," mi mamá says.

I can't stand to see the look on Pedro's face so I leave the room. But not before hearing arguments from Pedro, and sobs from Teresa.

Eduardo kicks my leg and I open my eyes. He watches me. "This has to do with Diego, doesn't it?"

And Melissa. "No."

Melissa encouraged Faith and Diego's relationship. Which meant I saw her often. We were the best friends who tagged along with the couple *enamorados.*

Melissa makes me remember him. I don't do well with surprise reminders.

But Melissa also makes me think of the water. Of that day. Of a time when I wasn't walking in a minefield, watching my every step. Diego's murder has taught me that one wrong move, one slight shift . . .

one step,
two steps,
BANG . . .
and an entire world can be blown to bits. Earthquakes can rumble the ground and split open the earth and swallow all that was once good.

It can make you see things in a different light. It can open your eyes to a new tomorrow. One filled with darkness and sorrow and so much anger.

"Liar."

My brother's voice disrupts my thoughts.

I am a liar.

Everything *has* been about Diego's death. Almost eight agonizing months ago.

"You have to let him go."

I clench my fists. *"Cállate la boca."* It's the nicest warning I'll give. And I'm only giving it because he's my brother.

"He was my cousin, too, you know."

"It's not the same."

And he knows it. Diego and I did everything together. We were the same age, eighteen, unlike my brother, who's older by almost three years. It's not like I lost a wingman. It's not like he moved away. He's gone. Permanently.

The night my cousin died was a normal night at *La Plazita*, a few blocks of street dedicated to Latino cuisine, culture, markets, dancing, and more. I know that because I'm the one who dropped Diego off there to meet Faith. A final destination, it turns out.

Diego wanted to surprise Faith that night. I think he planned on showing her a glimpse of our *Cubano* heritage. Faith was good for Diego in a way that nothing had been for a long time. I liked the change I'd been seeing in him.

No more cartel.

He'd left Cuba and the drug cartel he belonged to. On the run. Even though Diego was hassled by the MS-13 gang, who wanted to recruit him, he never joined. Diego went to high school and made good grades. Turns out none of it mattered because the cartel found him at *La Plazita* that night. One shot, and Diego was gone. Ripped and shredded and torn to bits, his heart

was

finished. . . .

Now I get it, why it tortured Diego not to get revenge on the men who killed his *mamá.* Now I know the need.

But I can't walk away as easily.

I never realized that I'd be dropping him off at his final resting place. I didn't know that I'd never get a chance to say good-bye.

If I had only . . .

If I had only . . .

But I can't.

Time won't stop for me. I've offered it everything, anything, but Time refuses to slow. To rewind enough, to give me a chance to do something different. Instead, I'm left with botched retellings of a memory I don't have. I didn't see it happen. I didn't actually hear the bullet *pop* from the barrel. I didn't watch it spin a perfect path, cutting through a crowd of people until it hit its target, slicing apart a heart. But *mi tío*, Diego's *papá,* told me the details, which were told to him by Faith. Because she was there to see it all.

My mind creates pictures for me. Diego bloodied. Nothing anybody can do to help him. Diego in a black bag. An identification tag like a price sticker attached to him, because this is the cost of a life on the run. One heart.

Stopped.

"Why are you holdin' on so tight?" Eduardo asks.

How could I possibly let go?

"Because nothing makes sense." I clench my fists. "How did the gang member get away?"

Wink, that was his name. Diego didn't join Wink's gang, so Wink led the cartel straight to Diego, their runaway member. Punishment. Join us or else, was the message, lethally delivered.

"What's it matter? Doesn't bring him back."

The watery, wobbly edge to my brother's voice tells me that he hurts over it, too, but he's dealing better than me.

"I have to find Wink."

I've said this before.

"Bad idea."

And that's his usual response.

But *mi familia* doesn't get it. I can't—won't—rest until Wink's found. Which means my life will consist of getting to know the streets and the gangs who run them. The exact thing I once wanted Diego to walk away from. But that's where Wink is, I'm sure. Hidden in a pack of wolves who are protecting their alpha.

That's where I need to find him.

Wink didn't pull the trigger that stopped Diego's heart. But he might as well have. It's because of Wink that Diego's gone. I can't let him get away. And if I knew the faces of the cartel members, I wouldn't let them get away either.

I know Wink's face. A memory.

Rain starts to fall. A quick drizzle. And then something more. The rain is speaking to us, becoming louder and louder. Heavier and stronger. Warning. Diego is lifting his girlfriend. Cradling her in his arms. Kissing her expectant lips. Melissa is staring at me. I'm thinking I wanna pick her up like that; taste her and not stop because those teasing kisses at the beach were not enough.

But I don't have time because someone speaks.

"Thought I recognized this car," he says, taking a step towards us.

Wink. Waiting in the parking lot for us as we exit the club after a night's worth of exhausting dancing. Suddenly, I'm not tired anymore. Suddenly, I can't think about kissing Melissa because she needs to run, and kissing her would keep her here. In the line of fire.

Wink isn't alone. He's the block of anger in the center of other gang members who flank him. He pulls a gun. Diego yells for Faith and Melissa to leave. Wink pulls the trigger.

And I'm bleeding.

I force the pain of a bullet ripping through my flesh out of my mind and concentrate on fighting, on helping Diego. I can't leave him alone to take the heat.

The cost of our fight that day is a permanent, almost perfectly circular scar near my right shoulder. The cost is Wink getting away. But more importantly, Diego making it through. It was worth it to help my cousin. He'd do the same for me.

This is the only memory I have of Wink. I hold on to it

with a vise grip. So tight, so consuming. I'm determined not to let this be the last memory. I'm determined to find Wink once more.

I wish there were a way for me to talk to Faith, to get a description of the man who pulled the trigger, but she lives out of the country now. I wish it were easier to contact her. I wish I could get in my truck and drive minutes away and have a conversation face to face. But I can't. I don't blame Faith for removing herself from all that reminds her of Diego.

I wish I knew how to remove my memories. Things didn't used to be like this. Before Diego's death, I made better grades. I studied harder. I actually gave a shit about school. I didn't have the wrath of hell coursing through me. I didn't know exactly what I wanted to be, but I wanted it to be something great. I had started to believe that life could be better for someone like me in the United States. Away from Cuba. Removed from constant turmoil.

I was wrong.

Cuba found a way to catch up to me.

And now, so has Melissa.

My mind is a slippery thing, sliding toward Melissa. Blond hair and tight body. Bright smile. Layers of confidence that she wears like clothes. The swell of her red lips.

Melissa is a catch-22. She is fun and good memories. But she is also a reminder that neither of us has that care-free existence anymore. I see it in her. I see the way her eyes trip over me and fall into what once was. I see the conflicted feelings in her stare, and I recognize them because I feel them, too.

Maybe there is a way to make this better. Maybe Melissa has Faith's number. Maybe Melissa can give me

Faith's address. I'd hop on the next flight. I need to hear the details from Faith. I need to know what the guys looked like.

Because I will find them. And they will pay.

Seeing Melissa has reminded me that I cannot put this off much longer. This is the motivation I need to track down MS-13. I will hunt them. Infiltrate their gang. It's a stimulant to my already overactive thoughts.

"Gonna go for a drive," I tell Eduardo, hoping he won't want to come with.

He watches me for a moment. Then says, as he's hopping out of the truck, "*Cuidado*. Some things aren't worth it, okay?"

I understand that, as my brother, he has to say that. But he's wrong. It is every bit worth it.

It takes me twenty minutes to arrive in Diego's old neighborhood. The one his *papá* still lives in, a neighborhood not far from my own. I think for a moment about stopping by, saying hey to *tío* Adolfo, but decide not to. I don't want my truck to be seen there. I don't want anyone to know I had a connection to Diego.

If this is going to work, I have to cover all tracks.

My past must be a ghost to them, invisible.

I park in a convenience store lot. Wait. Watch people hustle on the streets. I check my watch. Keep checking.

Seconds, minutes, hours.

It takes a while, but eventually I see it. Three guys with blue-and-white bandanas around their heads. The colors signify exactly what I'm looking for. Mara Salvatrucha 13 Gang, or MS-13.

The ones who gave up Diego to his old cartel.

The ones who will know where to find Wink.

Diego's run-in with MS-13 has taught me what I need to know about their gang. They recruit guys that they think will be strong members. They do everything as a so-called family, watching each other's backs. Dealing in drugs, car-jackings, robberies, initiation crimes, murders, anything that will gain them respect or money. The crazier the crime, the more respect earned.

I get out of the truck. Act as though I'm about to enter the store. Walk up to them. No hesitation.

Just like their members, every time they pull the trigger.

I knock into one hard enough to throw him off balance.

"Watch it," I growl.

He plays right into my hand.

His sneer comes first. Then his right hook. I block it easily. Throw a punch that lands in his ribs, hard enough to knock air out of his lungs and into my face. Another punch snaps his head backwards. He wobbles. Stumbles.

The guy next to him comes for me. I let him land one punch to my stomach. Then I drop him to his knees with a hit to the temple.

Easy, so easy.

I try not to think about the streets that taught me to fight like this. I try not to picture Diego's face. I need every ounce of concentration because the third guy is swinging at me. It's a good swing, one I barely escape. One that clips my jaw. Strong enough to maybe do damage had it met its target. But I'm behind him before he realizes what's happened. His forehead smacks the concrete. He doesn't get back up.

I walk to the one that's struggling to his feet. Make sure he sees my face.

Remember, remember, remember. Me.

And then I hop in the truck and drive out of sight.

I've shown them how well I can fight. They'll be watching for me. The next time I show up there, I'll be on their list.

For recruitment.

melissa ³

The small house I call home smells of roasted vegetables and chicken with rosemary. If I close my eyes, I can even smell my childhood. Scent is like that sometimes. Triggering. One minute I'm working at the beach, talking to Javier, and the next minute I'm walking through my front door, suddenly young again.

What I smell now is our usual choice for family dinner.

Family.

Six letters packed into one word that means everything. Sometimes the people are linked by blood, a lot of times by choice.

But family is tricky. Family has split personalities. Sometimes it goes by the name Love. Every now and again, by the name Betrayal.

We don't have a lot of family dinners now that everyone has grown up. Now that we all have responsibilities.

Childhood is the best time of your life, people always told me as a kid. What they didn't tell me was that it could also be the worst. My childhood was shadowed by panic attacks and nearly constant worry when Dad left. I worried about everything. School, family, what I would wear that day. Nerves made me feel withdrawn around other people. Like maybe I'd say the wrong thing or do the wrong thing, and then what if they laughed at me? It was Faith who taught me to let go.

"Talk to him," Faith says, *pointing to a crush of mine.*

We're thirteen. I don't know how to talk to boys. I've never talked to boys.

"What do I say?" I ask.

Faith laughs. "How should I know?"

We're both new at this.

"If I talk to that boy, you have to talk to his friend," I wager.

"Deal," Faith says, grabbing me by the hand.

Both of our palms are sweaty. Slick residue of fear. I'm not the only one nervous. That's what makes it okay. The fact that this is what normal feels like. I can finally learn to disable nerves. They don't have to control me. If only I take chances.

I took a lot of chances after that. That's how I became the extroverted me. That's what helped me to see the world differently. I loosened my grip on control and learned how to let life happen.

Because when life happens on its own terms, I am free.

Walls the color of lemons and floors covered in squared tile greet me. There's one kitchen, two people living here, and three bedrooms.

One memory of two people split by a third.

My tiny piece of this world is decorated with dark, licorice-black leather couches. Twinned vases of flowers stand like living columns on either side of the television. Frames with memories stuck in them. I pass a few on my way through the front door.

I'm being told, "Smile at the camera!" by some overly excited photographer. What they don't understand is that the girl next to me, my sister Megan, is pinching me. I'm seven. She's ten. This is how it goes with us, Megan picking on me in a way that I will later understand as being what sisters do to one another. I hated it then, or so says the scowl on my face, captured for all time. Paper caged behind a glass prison.

Funny how I miss that now. The scowl. The pinching. A time when my sisters were here and I didn't yet know the depths of Dad's betrayal.

Next. A series of photos.

My sisters and me having a water balloon fight. I turned nine today, though I don't feel any older. My hand is a cannon launching the balloon inside of it at the back of my sister Monica's head. Bull's-eye. The balloon breaks, drenching her in cold liquid. I'm laughing and turning to run and not realizing that my sister May is aiming a balloon directly at my face.

There's a blurry cake in the background of the center photo; it's dizzying to look at because the focus is on me, crystal clear. Pieces of broken balloon thrown by May float around my head like confetti. My mouth is open in shock, eyes squeezed tight, at the burst of water over my face.

I didn't realize Mom was taking pictures. I'm glad she did.

And that makes me wonder. Would I hold as many memories if the pictures didn't remind me? I'm not sure that I'd know as much about my childhood if there weren't these souvenirs of what once was. Are memories copied to mind, instead of paper, enough?

I've blocked a lot of them out.

What I don't see are photos of Dad. Better that way. He's not here anymore, so his ghost shouldn't be, either.

He doesn't belong here. Hasn't for some time. And if I'm being honest, he never really did.

Dad packed up the things that mattered to him. His clothes. His television. His tools. Certainly not us. Not Mom. Or me. Or my three sisters.

He took his things and piled them into his convertible like treasured jewels that he couldn't live without, and he left. I was eight.

I have to go, he'd said.

Please stay, I'd begged.

I didn't understand. Dads were supposed to stay with their families.

How long will you be gone? I'd asked.

But I knew. Even as young as I was, I knew that day would be a day of lasts.

We weren't close, Dad and me. He worked eighty-hour weeks. Left before I woke, came home after I went to bed. But Sundays, I'll always remember Sundays. Those were the days he stayed home. Sometimes we'd have his attention, my sisters and me, but it was never for a good reason. If we had his attention, it was because we'd done something wrong. Attention from Dad meant he'd be yelling at us, punishing us. Mostly, Sunday was game day. He preferred yelling at players on the television, a life that wasn't filled with dress up and cooking at tiny play ovens and teaching us how to ride bikes.

Still, it didn't make things easier, his abandonment.

I need to go now, he'd said that last day, desperately trying to pry my little hands from his arm.

Why? was my last question.

Do you know what love is, Melissa? he'd asked me.

I wasn't so sure that I did.

Dad took a step back.

Some day you will, he'd said.

He needed to do this for the love of his life, he'd said.

Which wasn't Mom.

I watched him leave, a million unshed tears gathering, gathering, gathering. Too many for my heart to handle. Too many for my eyes, too.

So down they fell.

That would be the last time I cried for him. The last time I ever saw him.

And he's such a liar, because I'm older now and I still don't understand. I look at Mom and think about the crinkles like creased paper at the corners of her eyes and mouth. She earned those lines. She laughed good and hard for many years to get them. She toughed it out day after day, even though not all of it was smiles. She stuck around while Dad traded us for a life with fewer responsibilities, while he substituted us for a young girlfriend with no kids. I look at Mom's million-watt grin, almost blinding, and I listen to her laugh, so contagious. And all I think is:

Beautiful.

So, no, Dad, age didn't help me understand your betrayal.

But it did teach me that I never want to be like him. And that we're better off without him.

A loud voice shatters my memories.

"Shit. Stupid stove."

Monica's cursing from the kitchen brings a smile to my face. Not an abashed smile. Not a smile that tries to hold back. But a full-blown smile.

I turn the corner.

Everyone's here. Mom, Megan, Monica, and May. Riffling through drawers. Mixing a salad. Preparing dinner.

"God, Monica, you suck at cooking," I say, entering the kitchen.

Monica tries to glare at me. The gesture is ruined by her laugh.

"Shut up. I'm getting better," she replies, holding up a pan of burnt something.

"Really?" I say, teasing. "What's that supposed to be, anyway?"

She looks at me like I should know what's underneath the black crust.

"Green bean casserole." She frowns at her creation, trying to puzzle it out. "But I think the cheese was in a little too long. When should I have taken it out?"

"About twenty minutes before it looked like that," I say.

She gives up and grabs a serving spoon. Begins scraping hot, burnt goo into the garbage. Two oven mitts on her hands. Two eyes staring at me.

I want to remake the casserole because it's tradition that we have it. I don't want to miss out because my sister cooks worse than anyone I've ever known. But I wait for Monica's approval.

"Might as well," she says, reading my mind. "You always make it the best, anyway."

I quickly wash my hands and get to work cooking beans.

"Hey, Lissa," May says, hugging me. "Good to see you again."

It's good to see her, too. Eyes the same shade as mine. Like the ripest blueberries. She's the one whose features are the most like my own, though we all look alike. Blond hair. Short. Muscles slightly defined by exercise and sports.

"Hey, May." Smile. "How's volleyball this year?"

May's played since I can remember. She made the college team, no problem. And her scholarship has helped ease the family's financial burden. Though dorms still cost money.

That we don't have.

"Good." She begins breaking off bean tips and tossing the inedible ends away before she adds the beans to the boiling water. "I thought my first year of college would be hard. Transitioning, you know how it goes."

"Hey, little sis," Megan says, coming to my side.

Megan's the oldest at twenty-one. Followed by Monica, May, and then me. We're all one year apart, but Megan's always been an old soul. I'm not sure that I've ever seen her wear anything casual. It's always pencil skirts and blouses, heels, and her hair in different updos. Even her pajama sets match.

Now graduated, she'll be in town more often. She landed a job at a local advertising group. Her bossy, organized personality fits perfectly in a place like that. I'm happy for her. She's found somewhere that she belongs.

I wish I could belong. Go to college like her. I applied. Got in. An acceptance letter came from the community college down the street, the cheapest path. The plan? Earn my associate's degree and transfer to a university afterward, if I want. If I have more money then. But unfortunately, all that had to wait.

Serving drinks helps pay for things I need. Like ridiculously high monthly medical bills.

Doctors and hospitals and surgeries.

Extra cash—hard to come by—goes straight into a savings fund. I won't start school until I have enough for both years. I don't want to go and then run out of money.

"Hey," I say.

Mom smiles at us the way she does when she sees every-one together. It's a smile reserved for when she's truly happy.

"I got it, Mom," Megan says, grabbing the knife from Mom's hand, chopping the carrots for her. Megan looks out of place almost, with her elegant attire, but I know she shops bargain and thrift stores, not name brand.

Megan gives Mom a gentle hip bump, shooing her out of the kitchen. "Go relax."

Mom deserves it. A moment alone, a moment to breathe. To not work grueling shifts. She picked up where Dad left off. She raised us alone and never complained about it, not once. She's not afraid to discipline, to love, to be there. She's everything I hope to be one day.

Because I know no one stronger.

Mom doesn't object, mostly because arguing with Megan is a losing battle. While we make dinner, she takes a seat on the couch. It's the least we can do after the years she's given us.

While the beans boil, I slather the bottom of a cooking dish with mushrooms and cream. They leave a gooey mess on my fingers.

So messy, so messy. My broken life.

Megan's watching me carefully. Something she's been doing lately, the couple of times she's visited.

"Stop staring," I sigh, not bothering to look up.

"You know I have to ask."

I wince at her words. I anticipated this. The onslaught, the inquisition that. Never. Ends.

"No, you don't."

May gives me a sympathetic pat on the shoulder. She's

been the best about everything. Not pushing me to talk. A beacon of light in a sea of dark.

"Have you been to the doctor recently?" Megan asks.

They know what I've been through. We don't keep secrets. Doesn't mean I want to rehash.

"Stop." I pack as much punch into the one word as possible. It doesn't stop Megan, but it slows her down.

The lines between present and past blur.

"You're going to be okay," the doctor says. "Breathe deeply."

There's a mask over my face. A calming drug is being introduced into my lungs. My back is against a bed that's soft like memory foam.

"Scared," I manage to say, though even that one word is difficult. My mind wants sleep.

And then I do the weirdest thing. I laugh. Nothing about this moment, about being wheeled into the hospital operating room, is funny. But these drugs, they make it seem okay for a minute. And I'm laughing because every other ceiling tile is a mural of something relaxing backlit by bright lights. A palm tree, sand touching water, airy clouds.

I'm thinking that the idea of painting the ceiling is brilliant because it does calm me. It makes me happy. It's obviously meant for the patients, lying flat, looking up.

The doctor and nurses have stopped wheeling me. They're looking down with serious faces and I want to tell them to look at the ceiling, too, because I think that might make them happy like me.

Why am I here again? I've forgotten. And I'm too sleepy to care anymore.

"Can you count to ten, Melissa?" the doctor asks.

"One, two, three, four..."

Blink.

"I only ask because I care," Megan says.

She doesn't need to explain. "I get that."

Please stop.

The thing is, I don't like to think about it. The incident that changed my life in the wake of Faith leaving. The surgeries. My mind clamps down and refuses to think about it. I need to let it out one day. I just don't know how.

"Are you okay, at least?" Megan asks.

I whirl around. Face etched in stone.

"Would you be okay if it happened to you?"

Megan has the decency to look embarrassed.

The beans are done, so I layer them in the casserole, not caring that they're too hot. Not giving them time to cool.

"And the scars?" Megan asks.

I hate the scars.

I hate the reality of what put them there.

I place the dish in the oven. "I said I don't want to talk about it."

I don't mean to snap at her. But I can't deal with it yet. Maybe ever. I don't know. I'm trying. I really am.

"Give me time," I say, softer.

As I move on to mashing potatoes, Megan nods. Mouth in a pressed line like she wants to say more, but will honor my request for space.

"Can I at least ask about Faith?"

Megan will always ask. Her personality is as calm as a puppy on caffeine. She's been this way since Dad left. The oldest, forced to grow up too fast. Forced to take on responsibility far too young.

"Sure," I say, because it's the lesser of two evils. "She's reclusive. Not talking too much. Still having trouble with everything. Understandably."

Megan nods again.

"Have you told Faith what happened to you?" May asks.

I wasn't expecting May to say anything. Her question catches me by surprise, which is maybe why I answer honestly.

"No. She has enough to deal with."

Megan doesn't push anymore. Nobody pushes. I go back to cooking in a stretch of silence that screams against my grated nerves. Reminds me of a truth I don't want to face. It upsets me that life is this way.

Unfair.

It's frustrating to try and understand why families come apart at the seams like old, worn jeans that people throw away for new ones instead of cherishing them and keeping them for the history that made those rips. It's draining to think about people who, through no fault of their own, are dealt a bad hand.

But then I realize that we are not permanent. None of us.

And life doesn't owe us anything.

4
javier

A clock on the far wall ticks to the tapping of my foot. I'm anxious. Watching seconds turn into minutes turn into hours, and all the while my life is swirling down the drain. These pieces of me are being wasted in a pointless class I'm sure I'll never use. Ethics. Really? Whatever. It's almost over.

I'm in a plastic chair under fluorescent lights that barely illuminate the paper in front of me. I'm holding a pencil with an eraser that's worn down to bits.

Like my patience.

I am wondering why any of this matters. Summer school. A teacher at the front of the room who obviously doesn't want to be here—or so says his slouching position and the book he's holding in front of his face. So says his silence and his numerous head swivels toward the clock.

What happened to the cool teachers who inspire students? The guy sitting at the front of the room? He is not that teacher.

He's given me and the other six people in this class an assignment to complete. Words blur into paper as white as my clenched knuckles. We have five minutes to finish. Five agonizing minutes until I don't have to be trapped in this room with windows we're not allowed to open and voices we're not allowed to use.

I wonder about the other people jailed in here with me. What happened to them? They missed credits, obviously. *¿Pero por qué?* Were they lazy? Sick? Not able to keep up?

Or were they like me? Attending a funeral. Getting family affairs in order. Not able to concentrate for shit in a classroom because every day a murderer is walking the streets. Who knows.

All I know is that Wink's free when he shouldn't be.

This is what I'm thinking about when I should be doing classwork. I can't help it. I haven't focused since *mi tío* called to tell me Diego was gone. Eight months ago. My grades have dropped to failing. And I can't find the energy to care.

Wink got away. He bested *la policía*. Probably figures things are fine as long as he stays far from the cops.

But he doesn't know.

He doesn't know that I remember him.

He doesn't realize that I'm coming for him.

And maybe that's okay. Maybe that works better. Maybe surprise will be my greatest advantage. Because I am a storm, brewing. Waiting for the right moment. I am the tornado that will drop out of nowhere and destroy everything that Wink has built.

Slow at first, then swirling faster. Momentum in the form of anger. Winds that lash out like whips, striking each of them, one by one.

I scribble answers to the ethics questions, but my mind is elsewhere.

The assignment is titled "Justice."

I almost laugh at the irony.

Justice. They want to talk about justice? Justice would

be Wink suffering the same fate he dealt my cousin. Justice would be the police pursuing Wink and not just letting the case drop. The Cuban government ending *El Cartel Habana* and not getting paid by its top members to overlook criminal activity would be justice. What does this high school class know about justice?

Justice is what I'll serve to Wink on my own terms.

Only two more weeks of meeting every Tuesday and Thursday. Only a handful of days until I've made up my credits. A high school diploma will be my reward. *Mi mamá* insisted that I get one. She reasoned that living in the States for the last five years has rained down opportunities that our homeland, Cuba, never would have. Now me and my eleven siblings have a chance at an education. She didn't want me to waste this chance. Why not go to school for free, she'd said. Not graduating was not an option.

Especially since she never graduated.

Mi papá had other reasons for wanting me to graduate. You can get a good job, he told me. You don't have to live on the streets of Cuba anymore. You don't have to struggle for food and fight with your fists to survive. You don't have to carry a gun and make hard choices like: *Will I join a cartel today, or will I die?*

You can be sure that you'll eat every day and you will never have to beg. You can lock your door and know that you won't hear the *pop, pop, pop* of a gun going off at night, ending a life outside your walls, because that's what happens all the time in Cuba. You have freedom here in the States, *mi papá* said. Don't throw that away was the message.

And it's true. Things are different in America. Sure, America has dirty streets and drugs and violence. But

America also gives people the option to live a clean life and go to school and make something of themselves. So I get what my parents are saying. I understand that this education, and the paper that says I've earned it, can mean something. But I'm not sure how much that matters now. My focus is elsewhere. A sheet of paper saying I graduated will never bring Diego back. It will never exact revenge on his killer. It will never find Wink for me.

Not everything is as easy as a sign-on-the-dotted-line and thank you and your application has been accepted and I've reviewed your resumé and welcome to your new job where you'll make money and live happily. Because it doesn't work like that. Diego's death has opened my eyes to the darker side of America.

It's a vision that cannot be undone.

One hour later, I'm sitting at the beach in board shorts the color of gunmetal. I'm drinking water because Melissa won't serve me alcohol. This job is good for her and she doesn't want to lose it, she told me.

Melissa's sitting next to me. I'm using every ounce of my control to not stare blatantly at her suit, which is a one-piece but somehow sexier than all the bikinis around me. Maybe because it's different from the normal attire. Or maybe because of the girl wearing it. But whatever it is, I can't stop looking at the neon yellow-and-brown tiger-striped suit; it looks shredded because of the slits that move from the top of her ribs down to her belly button. Goes with the tiger theme. Dips low on her back. Has cutouts on the side that show her hips.

At the sight of her, I'm dying.

My body is having a hard time staying in check. It

wants to respond to her wearing that. Sitting so near. Smelling sweaty, faintly like salt. Somehow sweat smells deliciously good on her.

I force my eyes to look anywhere else.

Ten minutes is the time she has to spend with me, on break.

"Do you remember?" I ask, staring at the water.

Not sure how she could forget.

"Remember what?" she asks.

Her voice commands my attention. I look up.

Melissa's a beautiful liar because her eyes are on my lips. Her words try to block the truth. Her stare gives her thoughts away.

I grin. "The water."

Like you don't know.

Give her a chance to act as though she's just now retrieving the memory.

"Oh, right." She bites her top lip nervously. "Yeah. I mean, sure. That day."

She's stumbling over her words. Her tongue's tripping over itself. I love watching her falter. Because it means something.

I lean in.

Melissa inhales sharply. Doesn't move.

I enjoy the effect I have on her.

"You wanna go somewhere? *Ven conmigo.*"

I really think she might. I need to get her somewhere quiet. Hopefully somewhere where she'll talk to me about Faith. Maybe Faith told Melissa the details of what happened to Diego that night. I don't know. But I intend to find out.

"Where?"

"I have a hotel room here." Her eyes go wide. "It's my twin brothers', Eduardo and Pedro's, twenty-first birthdays. We're here for a week. *Estamos celebrando.*"

It took me nearly a month's worth of building houses with the contractor I work for to save up enough to stay at a nice hotel. I never in my life thought I'd be staying in a place like this.

I only live thirty minutes away. Amazing how much difference thirty minutes can make. Roads that start with older, more run-down houses like mine slowly morph into million-dollar homes on the water.

I tried suggesting that I just drive out to *la playa* every day, but *mis hermanos* weren't having it. This is what my brothers wanted: a week on the beach. A week free of everything. And I have to admit, it is relaxing.

Melissa doesn't respond. She only stares at me, and I realize how forward that must have sounded to her. I didn't mean it in that sense. Not that I'd object.

"You can stop by for a drink. Or just hang out. It's quiet there."

Her expression relaxes. "I'm not off for another hour."

I sip my water. Watch her face. "Come by after."

I might conveniently forget mi mamá's *rule.*

A server, the guy from yesterday, tells Melissa that she has more drinks to deliver on the fly. He needs her help with cabana seventeen.

"I'll be right back." She says it like a promise.

My disobedient eyes don't care that I tell them to stare at the table. They find Melissa, balancing a tray overloaded with drinks. Guys flirt with her. One touches her leg. It's none of my business. Maybe she knows him. She passes the drinks out and smiles. They're still looking at her as she cuts a path through the sand back toward me.

"Sorry about that," she says.

One guy whistles. She laughs.

"This job," are the words mumbled under her breath.

"Is it worth it?" I ask.

Melissa tilts her head to the side. "Well, I've flirted with no less than twenty guys. Complimented even more girls. And made three hundred dollars in five hours. You tell me."

Can't deny that the money is impressive. *"Bien."*

A grin crawls up her face. "What room?"

My heart stampedes in my chest at the thought of Melissa in my room.

"Two-oh-four."

"One hour." She brushes my arm lightly. "I'll meet you then."

melissa 5

Ring, ring, ring.
    I wait as the phone rings three more times. I'm off work, still at the beach. Cell to my ear. Like most times, Faith doesn't pick up. She probably won't call back either. That's okay. I'll keep trying.

"Faith," I say into the phone, leaving a message. Hand cupped to my mouth to block out the sea breeze. "I miss you."

Most of my voice mails go like this. Me not knowing what to say, besides that I miss her. Me choking up because my best friend is lost to agony.

"I miss you so much."

I try to think of something more to say. My mouth is full of emptiness.

So I hang up.

Nothing left to do but wait.

I'm a tangled bundle of nerves. I'm jittery and breathing irregularly. And, God, why can't I stop fidgeting? I need to control myself. I unhook my hair from a clip. Let it fall down my shoulders. Recheck my pink sundress, looks okay.

Relax, I tell myself. *Breathe.*

I take the stairs two at a time. There's one elevator and a million guests. With luggage and people constantly going up and down, it's easier to climb. The air is musty in the stairwell, I guess because most people don't use it. It's a reminder of the times that I spent in the library with Faith. Dusty and old. It's not a bad smell.

As soon as I open the door to the second floor, I'm hit with a wave of fresh, humid air. I spot Javier's room. Last one on the end. A rectangle door and circle knob and untold shapeless questions hanging in the air.

What am I really doing here?

Why does Javier's gaze wrap around me so fiercely that I can hardly breathe?

What does he want from me?

His room is private. Vending machine alcove on one side. Windows on the other. No neighbors, except down the hall.

I know what it's like, being alone. Living in an empty house most of the time. I'd give almost anything not to be alone. To have Faith back, living a few doors down, coming over whenever. For my mom to not work as many double shifts. To have sisters who aren't away at school.

Alone is good until it turns into days that turn into weeks with barely any contact with other people. That's one reason I love my job. No shortage of people there.

ROOM 204 announce gold numbers hanging just above the peephole.

Knock, knock.

One, two, three seconds until Javier answers. One, two, three skittering beats of my heart.

"*Hola,*" he says, lazy grin on his face.

I want to touch his grin.

"Hi."

His eyes are the color of soil before it rains. His stare is trained on me.

"Come in."

His voice is the warmth of a summer storm.

I glance at his black shorts and red shirt. He's wearing a hat turned slightly sideways, easy style. Simple but coordinated.

One step into the room tells me that it's nice. Marbled countertops, fridge, and two-burner stove. Plush living room and hideaway doors that separate a bed and nightstand. Behind tan couches with palm tree patterns hangs a large painting. A lone sailboat against a backdrop of blue. Everywhere blue. The waves the sky the fish below. A flat screen television is attached to the wall facing the couch.

But despite the seeming luxury, I also know that this is just a regular room at the hotel. The expensive ones start on the fifth floor.

I try not to look at the bed, white comforter with green pillows and sham. I try not to notice the way it fluffs in a rolling pattern. I push back the need to know what it feels like.

Focus.

"Nice room," I say. Match his lazy grin.

I lower myself onto the comfortable couch.

"Wanna drink?" he asks.

"What do you have?"

Javier goes to the fridge. Bends. I no longer see his body over the top of the counter.

"Coke, sweet tea, *agua*, *cervesa*," his voice tells me.

He blends everything fluidly. Spanish and English.

"Sweet tea."

Faith and I took Spanish in high school. I remember enough to understand the basics, though I was never really that great a student. Some things come naturally to me, like sports and exercise. But not studying. That was always Faith's strong point.

Javier's head pops back up. He digs through the freezer for ice. Fills a cup. I don't miss the way his eyes slide across to me. I don't pretend that I'm not staring back at him.

I fear the way he makes my body feel.

Javier hands the cold glass to me. I take a sip before setting it on a coaster in front of me and force my hands not to shake. Make my spine sit tall. My eyes watch his.

His look.

God, that look.

I'm melting. Dripping into a puddle at his feet because his look is so, so, so

Piercing.

"*Gracias* for coming."

How could I not? Of course I came. Even though I probably shouldn't have. Even though I haven't dated anyone since my diagnosis almost six months ago. I slowly let my mind think the word.

Cancer.

I freeze. Such a jagged word. Sharp edges that cut through a carefully planned life. The life that cervical cancer killed. Like going to college, traveling, relaxing at the beach in swimsuits that don't cover my scarred stomach, these were my plans. Having kids one day. That'll never happen now. Having fun without the worry of life withering under the brutal fingers of cancer.

The doctor walks in, a folder in his hands. His face is rounded with a perfectly arched smile. I relax a little. Stop

tugging at my hair, a nervous twitch. A smile is good. A smile means that the abnormal area that they saw on ultrasound was probably nothing.

The results of my biopsy are what he holds in his hands. He flips a page in the folder.

One page. Everything will be okay.

Two pages. He sits in a chair.

Three pages. He wrecks my life.

"It's cancer."

He doesn't tell me how sorry he is. He doesn't tell me it's just a joke after all.

And I can't believe my ears because how could this be true? I can't have cancer. I'm only eighteen. I haven't taken a college course. I've never been in love with a guy before. I haven't been rock climbing like I always dreamed of doing. Or skiing. I haven't even made up my mind if I want to dye my hair this summer. Will I have hair to dye this summer?

Oh, my God, I have cancer.

The doctor waits patiently, allowing me to absorb his words.

"How?" is all I manage to ask.

He sets the folder down. "It's more common than people think."

But it's not common for me, Doctor.

"Does anyone in your family have a history of cancer?"

"I don't know. I've never asked. I didn't realize that I'd have to ask."

He's not smiling anymore. "You're going to need surgery, Melissa."

He hands me a form to sign.

"Immediately."

What's the point in dating during a time like this? Surgeries and medicines and recovery times. It's not fair to ask someone to understand. Though I'm in remission, the cancer could come back. My six-month checkup could reveal that the surgeries weren't enough, that I'll need chemotherapy or radiation.

But then I look at Javier and I wonder about roads not taken. I wonder how much fun they could be if only someone had the guts to explore them. I look at Javier and I decide that I don't know how to say no to him.

Life can be so short.

I wonder if maybe I should be seizing moments instead of pushing them away. I've wanted another opportunity to see him, but I never thought it would happen after Diego and Faith left.

"What have you been up to lately?" he asks.

Everything.

And.

Nothing that I can tell you.

"Not much. You?"

His jaw tightens. "Dealing."

I have an urge to reach out, to say something. If only there were something to say. Because the face of his pain is crushing.

But I don't say anything. Mostly because nothing I say can bring Diego back. I know from the experience of losing my dad—of him being gone for good—that no words are better than empty words. That looks of pity and small condolences do nothing to lessen the agony. But silence? Silence can heal. Because silence allows others a chance to speak, to vent, and that's a million times better than a crowd of "that's too bads" and "what a shames."

And then Javier says something that strikes a painful chord in me.

"How's Faith?"

He really wants to know? Well, then. Here's how Faith is. She's struggling. Barely answering my calls. Always making excuses for why she has to go two minutes after we start talking. She's avoiding me. I'm not exactly sure why, but I think maybe it's all too much for her, being forced to remember the life she had. She watched the boy she loved die. Something like that changes people.

It scares me.

And I worry about her. I wonder how she can sleep every night and not scream into the air from the memories. I imagine the nightmares that must ravage her dreams, the visions that must haunt her daily. I wonder how she doesn't bite into her pillow and let loose the agony in guttural cries.

Or maybe she does. I wouldn't know. What I do know is that the kind of friendship we used to have—spending nearly every day together, not holding one thing back—is nothing, not anything, like what we have now.

But I won't give up on Faith. Even if she only talks in small spurts about absolutely nothing. The weather and schools she's building and not much else. Even if she only says "hi" and "bye" and sometimes "how are you" in the middle. Even if she doesn't truly listen when I talk or realize how hard this is on me, how much it hurts not to have her here.

I won't give up on her.

Though sometimes, I think she wishes I'd do just that. I think Faith's pushing and pushing and fighting our friendship. Some days, I feel the block of distance that she's wedging between us, heavy like concrete.

But I'm stronger than her attempts at space. I will wait. And she will, one day, be better. And if by some chance it's all too much to bear, if she teeters from the burden, I'll catch her as she falls.

Because that's what friends are for.

Javier is still looking at me. I haven't answered his question. It's a loaded one, and I think he knows that. What I can't figure out is why he asked it. Maybe he genuinely wonders how she's doing. Maybe he's being polite.

Or maybe not. Either way, I won't mention Faith's personal demons. That's her story to tell.

"She's okay," I lie.

I will lie for Faith a hundred times if necessary. I will protect her fiercely. I will call her number every week no matter what. And I will leave messages even if she never listens to them. Because what she's going through is bigger than me and my wounded feelings. It's bigger than Javier's inquisitions.

Javier bounce, bounce, bounces his knee. His brows scrunch together and I wonder if he knows that I'm a liar. It looks like he might say more, so I switch the topic.

"I've never actually seen a room in this hotel before," I say. I've only heard people talking down in the bar about how nice the rooms are.

His face relaxes into something easy. Like maybe he's grateful for a reprieve from the memories, too.

"Me either, before now." He takes a sip of water and speaks. "But wait. Don't you work for them?"

"I work for them, sure, but only on the outside," I explain. "Taking orders. Serving drinks."

"Right."

I wonder what he's thinking.

His eyes zone in on my mouth.

I wonder if he wishes for my lips like I do his. The strongest of all currents, tugging, pulling. I wonder if, like me, he dreamed about the way I tasted long after my tongue left his. Javier never tried anything with me after that day, and I was too busy finishing high school and applying to colleges to think about why.

But I never forgot his lips.

Judging by Javier's comment earlier on the beach, he didn't forget mine either.

"What have you been up to?" I ask.

I wonder if he has a girlfriend. I don't know much about Javier, I realize. That needs to change.

"Summer school. Family. Work." His answers are short. Not enough.

"What's your family like?"

He laughs. "Big. Eleven sisters and brothers."

He shifts positions. One leg brushes against mine—

And everything stops, a hanging moment. Dangling from the sky, about to fall. I hold back a shiver. His touch. Just a touch. That's all it takes for my cheeks to drown in heat. My pulse hammers away at the skin of my neck, looking for a way out.

"I never forgot the water," I blurt.

I shouldn't have admitted that.

Javier grins. "I know."

I hate that he makes my bones wobbly and my blood rage. I love that he's here. I love the way his eyes watch me wherever I am. I love that he never forgot the water either.

"Are you with anyone?" I ask. Because something in me needs to know.

His grin spreads into a sly smile. "Would I ask you up here if I was?"

Good question.

"Not sure," I answer. "I don't really know enough about you."

He nods. "True. We should fix that."

Please. "Okay."

"And to answer your question," he says, inching forward, evoking a tremor from my trembling muscles, "I'm not with anyone."

My eyes don't leave his.

"Me neither," I say, though he never asked.

I've never been with anyone seriously. Dating. Fun. That's my thing. It's not that I never wanted a serious boyfriend. It's just that it never happened for me. Things always fell apart easily. Amicably, sure, but they fell apart nonetheless. I guess I don't really know how to hold stuff together.

"Mmm" is Javier's response.

I want to know what's happened to the air in this room, how he's so effortlessly syphoned it away. Because I can't find oxygen to draw into my lungs when he stares at me like that. My breathing becomes embarrassingly erratic. I'm trying to hush it, but with no other background noise to disguise the effect he has on me, I'm sure it's obvious.

Javier chuckles.

My cheeks demand his attention, drowning in red to catch his eye.

He hasn't touched me directly, I realize. All of this and Javier hasn't even tried anything. I can't imagine having enough strength in my joints to withstand a direct touch.

You are ruining me.

Please don't stop.

"You didn't talk to me much after the water," I say. "A few times at school, and at the concert. But nothing like that day."

His eyes narrow. "Back at 'cha."

True.

I could have gone to him. It's not like I've never hit on a

guy before. It's not like I've always waited for a guy to make the first move. That's how Javier and I ended up in the water, kissing. Because I went to him first.

"I wanted to," Javier says. "I wanted to talk to you a thousand times. When I'd see you at school flirting with other guys, it'd drive me *loco, mami.* But you weren't mine."

His.

And then the next thought. "You watched me at school?"

"Yes." He holds my stare. "I watched when you flirted with other guys. I kept my mouth shut and wished it was me. You watched me, too."

So he knew. He knew that my eyes often slid his way. I look away and chew my lip.

"Don't be embarrassed." He grins. "I liked it. I just don't share. So, you know, I figured it wouldn't happen for me."

Because I flirt? It's just my personality. Open. And I remember from sitting with Javier and his friends at school that he's the opposite of open. Only lets a few people get close. I think his past has something to do with that.

Will I be one of the people you let in?

"Doesn't mean I wanted them, those other guys," I say, speaking my thoughts aloud.

But I realize he had no way of knowing that.

"That's how I am," I explain. "That's why this job comes easily. I don't know how to be different. It's all for fun. Nothing serious."

He nods like he gets it. "Good to know."

Javier doesn't say much. Clipped sentences and hacked-off words. I want to know more.

"What happened in Cuba?"

I must have said something wrong because Javier leans away from me. Diverts his eyes.

"Why?"

Because if I knew that, I'd know you better.

"Faith said you and Diego had it rough. I don't know much more."

Which is the truth.

"Cuba," he says, like the word tastes bitter in his mouth, "is the place that gave me life, where it all began."

Pause.

"And nearly ended."

6
javier

Melissa wants to know about my life in Cuba. I can think of many words to answer her.

Home.

Hell.

Love.

Fear.

I can't find it in me to hate the country of my birth. But, damn, it's a rough place to survive. I can't call it living. Not in the streets I came from. Those alleys are places that steal lives and spin dreams into nightmares. It's a place of monsters made real and fear around every corner. It's a place where *living* isn't an option. In Cuba, you *survive*. Make it through one day at a time. Hoping to eat, to scrounge food. Hoping to not get jumped or shot or hooked on drugs. That's the Cuba I know.

"If I tell you 'bout Cuba," I say to Melissa, "will you tell me the truth 'bout Faith?"

There. I called her out on it. The lie she tried to pass off as truth a moment ago, telling me that Faith is "okay." Not looking me in the eye. Not sounding convincing at all.

Melissa doesn't seem surprised.

"I can't," she says. "Faith is my best friend. It's her story, you know?"

Fair enough.

"Then I wanna know 'bout *your* past."

Where do you come from, mami?

Everyone has something to hide. And this has to be an even trade. She needs to know that whatever I tell her cannot be repeated. So I'll need something of hers to hold for assurance. This is the way my thoughts work. One secret for another.

My demons for yours.

And if I'm being truthful, I know that I'm nervous, because some people are too far gone. I wonder, after I tell her, will she think I'm one of them? Has she lived a life anywhere near as twisted as mine? Only those with the deepest scars know how to navigate the scars of others. Because they've had to learn how to walk on their own.

When she doesn't say anything, I let the truth come out.

"Please, Melissa. I have to know 'bout you. I have to know how close you are with Faith. I need this. I *need* your help."

I need to make sure that she's still in contact with Faith. I need to know everything Faith knows about the night in *La Plazita.*

"I have three sisters and a mom," Melissa says. "Sisters are off at college, except for summer when they come home to visit. One just graduated, actually. We're close. I miss them. Mom works a lot. My dad left us for another woman. He's never come back. I've never spoken to him since."

She pauses, looking uncomfortable.

"I let Faith get hooked on drugs a while back because I

wasn't paying close enough attention. It's not my fault, no, but I should have understood that I wasn't the only one drowning in pain. It changed my life. Made me realize that there's a world of people out there dealing with different issues, and all of them are equally horrific. I learned how to be there for someone in need. For once, someone *needed* me." She blinks. Watches my face. "You are the second person to ever say that they need me."

I'm not expecting something so raw, so blunt. Straight to the point. And I want to laugh because she's incredible.

"Cuba is a wasteland of violence," I say. "At least, the part I came from. You had two choices. Stay there or flee. Stayin' meant a life of cartels, drugs, and very little chance of survival. So we left five years ago. Diego was in a cartel." Melissa sucks in a breath. "It was the only way for him to live. He always followed orders. Until one night. He didn't do a job they wanted him to. Within hours his *mamá, mi tía,* was murdered."

I realize in that moment that I can't say more. I didn't want to say that much, but Melissa needs to understand the importance of me talking to Faith, of me understanding what happened the night Diego died.

I'm choking back emotion. All that time, I was so focused on helping Diego accept that his *mamá* was gone and that it wasn't his fault.

But now Diego's gone, too, and I feel his pain.

Six thousand fingers ripping my heart to bits.

I feel the tendrils of revenge calling to me. I know what it's like to be an insect wrapped in a spider's web because revenge has cocooned me. There's only one way to break free.

Free, free. What is that, really?

"Melissa, I need to know about the men who killed

Diego." I grind my teeth. Hold back my anger. "I think they're the same ones who murdered *mi tía*."

That's all I'm willing to say. I don't know how to be anything other than guarded. I have a million more demons. But I won't tell Melissa that. I'm not sure she'll understand. *Her home isn't as brutal as mine.*

I see it in the way her eyes trust easier, in the way she can sometimes seem so free. I don't know how to completely let go like her. My home never allowed such things.

Melissa's blue eyes are a pinwheel of emotions. Spinning me around, though I'm locked securely in place. I fight the desire to run. Her stare is uncomfortable because it's too intimate. Like she *sees* me. And the feeling is foreign. My body automatically wants to reject it.

But I control myself. This isn't Cuba. And Melissa's not the enemy.

"I don't know anything about that night," Melissa says.

Faith it is, then.

"I need to find a way to talk to Faith," I say.

She sips her tea. "That's why I'm here?"

She doesn't sound hurt. More like resigned. Like this is an accepted fact. Like it all makes sense now.

My opinion has always been that my kind, Latinos, don't mix well with her kind, *gringas*. It's how I've been taught. Maybe that's part of what held me back, after that day in the ocean. Maybe the other part is because *mi mamá* would kill me if I dated a *gringa*. And as much as I love *mi mamá*, I'm thinking now, here, sitting beside Melissa, that she couldn't be more wrong. I've just never had a reason to argue her point.

So I let Melissa in on one more secret.

"That's why, yes." Truth. "But also, you're here because I don't wanna stay away from you this time."

melissa

Music blares inside my car at an obscene level as I drive home from the beach. I'm hoping that if I crank it loud enough, it'll drown out thoughts of Javier. Of his rounded lips. Of the way his eyes tear me up inside.

I can't understand the way he looked at me with such intensity. I was almost willing to tell him anything. I don't talk about my dad. Faith knows because she was there when he left. Her mom left her at the same time. We held each other up. Stood together. Fell together. But no one has convinced me to speak of him since then.

Except for Javier.

I'm trying to forget Javier's touch, the gentle brush that ignited my nerves in the best way.

Does he understand the power in his hands?

And I'm thinking, he doesn't see the potential he has to ruin me.

And I'm whispering, *how did he get to me?*

And I'm wondering, what, exactly, happened to Javier to make him so rough.

Because I'm thinking it didn't start with Diego's death. But maybe Diego's murder was the final catalyst for Javier's change. Faith once told me that Diego's family has a darkness about them. I didn't understand then. I'm starting to now.

Javier—with his sharp eyes, with his hands so right, touching me but not directly, twisting a need in me, but not knowing it—has me hooked.

I force myself to think of something else. The warm night's breeze. The smell of sulfur water and Florida air. The humidity that causes beads of sweat to bloom across my skin. I'm telling myself that Javier didn't mean anything rude by asking me there, though he admitted to needing information from me.

At least he didn't lie.

I thought Javier wanted to see me. Maybe get to know me better. Since he remembered the water, I assumed that his invitation was about us. Maybe we'd lounge in chairs on the balcony under the moon. Maybe watch the water. I imagine what it'd be like to taste his lips again.

I didn't think I'd be there to talk about Faith.

With the gear in park, sitting in my driveway, I command myself to think of anything other than him.

No such luck. The front door cracks open. May's head pops out like a Jack-in-the-box. She gives me a strange look, and I remember that my music is still blaring. I turn it off. Walk to her side.

"Wanna talk about it?" she asks.

I give. "Okay."

This is what we do, my sisters and I. Share everything. No secrets. No limits—with the glaring exception of my surgeries. It's how our family is. I'm maybe the closest to May, but everything eventually gets distributed. I don't mind. I like the openness. There's a freedom to letting your secrets go, allowing your lips to speak them. When you watch the letters form words that burst out of your mind and float into the air, it's not as stifling. This way, none of us bears the burden alone.

We walk to our bedroom, the room May and I have shared all our life. It's directly across the hall from the room Megan and Monica shared.

X marks the spots where memories were made. The chair in the corner, a checkered sailor print in blue and red, was where May cried for hours after a boy broke her heart. The writing desk that got us both through endless nights of homework. The trundle bed, now tucked under the full bed, is where I used to dream of Dad coming back. There's the closet where May loved to hide, jumping out at me when I came in, winning a terrified scream from my lungs. She'd laugh hysterically because no matter how many times she did it, it always worked.

My eyes sweep to the bookcase, where I shelved my journal, stuffed it between tales of adventure. Think about the fact that May knew where it was but never read the lines without my permission. I take in the television that May left on every night. The low volume helped her fall asleep. Think about the fact that I sleep with it on to this day because it helps drown out the noise of my thoughts long enough for me to drift into dreams.

May looks around like she remembers, too. Offers me a smile.

"Good times, right?" She laughs.

"Mostly, yeah," I reply.

My eyes travel to the skylight. Since we're the younger ones, Monica and Megan automatically got the bigger room. But we never minded, May and me, because it meant that we got the sky view.

May follows my stare.

"Totally worth it," she says, like she knows my thoughts. And it was. To be cramped together all those years. To not have the distance that too often separates families. To know that the vastness of the sky was only a peek away.

May's staying in the room with me until she returns to college in three weeks. Her bags crowd the corner by our closet.

"Come," she says, patting a spot on the striped comforter. I lie next to her on my back, watching the stars twinkle through the skylight. Mesmerized by how they shine so brightly despite the darkness around them.

I want to know your secret. I want to store that much light.

"Is it the cancer that's bothering you?" May comes right out and asks.

It's always bothering me, every day. Not in a painful way; that passed a couple weeks after my surgery. Symptoms are gone, too. The only thing left is hormone pills. Headaches that sometimes accompany them. What worries me is the scare that it could come back. My greatest fear. But that's not what's upsetting me tonight.

"You can talk to me about it," May offers.

The door to my heart slams shut. "I can't talk about the cancer, May."

Disappointment in her eyes.

"Not yet," I say.

May, like the rest of my family, only wants to help.

"It's not about cancer this time," I say.

And as long as it's not about my diagnosis, May knows I'll talk.

"Spill," May says.

So I do.

"There's this guy," I begin. May smiles. "I met him a while ago."

I pause. Try to figure out how to describe Javier to my sister.

"Boyfriend?" she asks.

I jolt at the thought. "No."

"Does this guy happen to be hot?"

I smile. My sister doesn't beat around the bush. She kills it. No reason to waste time.

"He might be."

I can't stop grinning, though I'm trying. My lips are a pair of traitors. Following each other's lead.

"Hmm, so this maybe-hot boy, what's his name?'

"Javier." His name is delicious in my mouth.

"Javier? Is he Latino?" she asks.

"Yes."

Spanish and English all in one. Me and him, an interesting match.

"But you're mad at him," she says.

Yes. "I never said that."

She laughs. "You didn't have to. Your music was enough. You always play it super loud when you're angry."

The advantages of having a sister who knows everything.

"Okay, yes. I'm frustrated," I admit.

"What does Javier look like?"

I turn to my sister. "What does that have to do with anything?"

"I want to picture him in my head while you're talking about him."

I sigh. "You're so weird, May."

"You love my weird."

Images of Javier slam against one another in my mind.

"Tall. Dark hair and eyes. Tattoos, but he only got those recently. And his lips," I waver at the thought of his lips, "are perfect."

May arches a brow.

"I don't know, May. There's something in his eyes. There's something about his way. It's so," I search for the right word. "Sad."

Taking a deep breath, I tell May everything. I explain Javier's relation to Diego—she knows all about Diego and Faith.

I think about how hard it must be for Javier to know that more of his family is gone. Murdered, like his aunt. *Lives taken before their time.*

I wonder how this world can be so careless and greedy, taking, taking, taking by whatever means necessary. I think about how evil has so many faces and goes by so many aliases. Drugs. Cartels. Murder. Hopelessness. Violence.

I hate that Javier has no choice but to accept that life hasn't been good to him. That this is the way things are. Like the sky is blue and the sun is yellow and your family will die too young. No big deal. Move along. Accept your fate.

May looks conflicted. Like it pains her to hear it, too. She goes with something positive. Lightens the mood.

"So you met him a while ago, but all you ever did was kiss?"

"Yes."

"And now he's back?"

"It seems."

May smiles. "Go for it."

The fact that he wants to know about Faith bothers me, though. I say it out loud, listening to the words experimentally.

"What do you think of him asking about Faith?"

I feel her shrug. "Can you blame him? I mean, if it were you, wouldn't you at least ask? Wouldn't you feel the need to try?"

And I realize that, yes, I would want to gather as much info as possible. And no, I can't deny Javier that truth.

I need to lead him to Faith. Because she's the only one who can answer Javier's questions. But, I wonder, what will happen to Javier once he knows?

"You think I should give him Faith's number?"

"I think he has a right to know about his cousin's death, yes."

Closure, I think.

"What then?" I ask.

"Then," May says, a glint in her eye, "you make that boy remember what your lips feel like."

8
javier

I can't stop thinking about Melissa.

When she heard me confirm last night that I'd asked her up to my room to get information, she took off. Not that I'm surprised. I can only hope that she'll see the importance of what I'm asking and come back.

Six more days.

That's the amount of time I have at the beach with *mi familia.*

And then it's time to find Wink.

My family shuffles around me, preparing for a sunset dinner. I don't pay them any attention until my brother Pedro's palm smacks me upside the head.

"*¿Que pasa contigo?*"

I shoot him a look. He and Eduardo are identical, with their shaved heads and matching faces. Brown eyes and pudgy noses. The only difference is the small off-center mole below Pedro's bottom lip.

"What's wrong with you?" he repeats in English. "It's like you're not even here."

Most of my family members speak a combination of Spanish and English now that we've been in the States a while. Except for my youngest brothers. They speak mostly

English, because that's what's spoken in American schools, despite the rest of us trying to make sure they know Spanish, too.

"Maybe he's thinking about that *chica* from today," Eduardo says, laughing.

My friends laugh along with him. I've invited them today; the six of us—me, Ramon, Esteban, Juan, Rodolfo, and Luis—are often together. Ramon and Esteban are brothers and have similar looks—slight overbites, wide eyes. Juan is a walking painting, covered in tattoos. Rodolfo is all smiles, one dimple poking through, creating a pocket in the side of his cheek. Luis and I are similar in size; we hit the gym together. Freckles spot his face like a dash of pepper.

I've known them since I moved here. Latinos, like me. They know about Melissa. They've always known about Melissa. They were there that day on the beach.

The first time she kissed me.

I need to not be thinking about her lips right now.

Mi mamá's head snaps up, suddenly interested in our conversation. *"¿Que chica?"*

She wants to know what girl. I'm not ready to share Melissa with my family. I fear what *mi mamá* will do with that information. Most likely run Melissa off. For my own benefit, *mi mamá* will say.

Mi papá is staring now, too. A grin on his face. He knows what it's like living with the world's nosiest women. It's almost like he's telling me *good luck*.

"No one," I say, prepared to kill my brother for mentioning her.

"Somebody," she says. She speaks with a heavy accent. "If you're that red about her."

Right on point. I feel my cheeks flame.

"No one, really." Not sure she's convinced, but she lets it go.

"How's school going?" she asks, changing the subject.

It's more than one question—I can see that from her look. *Mi mamá* has a way with words, and she knows us all too well. She knows exactly how to make us squirm.

I struggle to sit still. Because I realize what this really implies.

I'll answer: *Bien.* Almost done.

And then she'll say: What's next?

It plays out just as I imagined.

What's next? I think about telling her the truth.

I'm going to find Wink and the men who killed your sister. When I'm done with them, they won't ever do this to anyone again.

Instead: "Not sure." Shrug. Purposefully noncommittal. Because that's how I am most of the time.

She knows this, and so she pries. "Not sure?"

I don't need anyone to worry about me. I can't afford to have people wondering about the changes taking place, asking why I'm locked up even tighter than before. If anyone is going to see through me, it'll be *mi mamá*. I can't seem to hide from her. I'm not in a place where offering information is an option. Because she would stop my plan from happening. *Mi mamá* would do anything to make sure I don't follow the same path as Diego. Her love for her children is fierce. Almost to a fault. Almost to a point that it drives us crazy. She won't let me end up like *mi primo.*

Dead.

Withering skin and brittle bones.

My hands clench the picnic table bench beneath me.

Mi mamá sets three tables; we've secured the plates and napkins with drink cups so they don't fly away in the stiff breeze off the ocean.

"What are you hiding, *mi hijo?*" she asks.

"*Mamá, porfa.* It's Eduardo and Pedro's birthdays. Not today."

I don't usually argue with her. None of us do. Including *mi papá.*

Unable to meet her eyes, I stare at a multicolored umbrella above our table. The ocean eats at the shore, filling its mouth with sand before the force of gravity drags the waves back out, an unavoidable cycle of existence.

Unavoidable. I know the feeling.

I'm grateful for *mi papá's* bravery, for his willingness to move us to the States. Nothing short of a miracle that we arrived unscathed. My country doesn't let its people go easily.

I'm grateful, really. But I'm also pissed. Because I was thrown into this American life that isn't as easy as it seems, that makes promises and then betrays them. I'm supposed to feel safe and warm and like everything is better, but I've never felt safe. Not anywhere. A childhood like mine doesn't grow into something safe, no matter where I'm placed.

So I make the best of it. I try. I make a few friends and welcome Diego here and I think for a minute that things might actually be okay.

But they're not.

America is kind of like Cuba. Only America is dressed in prettier clothes. It's robed in a promise of freedom, but tell me, someone please tell me, how being locked in a coffin six feet under equals freedom. Because I'd love to know.

America is a liar.

And I think that I won't be able to go anywhere and feel okay.

"Girls, pour drinks," *mi mamá* says to my three sisters, Maria, Tatiana, and Alejandra—fifteen, twelve, and nine years old.

This is how it usually goes. The girls in the family cook and take care of the rest of us boys.

Mi mamá looks at me, ready to continue our conversation.

"Can I help?" I ask.

I'm dying for any distraction from the stare *mi mamá* is boring into me. Maybe if I'm busy, she'll let it be.

"Offering to help?" Eduardo asks under his breath. "Red flag."

Hopefully, *mi mamá* didn't hear him. I learned early on that asking to help is borderline offensive to the women in *mi familia*. But I don't know what else to do. Usually I'd leave. Offer up some excuse about where I have to go. But I'm stuck at the beach. It's a celebration.

My sisters send a sharp glance my way at the mention of me helping. They learned from *mi mamá*. They take great pride in knowing that they can care for us. *Mi papá* explained it to me one day. Asking to help is almost like suggesting they're not doing a good job, he told me. They only want to hear compliments.

One miserable day a few years ago, I suggested that mashing the chunks out of the potatoes might make them taste better. I'd tried them that way once at school and I liked it.

Big mistake. Maria yelled at me that she knew how to cook mashed potatoes just fine. Weeks went by without a word from my sister, her feelings hurt. I had to eat a whole bowl of Maria's mashed potatoes to get her to forgive me.

You think you like potatoes with no chunks, *mi papá* had said, but the trouble it causes you to mention it will change your mind.

I apologized to Maria and told her that her potatoes were perfect. I've never complained about their food since then.

Any chance that *mi mamá* didn't hear Eduardo goes out the window as soon as her words reach me.

"You're definitely hiding something."

My brother nudges me, but I'm not in the mood for his shit so I nudge him back. Hard. He kicks my leg under the table.

"What the hell is your prob—"

The words die on my lips. I realize why he's nudging me. My eyes find what has stolen his attention.

Melissa.

Nothing good will come of this.

Melissa sees me and smiles. She's not in a bathing suit, which makes me think she's off work. My eyes follow her body. Tiny shorts. A loose fitting thin top that ripples in the gusts of ocean wind. A girl that looks nearly identical to Melissa stands beside her.

I compose myself and brave a peek at *mi mamá*. She's watching me intently.

Melissa turns a path in the sand, cutting her way toward me.

She has no idea what this means. She doesn't know the women in this family. Melissa doesn't understand that she is prey, heading straight into the lion's den. And everyone knows that it's the lionesses that fight and kill for the pride.

I have to stop this. But if I go to her, *mi mamá* will know.

I hate that Melissa's not mad anymore about our talk yesterday. Maybe if she were still angry, she wouldn't be walking this way. She wouldn't have to see what happens next.

I can't let my family rip her to shreds. *Mi mamá* has no problem telling a white girl that she has no place with any of her sons.

There's really only one way to handle this without causing irrevocable damage at the hands of *mi mamá*.

Melissa stops at the side of the grill where *mi mamá* is cooking the meat.

So close, so close to the one who will destroy this.

I look out at the water like I don't see her. Hoping it'll help.

It doesn't.

She comes closer. Mere inches from the bench where I'm siting. My brothers check out the two girls. My blood boils.

"Hey," she says, eyeing only me. She doesn't see the danger. If I want anything to do with this chick, I need to get her the hell away from *mi mamá*.

"Hey," my lips say.

Bored my tone says.

This needs to be convincing.

"Didn't expect to see you." Melissa glances at my family. "So many of you."

Most of us look alike is my guess at the meaning behind her statement.

"Okay," I say.

Melissa looks at me strangely. Like she expects me to say more.

"Can I help you with something?" My tone is fluid. No hiccups. No reason for *mi mamá* to think I'm interested.

Melissa's eyes narrow. "Um, no. I guess not."

My gaze darts to *mi mamá*. Hopefully, Melissa gets the point. Panic sets in. If I let Melissa stay, *mi mamá* will destroy everything. But if I let her go, I might never get the true story from Faith about what happened to Diego. I'm risking losing my best lead about the night *mi primo* was murdered.

But then *mi mamá* takes a step toward Melissa as if to get close enough to ask who she is.

I make a gut reaction decision.

"See you around," I say.

Melissa kills me with her stare. Murdering any hope I had.

"Not likely," she replies.

And leaves.

After seeing the look on Melissa's face, I realize that I might not be able to come back from this. I tell Melissa that I want her, and then I shove her away. She's right to be angry. She's right to want to get away from me.

She really, absolutely should.

melissa 9

"**I**s that the guy?" May asks.

My breathing is all wrong. Anger is eating holes in my composure. I'm walking away fast and not looking back at Javier.

"That's him," I reply.

"Definitely sexy," May says. "Not sure that he's into you, though."

She doesn't mean anything by it. I would think the same thing if I didn't know him better.

"He is," I say. I remember his lips molding to fit my own. I remember the way his heart bashed against his chest, responding to my nearness. "But something's not right."

May looks at me with kindness. "Are you sure, Lissa? I mean, could he have been lying?"

Possibilities spin, a whirlwind in my mind.

"Maybe," I admit.

Her brows knit together. "Or maybe he was expecting someone else and didn't want you to stick around?"

The suggestion makes me queasy. I don't want to think about Javier with someone else, though I have no right to care either way. He said he was single when we talked in the hotel room, but still, it rips at my insides. Too tough to digest.

May gives me a hug. "Sorry, babe."

I should have talked to him more after that day at the beach. I should have approached him at school.

I shrug it off like it's no big deal. Like my mind isn't racing at the possibility of Javier and another girl.

The taste of regret is bitter.

I want to turn around. To go back and ask him what his problem is. But I won't. I'll keep walking and pretending that I haven't been punched in the heart by the force of his dismissal.

"I thought he liked me," I whisper.

My thoughts don't matter now.

"Maybe he does," May says. "Guys are weird. He might really like you, but that doesn't mean he's not interested in other people, too."

She's right, of course.

We take a seat on a padded cabana. Watch the water froth at the shore, the tips of the waves almost reaching us. Tiny clams are propelled out of their hiding spots in the sand by the force of the tide. The unlucky ones are eaten by waiting birds. The others re-bury themselves quickly. But their time is limited; in a minute, the ocean will make them vulnerable again.

I know how they feel, battered and worn.

A hundred times today I've thought about Javier's story. Wondered at the details. Wanted to know what brought him this far. And why his eyes hint at a life unmentioned.

He's hiding something.

I think about how hard Diego's death has been on Javier. I wonder if he feels guilty. I wonder why the need to find answers rests so heavily on Javier's shoulders.

Sometimes life doesn't give out answers.

I want to tell Javier that fair doesn't exist, and that going to Faith for information might only increase his pain. I can't promise that she'll want to talk about it. I can't guarantee that she'll have anything to say. That she'll even answer the phone.

"Don't worry," May says, motioning to the ocean. "You know what they say. More fish in the sea."

I'm not sure that I'm interested in the others.

"Speaking of." May whistles at a group of guys fishing on the beach.

I laugh.

When the three guys hear May, they leave their poles rooted in the sand and head our way.

She winks at me. "You're welcome."

The guys stop in front of us. One catches my eye. Light skin and olive eyes.

"Hi," he says, blocking my view of the setting sun.

May nudges my arm.

"Hi," I reply.

She smiles, approving. "Which one of you boys wants to show me how to fish?"

The remaining two offer at the same time.

"Both of you it is," May says. My sister knows how to charm any guy. I learned half my flirting skills from her.

Olive Eyes sits next to me.

"Aaron," he says, grinning.

"Melissa," I offer back.

I look over at my sister. She has a guy on each arm, leading them down to the water.

Aaron follows my gaze. "Friend?"

"Sister," I correct.

My eyes rake across his body. Defined legs. Muscles that speed bump over his stomach. Beach-wavy hair.

"You guys live here, or just visiting?"

I get this question often. It's understandable, since Florida's beaches are usually packed with tourists in the prime seasons.

"Local," I answer. "You?"

He reaches a toned arm behind his head, lying against the back of the cabana.

"Same." Eyes on the water. "Your sister knows how to fish already, doesn't she?"

I grin. "What would make you think that?"

Aaron's gaze lands on me. He catches my grin. "Because she just cast like a pro and you live in Florida."

"Not all Floridians know how to fish," I say.

He smiles. "But most do. And it's obvious that your sister does."

My cheeks heat up as his statement settles. He knows she left us alone to talk.

"What are you up to tonight?"

Nothing. "Not sure. Why?"

"We're having a bonfire on the beach. You should come."

I should. I should forget about wanting Javier. The image of his face makes my insides flip.

"What time?"

May comes running up, a fish hanging off the line. That was quick.

"Look, Lissa! I caught one." I can't tell whether her excitement is real or feigned, but I know for sure, since May used to go fishing with friends, that her next words aren't. "First time!"

The fish squirms on the hook. Poor thing.

"Good job." I laugh. "Beginner's luck."

Aaron bites back a smile.

"Want to go to a beach party, May?" I ask.

My sister doesn't hesitate. "Sure! What time?"

The sun slips below the horizon, promising a night of distractions. Here, I don't have to worry. Here, I can flirt and have fun and see so many faces that Javier's won't matter anymore. I look to Aaron for an answer.

"People will show up in a couple hours, probably," he says.

May hands the pole to one of the guys standing next to her. "Great. We'll run home to get ready and come back."

Aaron turns to me. Lips curling upward, suggesting that he's happy with May's response.

"You have a phone?"

I reach into my pocket. Pull out my cell. Aaron quickly programs his number in.

"Call me when you get back."

I nod because his stare steals my words.

My thoughts flash once more to Javier. I look around, half expecting him to be there. Hoping that he changed his mind about blowing me off, that he'll leave whatever he was doing. This is his chance to make things right.

My eyes take in everything around me. Gray clouds smeared across the sky. The moon brightening at the first signs of night.

And Javier.

Nowhere to be found.

Back at the house, May and I get ready for the beach party. I pull off my outfit. Standing in nothing but matching underwear, I reach for a suit, shorts, and shirt. May sucks in a breath that draws my eyes. My lungs deflate. The look on her face, God, I hate it. Because I know that look. It's . . . pity.

May is staring at my scars like she feels sorry for me. The pink lines that mar my skin. That rip a pretty picture to bits. Just above my pubic bone. Inside my belly button. One right below it.

I cover them with one hand. Ashamed. Tears prick my eyes.

May looks up. Knows that I've seen her.

She flinches. Like the scars hurt her. It's the flinch that gets me the most.

"Oh, Lissa." My sister's voice in my ear. Her arms hugging me like maybe she can hold me together, all my broken pieces. "I'm so sorry this happened to you," she whispers.

I draw a hand to my heart. Try to stop the sobs.

"I've got you," she says. "You're never alone. Not ever."

So I let it go. All of it. The emotions that beg to be freed. My shoulders sag and my lungs heave with silent cries.

May lets me cry. Doesn't bother with the wetness on her shoulder or the weakness in my bones. She lets me cry and cry. Every tear that needs to be set free.

"We don't have to go anywhere tonight," she says. "We can stay in. I won't leave your side."

What I need is to get out and forget my diagnosis, my scars, Javier. All of it.

"We can do whatever you want," May offers.

Whatever I want? Right now what I want is to get out of this house.

And forever end these tears.

10
Javier

Pedro hands me a beer. Not my first one of the night. Usually a guy with my body type, over six feet tall and two hundred pounds, can handle several beers, but I don't drink a lot so I'm feeling a little wasted. It's a good kind of wasted, though. The kind that numbs awareness. That makes me not worry as much about the fact that I blew Melissa off and probably ruined any chance I had with her—not to mention any chance of hearing from her what happened to Faith.

It's not that I'm cool with how it all played out, but I'm glad that she didn't meet *mi mamá*. That would have been worse.

I get up and concentrate on not stumbling in the sand.

"Where you goin'?" Pedro asks.

"To piss," I mumble, not caring that only one half of me is obscured by the patch of sea grass where I've stopped.

My brother laughs. "Haven't seen you this way in some time, *hermano*. You sure that *chica* didn't get to you?"

"Her name's Melissa," I say, zipping up. "And what *way* are you talking 'bout?"

I plop back down on the blanket laid out on the sand.

"Drinking like this," he says. "You trying to forget?"

Her mouth. Dios mío.

Her skin. So soft.

Her look.

I gulp more beer.

Pedro doesn't back down. "You're trying to erase her."

Yes. "Maybe."

"That's what I thought."

So what? I'm trying to forget. Nothing wrong with that. I remember many nights of Pedro trying to forget after *mi mamá* drove away the only white girl he ever had the nerve to like.

"I get why you did it, though," he says, serious.

Of course, he does.

"You know how *mamá* is. It's not worth the trouble."

Mi mamá is exactly what got me into this mess in the first place. I wish she could just be cool about the girls we pick. I hate that I can't flirt back with hot *gringas* who make it obvious that they're interested. I don't like crumpling strips of paper with phone numbers on them just because I know it would never go anywhere, thanks to *mi mamá.*

"I should've been smart 'bout it like you. Pushed the *gringa* away before I got in too deep."

He hands me a water bottle, but I shrug it off.

"Damn, Javier. This is supposed to be my birthday week. You gonna make me babysit you tonight, aren't you?"

"Fuck you talking 'bout? I don't need a sitter," I say, the words slurred. "I need a new memory."

Pedro shoves the water at me again.

"Do yourself a favor and drink this. You can thank me tomorrow."

Fine. I chug the water. Stop once to burp. My stomach sloshes and I think I might puke.

"*Cierra los ojos*. It'll help."

I take Pedro's advice and close my eyes. At this point, I don't care to watch the world spin around me. I let the background noise—a lapping ocean, screeching gulls, music—drown out my awareness.

And when sleep knocks at the door to my mind, I gladly answer.

I don't open my eyes again until sometime later. The night has grown colder; the sky has darkened. I look to my left. Find Pedro talking with a few of our friends.

"Time is it?" I ask. Slowly, I sit up.

The beers have worn off some. I feel an appropriate buzz. Enough to take the edge off, but still think straight. Enough that the world is no longer twirling. I don't feel like I need to puke. But I'm not completely sober, either. *Perfect.*

Pedro glances at his watch. "Midnight."

He hands me another water. I drink most of it.

"*Gracias*," I say, feeling guilty that I made him stick by my side.

"You good?" Pedro asks.

I nod. "*Lo siento.*"

"What do you say we hit up the party down the way?"

I glance in the direction of a blazing bonfire.

"*Muchas chicas*," Pedro says. He's offering me exactly the distraction that I need.

"*Vamonos*." He doesn't need to ask twice.

The salt water is warm where the sand is cool beneath my feet. It takes only a few minutes to walk to the shore party. At the outskirts of the firelight, a guy I've never seen before holds out fresh beers, stopping us as we approach.

He says, "Welcome. You bring anything other than alcohol and the cops find it, it's on you."

His message is clear. I don't do anything other than drink. Not that I'd blame anyone else if I did.

"Got it," I say, taking a beer from his outstretched hand.

Luis takes the other beer he offers. My brothers grab drinks from the table behind the welcome dude. He looks at a few of us—namely Juan, Esteban, and Ramon—like maybe he's wondering if we're old enough to drink. He doesn't question it, though.

I've never understood the legal drinking age in the States. In Cuba, as long as you're sixteen or older, people don't care. And if I'm being honest, most people don't care even when you're younger than sixteen. I'm not sure that my country has a legal age.

The United States.

A million rules.

To break.

My eyes, on impulse, take inventory. Bodies lounging in the sand. Speakers stacked atop one another, music pouring out. So many girls.

No danger noted.

"*La playa* always has the best parties," Eduardo says, smiling at some *chicas* walking by.

There's more people than I expected. Half of them female. A fifty-percent chance to forget the way I blew it with Melissa.

My friends get to work immediately. Ramon approaches a *gringa*. "*Hola, muchacha. ¿Cómo te llamas?*"

"English," she says.

I'm partially surprised that she stops, gives him the time of day. Ramon runs girls off, mostly. True to form, he starts saying something about her skirt being pretty and how he'd love to get in it. The girl walks away, clearly annoyed.

"I don't understand how you ever get women," I say, laughing.

"That's 'cause you haven't seen my charm." He smiles.

"Sleaze isn't the same thing as charm, Ramon," Luis says.

"Is in my world," Ramon replies. Eyes another girl. "Later."

He takes off. On his way to being shot down again.

"Wanna scope it out?" Luis asks.

I follow his eyes to another part of the party where a group of girls are huddled together, laughing, wearing nothing but small suits.

"Sure," I say, keeping pace beside him.

The girls look up as we approach.

"Hi," a few say at once, taking us in.

I don't have a hard time with girls. But I choose wisely. If they're white, it's Luis's territory. He knows I only date Latinas.

One of the girls looks like she might have Latina blood pumping through her veins. I ask just to be sure.

"*¿Tu eres* Latina?"

"*Sí,*" she answers, smiling.

"*¿De dónde eres?*"

I'm watching her features. Honey brown eyes. Matching skin and hair. I try not to think about how Melissa is a splash of color in my mostly homogeneous world. Blue eyes. Light skin. Blond hair. A rainbow of sexy when I'm used to something different.

Stop.

She tells me where she's from. "Colombia."

I claim the spot next to her.

"*Soy* Javier. *¿Cómo te llamas?*"

"Mariella."

"Ella," one of the girls says, rolling her eyes. "How are we supposed to understand you?"

I eye her *gringa* friend. She's not talking to me, but I answer anyway. "Learn Spanish."

Mariella laughs. Her friend's eyes narrow; she's not amused.

"Why should I learn Spanish when you clearly speak English?" she asks. "And Ella, you always speak English around us, remember?"

She keeps calling her that, Ella. I'm guessing that's her Americanized name. An abbreviation of her heritage. And I can't help but think, *bullshit*. I don't see why names should have to change like that. I wouldn't tweak mine to fit in. A name is a link to who you are. Regardless of who thinks it sounds better a different way.

And another thing, what's with this *chica* butting into other people's business? I don't remember asking her what she thought about my language.

I don't like a lot of things about Cuba, no. I don't think Cuba's safe, no. But I'm proud to be Latino.

"Well, he speaks Spanish," Mariella explains.

"Right, but we're in America," Clueless says.

I decide then that I don't like her friend.

"Anyway," Mariella says, tossing ringlets over her shoulder. They bounce like a springboard. "*¿De dónde eres?*"

"Cuba."

The word is memories on my tongue.

Clueless starts complaining to another friend about how

she feels left out. How it's rude to speak another language in front of people who don't understand it.

Why is Mariella friends with people like this?

"Wanna go for a walk?" Mariella asks.

In English. That way her friends get the point.

"Definitely."

I wipe sand from my shorts while her friends spear us with daggerlike stares. Mariella ignores their rudeness. Warm air wraps around my bare chest as we walk across a floorboard of broken shells. When we get far enough away she says, "So you speak English, too."

"Yeah. Just not in front of people like that, no offense."

She shrugs. "They're not so bad."

How is she cool with them?

"Being in America doesn't mean people have a right to tell you who you are," I say. "It doesn't automatically change things."

She watches my face. Sidesteps things that have been washed to shore by the pounding waves. A collection of coral strangled by seaweed. The remains of a jellyfish. Pieces of fishing net.

"It's just easier. To give in to this new life. It's more accepting, you know?"

No. I don't know. Listen to friends who shun your first language? Who tell you how to speak? Who Americanize you, change your name? Sure, maybe it seems more accepting. But only if you can let go of a part of yourself. Which I'm not willing to do.

Mariella waves to a few people in passing. One dude says, "Hey, Ella."

And I can't walk any farther. I'm tethered to this spot, my feet unmoving.

What the hell?
My breath speeds up. Heart hammers.
Breathe.
I'm so close, so close, so close to losing it.
Breathe.
Not because he said hi to Mariella.
But because of who he's got tucked under his arm.

11
melissa

My world wobbles like a seat atop a Ferris wheel. Every now and again, my stomach drops out and I have to remind myself that I'm not on a ride. The air out here is warm and damp and I desperately want to jump in the ocean, run through the waves that nip my feet, begging me to take a dip. The water is enticing. Refreshing. Maybe it'll dull my buzz. I really shouldn't have drunk that last beer. But I had to. After my breakdown in front of May tonight, I had to erase the tears. Fill them with this numbness that helps ease the emotional ache. Just tonight.

I'm grateful to the arm that's helping hold me up.

"What the fuck," I hear someone say. Harsh. Sobering, with a dangerous note.

I look up.

Of all the people, it had to be you.

I swallow. Look him in the eyes.

"Hi, Javier," I say, forcing my voice to be steady.

He's the one that blew me off, I remind myself. He's also the one standing beside a beautiful girl. Guess May was right. He must have been waiting for her. His dismissal makes more sense now.

Anger turns to sparks, catching fire in me.

Javier's stare is crippling. Like he wants to yell at me and undress me, both.

"What are you doin'?" he asks, jaw tight.

Moonlight curves around his neck. The stubble there. Deliciously enticing.

"Hanging out." Smile. "You?"

He looks at Aaron's arm around me. His fists clench.

"Same," he says.

The girl next to him looks at us in confusion.

"You know this guy?" Aaron asks.

I'm not sure if he's talking to me or the other girl, but I answer. "Yes." At the same time that she says, "Not really."

Wait.

She doesn't know him?

"I need to talk to you," Javier says.

"No thanks."

How's it feel to be blown off?

His brows draw together. I lean into Aaron more. Press my face to his shirt.

Javier takes a step towards us. "What you're seeing is not what you think," he says.

I glance at the girl next to him. "Seems clear to me."

The world tilts again and I'm reminded that I drank too much. I close my eyes.

"You okay?" Javier asks.

Not really. "Sure."

He sees through my lie.

"You're coming with me," he says, his words suddenly in my ear.

Snap. My eyes are open. Staring at his face. So close to mine that I can make out the individual eyelashes that frame his angry eyes. There are tiny freckles across his cheeks. I didn't notice them before. I can't believe I didn't notice them.

Aaron stares at me. Suddenly looking like he's in over his head. He takes a step away at the same time Javier takes a step forward. Now it's Javier balancing my woozy legs.

Not wanting drama, Aaron says, "This okay with you?"

I should say no. I want to say yes. I should tell Aaron to take me far away from the boy who makes my heart beat erratically. My pride is frayed. Saying yes would only make this worse.

But what I do is nod.

Javier doesn't hesitate to take me away. Aaron turns to leave with the girl that Javier came with.

"*Mujer,*" Javier says, putting space between us and the crowd. "What are you doing with that *pendejo?*"

"He's not so bad," I say.

Javier stops. Tips my chin up toward him.

"You want that guy, *mami?*"

And I can't for the life of me find my voice. No, I don't want that guy. He was a nice distraction. But I never would have gone with him if Javier hadn't blown me off. I break his stare.

"You want that girl?" I ask, watching as Aaron and the girl walk in the opposite direction.

"What I want is for you to look me in the eyes and tell me why you're drunk and feelin' up some dude."

"What I want is for you to want me like I want you!" I clamp a hand to my mouth. Regret slaps me in the face.

Javier pulls my hand away. His stare takes in all of me. My eyes. My lips. I'm embarrassed by what I said. I'm embarrassed by my ridiculous heart, which thumps loudly, echoing his every touch.

"You want me, *mami?*"

Yes. In the deepest parts of my bones, yes.

Silence.

"Answer me." His voice is demanding.

"No," I say, stubborn.

A grin crawls across his face.

"I owe you an apology," he says. "I couldn't talk to you earlier. Wanted to. But I couldn't. You understand?"

"Not at all."

Javier's warmth reminds me of the water. Of wanting to jump in. I'd do anything to cool off.

"If I explain it to you, will you remember in the morning?"

"Probably not," I answer honestly. "But then again, you're hard to forget."

I wince. What is with my traitor lips?

Javier laughs. "In that case, I'll tell you one day. Maybe."

Whatever that means.

"Let's go in the water," I say, voice slurred.

I don't wait for Javier's reply. One step, two steps, three steps in. The ocean laps at my knees, instantly cooling. I don't bother to remove my shorts. Javier eyes my suit. White with tiny pink hearts splattered across the fabric.

I can't let him see the scars.

I sigh. "Much better."

Four steps, five steps, six steps in.

Strong arms wrap around me. One hand rests just below my belly button. *Too close, too close, too close.* The other sits lightly on my exposed hip. He must be wearing a metal ring because I feel it against my side, cool on my flesh.

And suddenly I can't breathe. Another flashback.

The cold steel of a knife presses against my stomach. I feel that much, even in my drug-induced state. The doctor

*asked me to count to ten. I've reached four, the last num-
ber I can muster. There's too much fog in my brain. The
doctor's saying something about proceeding. That they
need to get it out.*

"Stop," I say to Javier. I turn. Take two steps backwards.
The water rocks against me.

He looks at me funny.

"You can't touch me there." Barely a whisper.

His eyes narrow. "Can't touch you where?"

I should tell him everything. I should spit it out and send
him running because what am I really doing here? What
do I hope to accomplish? There's a chance he won't want
me once he knows.

"My lower stomach."

Javier's eyes travel down my body, but his inquiring
look is blocked by my bathing suit. He can't possibly
know from the outside what I'm hiding. I can't stand
Javier looking anymore, so I turn my back to him. Try to
differentiate the dark horizon from the line of the sea. I'm
ready for his questions. Because surely he has some. I'll
shut them down, of course. But I'm ready.

Only, he doesn't ask. He doesn't question what I'm hiding. He doesn't let my hesitance stop him from bringing
me near.

"Okay," he replies, pulling me closer. Wrapping his
arms around me just below my breasts. Not touching my
lower stomach at all. His respect is comforting. His hard
body is perfect and warm, enough to make me forget.

"*Mami*, you smell so good," he mumbles into my hair.

I turn to face him. His shirt is off. I trace the tattoos
across his chest with daring fingers. He shivers beneath my
touch, and a groan escapes his lips. I want to feel him
more. I want to know if he has tattoos in places I can't see.

My exploratory hand lands on three words. Directly over his heart.

Descanse en Paz.

Rest in peace.

I know what the words mean because someone spray-painted them, along with a picture of Diego's face, on the concrete sidewalk near our school right after he was killed. I looked them up. I haven't forgotten the meaning since.

"I miss him, too," I say. Honesty raw in my voice. "I miss the way he made Faith free. I miss the way he didn't care about image. How he broke every rule. Because some rules are meant to be broken."

Javier tenses against me.

"You're a lot like Diego," I whisper. "But you're different, too."

"Let's not talk about that," he says.

My eyes find the moon. Lonesome in its secluded patch of sky. One sliver away from being full.

I feel one drop away from being empty.

Javier's voice trickles into the air. "I don't like seeing you with that guy."

His fingers wrap around my ribs. I tremble.

"You belong with me."

And as soon as he says the words, I know them to be true. At least for now, this is exactly where I belong.

Javier's calloused palms travel up my back. The only other time Javier has held me was in the water. Here. Like this.

It's as though he's remembering, too, because he tilts my chin up. Zones in on my mouth. Firecrackers explode in my veins. I want, I want, I need his lips. His tongue. I want to take our time because there's no reason to leave this moment.

"One day," Javier practically growls, his hands tightening on my back. "One day I will taste you again. But not today. Not until you're sober."

Disappointment is an anchor pulling me under.

"But why?"

He puts a finger to my mouth. Rubs it gently against my bottom lip.

"Because, *mami*," he breathes. "I need you to remember. Every. Last. Second."

12
javier

I didn't expect it to be so hard, leaving Melissa with her sister last night. Not kissing her perfect lips. The way she drew air in and out, almost panting when I touched her mouth with my finger.

I wish it were my lips instead.

I nearly lost it. But somehow I did it. I walked away. One foot in front of the other. Totally wound up and barely able to keep it in check, but I walked away.

For once in my life.

I normally enjoy all girls have to offer, no strings attached. I'd like to pretend I'm chivalrous and treat every *mujer* to dinner and a movie. But it'd be a lie. Girls are fun. I've had enough serious in my life to last a while. Seriously starving, seriously almost dying. On a daily basis.

Seriously running for my life to a new country.

Plus, there's *mi mamá*. It's not that I'm scared of her. I'll take a stand when it's worth it, but she makes it easy to weed through the bullshit. Some things just aren't worth the trouble.

But Melissa? She does something to me. She just might be worth it.

Chunk by chunk, I'm being stripped clean.

And now here I am, at the beach again. Chilling with my boys. Trying hard not to watch her body.

"Just look already," Luis says, breaking my staring match with the ocean.

"At what?" But I already know.

Luis laughs. Leans back on his elbows in the sand and nods toward Melissa. "You know what. So you gonna look? Or you gonna murder the ocean with your stare?"

"The ocean," I say. Because I have no other choice.

"Losing game," Luis mumbles.

I want to stare at her. But I can't. Because I'll end up in trouble. The way she flirts with guys, the way they touch her skin—it's enough to know about it. I definitely can't watch it play out.

"You ever gonna admit that you like her?" Rodolfo asks.

"I like her," I say. No hesitations. Catching them all by surprise.

"Damn, man. Thought that'd take longer." Rodolfo laughs.

"Nah," Ramon says. "You remember them in the water that day? I knew he'd be a goner. Shit, if I got to touch a *cuerpo* like that . . ."

One look from me. Ramon shuts his mouth.

"Still," Rodolfo continues. "What's the problem with lookin', then?"

"Maybe she doesn't want him back," Ramon says.

"When have girls not wanted him back?" Juan asks.

"It looks like now," Ramon says.

He has guts. Talking to me like that when I've finally admitted I like a girl. First time. He should've learned his lesson when it comes to pushing my family. Diego already taught Ramon that the guys in *mi familia* are hotheads. Especially about women.

"Shut the fuck up," I growl.

Ramon only laughs. Enjoying himself.

I'm thinking about ordering water or something just to get Melissa over here. But I won't.

Pride is a monster living within.

I pick up a Frisbee and walk toward the shore. Luis follows. I throw it hard. Letting go of my aggression with each flick of my wrist. Watching the disc spin a path through the air and land far away. Again and again I throw it. Each time, I feel a little less wound up.

Luis says something about how he bets I can't throw it all the way to the sand dunes. The dunes are far, but not impossible. Ten dollars. I take the bet. Because I'm competitive like that. But I know right away that I've thrown at the wrong moment. The wind takes it off course.

I owe Luis money.

Money that I don't have to lose on a bet. Plus, I hate losing.

"Double or nothing says I'll throw past the dunes this time."

Luis considers my bet. Shakes on it.

This time when I aim, I know I've got it. Until I hear her voice.

"Stop it," Melissa says. Serious.

I turn toward her serving section. A line of cabanas occupied mostly by a group of guys our age. Maybe older. A few cabanas on the end are taken by a family with small kids.

I zone in on the guy grabbing Melissa's hips. He's trying to pull her down onto his lap.

"Let go," she says.

Frisbee forgotten, I run to her. She doesn't see me.

"I said stop it," she demands. Louder this time. She's pushing at his hands, but she's not strong enough. There's a look in her eyes. Like pure fear. Like this guy touching her is more than just making her mad. She's scared.

His friends only laugh. Like her discomfort is funny.

I'll kill them.

I'm a weapon. Charging out of nowhere. I don't use restraint when my fist meets his face. He lets go of Melissa; crumples in a bloody heap, his nose broken. I know because I've been trained in the art of breaking bones. I turn to his buddies. Ready. But none of them challenges me.

I grab Melissa and haul her away. I'm almost positive that if I weren't holding her, I'd still be hitting him. I'm trying not to shake from adrenaline.

The lead server from the other day runs over. He surveys the scene.

"What happened?" he asks.

Everybody blinked, that's what happened. See how quickly things can go wrong?

I take deep breaths. Try to cool down.

"She said 'let go.' He didn't." It's the only explanation I offer. Nothing more needs to be said.

I'm thinking the guy is going to throw me out of his little patch of the beach. Surely I've broken some set of rules. I'm so sure that when he puts his fist up for me to bump, I'm momentarily confused.

"Thanks for looking out," he says.

Melissa is staring at me with this expression. Like she

doesn't understand what just happened. Like she didn't realize that the hands that held her in the water could also break bones. There's red on my knuckles like smudged cherries. Pretty sure the blood's not mine.

I don't know what to do. I won't apologize. Because I'm not sorry. I'd do it again. He deserved it.

And for the briefest second, all I can see is her.

This bonita chica *who stirs something deep in me.*

I hate that other guys touch her. I want to break every bone of every hand that dares to disrespect her. But what I really want is to lean into her smell. To breathe her in. To watch the way her body reacts to me.

So I do the only thing I can in that moment.

I leave.

Because if I don't, I'll kiss her. Right here, in front of everyone. An act of claiming. And I'll enjoy every second of it.

Mine.

The word slips through a crack in my thoughts. Infiltrates my mind.

Mine.

I only wish it were true.

melissa 13

Brock pulls me into the small office that's really nothing more than a storage room on the bottom floor of the hotel. The smell of lemon is strong, thanks to a plug-in air freshener. An AC hums to life as we close the door.

"Wanna tell me what happened out there?" he asks.

Brock reaches for papers in the top drawer of the desk. I know what they are. I've filled them out once before.

"I don't need an incident report," I say, motioning to the form.

"But it's company policy," he says.

I don't want to involve Javier.

"Is there a way around it?" I ask, hopeful.

Brock's eyes travel to my sides, where the guy grabbed me. "Do you have any marks?"

Not any worth mentioning. "No."

Brock's eyes trek back to my face.

"You're not in trouble," he says. "The form isn't anything bad, but it's standard procedure whenever a customer gets sticky fingers."

"Good," I say, relieved. I can't lose this job. "So, do you think we could let it slide?"

"Maybe if your boyfriend hadn't punched him, I could. But since the other guy's bleeding, I'm gonna have to fill it out. We can't be held liable."

I nod, understanding. And mumble, "He's not my boyfriend."

Brock grins but presses his lips together like he's trying to hide his smile. "Does he know that?"

"Yep."

He hands me a pen. I start filling out the paper. When I get to the part about what resolved the issue, I stop.

"Um, do you mind if I leave Javier out of it?"

I'm really hoping Brock won't make me tell the whole truth. The last thing I need is for a customer to file an assault and battery complaint and get Javier arrested.

"I suppose he could've just been a guy passing by. Someone without a name," Brock says.

I shoot him a smile. Brock is always doing this, has been ever since I started waitressing. Looking out for me. He's kind of like the brother I never had. One year older. Knows May. They had something, once upon a time. Now he's a friend that she still talks to occasionally. Someone who offered me this job when I needed money. Someone who cares about how the servers are treated. Who protects us from jerks.

"I saw May today," Brock says as I scrawl my story across the lines.

I'm not sure why he and May aren't together, come to think of it. She never said why they broke up, just that it ended a year ago. And when he dropped off some of the things that she'd left at his house, he didn't bother to give her heart back along with them.

"She looked really good."

I look up at Brock and he has this grin.

"Haven't talked to her in a couple weeks," he says.

I wish they'd get past whatever it is that separates them, because I think Brock would be good for May. Protective and sweet. His demeanor is hard and soft in some spots that he only ever shows a select few people. Like when he encourages me to go to college, saying that he'll give me shifts to work around my class schedule. Or when he takes moments to help little kids build sand castles on the beach. Or when he brought May flowers on random days just because he thought she was beautiful and deserved it.

"You guys should do something sometime." It's not my place to say, but since I know that May never really got over him, and since Brock lights up every time he mentions or sees my sister, I figure it couldn't hurt.

"I don't know," he says.

"She's not seeing anyone," I offer.

He doesn't say anything more.

I finish the form and sign at the bottom. Brock signs, too.

"Word of advice?" he says.

"Yeah?"

"If he's good to you, keep him around. 'Cause guys that look at a girl the way he looked at you, and defend them, even though he might have had to take on that whole group you were serving, aren't usually guys who are messing around. You know?"

There he is with the advice again. He could tell me to run from Javier. He could tell me a lot of things. But instead he says to give Javier a shot.

"Thanks, Brock."

We stand to leave.

"One more thing."

I wait.

"He may not be your boyfriend now, but I'd bet money that he will be soon."

14
javier

My black Ford pickup is nothing special. Old. Not a thing worth stealing. Still, they huddle around it like there's something valuable inside.

MS-13s. Four of them. Watching me. Probably wondering whether I'm coming out on my own or if they'll have to bust the windows to get in. They won't let me leave, that's for sure. Not that I want to. I came here on a mission. It's the only way.

Gang members start a slow crawl around my truck. I made sure to park near the convenience store.

A method to my madness.

I'm in the same part of town, near Diego's old place, where they last saw me. Only this time, I'm parked in a back lot. There's one other car in sight, abandoned with a flat tire.

Danger whispers my name.

Things could go wrong. The MS-13s could make me pay for the state I left their boys in. They're all strapped. Any one of them could pull a gun.

Every detail matters. The way I chose a discreet location, the way I left a trail of fresh images—my truck, my face, their blood on the ground—all so that they'd recognize me the next time I came. Each move I made was intentional. The MS-13s are a gang, sure. But they're also a pack. Hunting down those they want to dispose of.

And those they want to recruit.

One member kicks the front bumper. Another kicks the passenger side door. Warnings, telling me I need to step out, that they have something to say. Most likely, with their fists.

When I don't move, they kick my door. The truck rocks. Their scowls deepen into something more like grins. A challenge. This is fun for them. Seeing how scared they can make me.

There's nothing they can do to me that'll be any worse than what they did to Diego. His memory is fuel. I almost smile back.

They kick harder. I'm not worried about the truck. It's not the truck they want.

If revenge was all they were after, I would have already been in trouble. Beat up. Shot.

But this isn't revenge.

They're playing into my hand.

Like I'd hoped, this is a recruit.

I refuse to fold.

I'm looking around like I'd planned to meet someone here. It's an act, but they don't know that. They don't know that I'm different from the dealers that frequent this area, cars meeting in the cloak of night. Laws being broken with the brush of hands. I'm just another person in the wrong place at the wrong time, my little act says.

You won't know what hit you, my big secret whispers.

They're moving closer. Making it obvious that I'm a few seconds away from losing all of my windows.

Five. Guns that I know of. Theirs and mine.

Four. Guys circling. A slowing pace.

Three. Taps on my steering wheel. I'm almost ready.

Two. Steady breaths. In and out.

One. Person's revenge. Almost served.

Zero. Time remaining.

I open the truck door. They take a step back. So they remember my fists, I decide. Their immediate guardedness is indication. So is the fact that they've pulled guns.

I give them a chance to get into position. Wait for them to speak. My eyes dart to the ways I can get out of this mess after my message is delivered.

They've circled me. Probably hoping one of them will be able to attack my blind spot. It's smart. What I would have done. But I don't give them a chance. I circle, too. Slowly, like them. That way there's never one part of me that's left still.

I'm the bull's-eye in the center of their target board.

My gun stays tucked away. For now. It's only for emergencies. Until then, it stays out of view, hidden in my waistband, covered by a loose black shirt. Maybe they suspect I've got it. But if I've played them well enough, they probably won't. I'm wearing no gang colors. No visible tattoos. No indication that I belong to anyone. But they don't understand that none of that matters.

Cuba has already made a monster of me.

It's now, in moments like these, that I'm reminded of my home. Of constantly being on guard. Of not knowing what it means to relax. I can't afford to relax around them. I can't take even one second of concentration away.

In some ways, they all look the same. Full body tats. Blue-and-white bandanas—the colors of El Salvador, where the gang originated; some sticking out of their pockets, some on their heads. All Latino.

But in other ways, they're different. Like the biggest one, who favors his right leg. Suggestion of an injury to the left. I'll remember that if I have to take him down. Another one has a healed bullet hole in his neck. I can tell because I have a similar scar on my arm. Scars are often more tender than regular skin. Offer easy access to pain.

I continue to assess weak spots. I decide that my biggest threat is probably the smallest one, who bounces back and forth on the pads of his feet. Ready. Eager to get to me. And probably the quickest.

"We've been waiting for you to show back up," one says.

Good.

"*¿Hablas español?*"

"Of course, I speak Spanish, *puto.*"

He smiles.

"That fight," he says, never taking his eyes off of me. "You do that often?"

"*No. Sólo contigo.*"

He doesn't need to know that I'm lying. That I've fought many times.

"*Mentiroso,*" he says.

He's calling me out on my deception. With good reason. I shrug.

They're getting the point now. That I have something to hide. They just don't know what.

They'll never know what.

Not until I find Wink.

This is what they want, anyway. Members who can fight. Members who come from something dark. They don't accept guys with picture-perfect pasts. They'd never survive this lifestyle. They need danger, they need to recruit guys who can handle it.

"You belong to someone?" the big guy asks.

But they already know the answer.

"No," I confirm.

He smirks. "We should change that."

Two of them lower their guns. Realizing that I'm not going to attack them without being provoked. Not like last time.

"Why'd you fight us?" he asks.

I've decided that he's the leader. But who, I wonder, is *his* leader?

My mind flashes to Wink.

"*Porque estas en mi camino,*" I reply.

They got in my way. As far as they know, it's as simple as that.

Nothing is as simple as that.

He laughs. "*Sí,* you'd fit in just fine. Question is, do you want to?"

They're asking first. Do I want to join them?

"What's in it for me?" My words are making my act all the more believable. I know exactly what I want.

His smile disappears.

"We'll let you leave here alive."

Figured it'd be like that. Either I join. Or I die. It's the same choice they gave Diego.

I won't go that easily. This is the part where I deliver my message.

"I wanna meet your leader first."

His proud chest puffs out. "You're lookin' at him."

"The one above you," I clarify.

His eyes narrow. Suspicious. "*¿Por qué?*"

"Because I'm not gonna be some lowly fight guy. If I'm gonna join, I want in deep."

It's not a lie. It's the only way I'll find Wink.

"Don't think I care what you want," he snarls.

I'm provoking him. Basically telling him he's nothing. Just someone low down on a chain.

This time I do smile.

And then I hit him. Fast. My knuckles smash into his cheek. Taking them all by surprise. Before they realize what's happened, I have my gun trained on his forehead. Directly between the eyes.

He stiffens. His breathing speeds up.

His guys draw near, circling tight around us.

"Don't," I warn, clicking off the safety.

They get the message. Back up.

"Here's the deal," I say to the guy in front of me. "You're gonna go back to your leader. Tell him he has a chance at a strong recruit. But only if I get to meet him. Skip all this bullshit of startin' from the bottom."

"And if I don't?" he says, eyes steel.

I laugh. Menacing. "Then I pull the trigger."

He watches my finger tighten.

"You won't shoot," he says, but I hear his indecision.

"You wanna try me?"

I've shot someone before. In Cuba. A cartel member came for us, *mi familia*, demanding that *mi papá* hand over his oldest sons for recruit. When *mi papá* said no, they went for him, their fists crunching his ribs. I didn't think twice. I ran to where our guns were hidden. Grabbed one. Remembering what *mi papá* had taught me, I aimed. And shot. One guy came away clutching his leg. Bleeding. Smiling like an animal. He wasn't mad that I'd shot him. He was *glad*. He saw it as potential.

They let *mi papá* go. Turned to me. *That one*, the cartel member said in Spanish. We'll be back tomorrow for the two oldest and that one, he'd promised.

They wanted the twins because they were teenagers, old enough to train. And they wanted me because I showed something they liked. A willingness to shoot.

He hobbled away with the others.

That's the last day I lived in Cuba. *Mi papá* didn't hesitate to leave everything behind. Knowing that if he didn't, he'd lose his sons to a cartel.

The gang member's eyes waver. Deciding.

Moment of truth. Silence is a thick blanket descending on the air around us.

"I'll see what I can do," he says to the barrel of my gun.

I quickly spin the gun at the others. A warning for them to let me go. They step back. Allow me an opening. I take it. Jump in my truck and gun the engine. I drive away, hoping that this is the key that will help me infiltrate their gang.

The exact chance I need to take Wink down.

15
melissa

I dial Faith's number and wait for the phone to ring.

The whole time I think, *I wonder what she's doing at this exact moment.*

Does she ever see the phone ringing and not answer it on purpose?

Do I remind her of the boy she lost back in the States?

Why won't she answer more often?

Maybe this time will be different.

It isn't.

I knock hard enough that a middle-aged woman pops her head out of a door down the hall. When she sees that I'm not knocking on her hotel door, she shuts it.

I sigh, disappointed. Javier's not here.

I try knocking one more time.

Nothing.

I already searched the beach. He wasn't there either.

Where are you, Javier?

The *ding* of elevator doors followed by several people laughing catches my attention. I look up. Bingo.

Out steps Javier and his friends. I met some of them at a

club a while back. I glance at the guy next to Javier, who looks like he could be his brother.

Javier's smiling at something they say and even though I have no part in their conversation, I smile, too. I like the way he looks now. Not so . . . sad.

"Hey," his friend says. Takes in my outfit. A tight sundress. Hair in a messy bun.

Javier looks up. Eyes lock with mine.

"Nice," his friend mumbles.

Javier glares at his friend.

Grin from the other guy. "Relax, man. She's yours, I get it."

"I'm not his," I say. Impulse.

Javier's buddies laugh.

"Sure," says the one that looks like his brother.

Javier comes up and puts an arm around me, contradicting my statement.

"What are you doing here?" he asks.

His buddies lean against the wall, all in board shorts, bottlenecks in their hands. A couple of them are carrying twelve packs.

"Coming to see you," I say.

He runs a hand down my back. I shiver.

"If you're gonna make out right here, then at least give me the keys," his maybe-brother says.

"He looks like you," I point out.

"That's 'cause he's my brother."

Thought so.

"Pedro, this is Melissa." Javier introduces us. "Melissa, this is everybody."

He goes through a list of several names. I've forgotten them all already, except for his brother.

"Happy birthday," I say, extending my hand to shake Pedro's. "And nice to meet you."

Pedro takes my hand and kisses the back of it, staring at Javier with a wicked grin.

Javier yanks my body closer to his, which pulls my hand out of Pedro's grasp.

"Just what I thought," Pedro says, but he isn't talking to me.

Javier and his brother have a staring match, some unspoken conversation.

I glance at Javier. He doesn't look happy.

"We goin' in or what?" Javier's friend asks. He looks at me. "On second thought, what about your room, Pedro?"

Thunder booms outside. I'm guessing that's why they're choosing to hang out in the room instead of on the beach. I'm off today. It would have been too slow to make money with no one braving the Florida summertime storm, anyway.

"Eduardo has a girl up there. He'll kick our asses if we barge in," Pedro says.

"Do you need me to leave?" I ask, feeling like an intruder.

"No," Javier says immediately, to the amusement of his friends.

"Looks like both rooms will be busy," one mumbles.

I don't miss his insinuation.

"I was just going," I say.

The last thing I need is for them to think I'm only here for that.

"No, you weren't." Javier's words in my ear.

I can't leave when he looks at me like that.

"And if you ever talk about Melissa like that again, Ramon, I'll fucking kill you."

His friend shuts up, but doesn't stop smiling.

Javier's hands leave me. Fish in his pockets. He comes up with a room key. Unlocks the door. Everyone pushes past us, finding spots to sit. The couch. A chair in the corner. Bar stools. I don't know where I fit in this. There are plastic patio chairs, but not really any space to put them in the living room. His brother grabs one, shoves it in the only free area left, leaving just one chair.

"I should go," I say.

Javier takes off his hat. Runs fingers through his messy hair. "Not a chance. So don't even think about it."

I kind of love his demandingness.

"But there's nowhere for me to sit," I point out.

Except the bed, my mind tells me.

"I don't care. I want you here," Javier says. "One of them can stand if you need to sit. Don't go."

I smile. "Okay."

Javier leads me straight to the bedroom and my heart spasms. He pulls the hideaway doors shut just as one of his friends turns on the living room television. We're officially alone on this side.

"What'd I tell you?" A friend says from the other side of the door.

Javier's gaze darkens. "Did I just hear what I think I did, Ramon?"

"Nope," Ramon answers through the closed doors. Muffled laughs.

The television volume turns higher. A game's on. Soccer, from the sounds of it.

"Sorry about them," Javier says, opening the blinds.

The dark sky casts an eerie shadow across the bedroom. Lightning flickers like camera flashes going off. Capturing a moment between Javier and me.

"You look too sexy, *mami*," Javier says, crossing the room. "You in this dress is bad news around my friends."

I glance down at my dress. Simple. But I'd be lying if I said I didn't dress to catch his attention.

"And even though they're good people, they're *hombres* and they look," he says.

"You don't like them looking?" My voice is innocence mixed with a challenge.

Pieces of loose hair fall into Javier's eyes. He swipes them away. Pulls me against his chest.

"No, I don't," he says.

I like the way he claims me in front of his friends. The way he claims me now. No shame.

Not like the day I saw you with family on the beach.

"You don't like them touching me either," I point out, thinking of the way he yanked me away from Pedro.

Javier's muscles clench against me.

"Not one bit," he says.

The television is loud. I jump when the guys suddenly yell, "Goal!"

Javier laughs. "We like soccer," he says. "You like sports?"

The fact that he has to ask reminds me how little he knows me.

"A lot," I admit.

Javier's eyes light up. "Do you play?"

"Probably not as good as you," I admit. "But yeah, I know the basics."

He shakes his head, smiling. "A chick who plays soccer? I've won the lottery."

"Hardly," I say. Quick to knock him down a peg. I'm not the whole package.

If he only knew.

"What happened the other day?" I ask, not able to shake the thought. "When I saw you with your family on the beach."

Javier freezes. His hand stops its journey up my ribs. I love when he touches me like this, but I have to know.

"Let's not talk 'bout that," he says.

I know what it's like to not want to talk about things.

I swallow my pride. "Were you waiting for that girl?"

Javier looks me in the eyes. "No. Is that what you thought?"

I nod.

"I definitely wasn't waiting on her. I had just met her."

Good. "So why didn't you want me there?"

He winces. "I did want you there."

"No, you didn't," I say. "So what was the deal?"

"What's the deal with your stomach?" he says.

I step back. He didn't just say that to me. He didn't just come out and ask me. You can't outright ask a person about something so personal. Doesn't he realize what this means?

I have an urge to run.

"Not that," I say.

"You tell me and I'll tell you," he offers.

My hands tremble. Anger announces itself in the form of tremors.

"You can't ask me that," I say, my voice shaky.

"Whoa," Javier says, stepping toward me. "Are you okay?"

"No," I reply. "No, Javier. I am not okay. It is not okay to ask me that. You can't do that ever again."

His hands go up. A peace offering.

"Sorry." His voice is gentle. "Didn't realize it was this big."

I don't stop him when he approaches me.

"I'm going to touch you now," he whispers. "But not on your stomach."

I can't move.

"I don't know if someone hurt you," Javier says, his jaw tight. "Or what happened, but I'm here. I won't push it again. I promise."

And I believe him.

He pulls my head into his chest. Wraps me in his arms.

"I'm sorry," I say. "But you just can't . . . I don't know how . . . I'm not ready. . . ."

"It's fine," he interrupts.

"Thank you," I say. "And thank you for yesterday, too. I actually came here to thank you for saving me from that jerk on the beach. You broke his nose, by the way."

"I know," he says. "He deserved it."

"True." I sigh into him. "He told the hotel that he expected them to pay for his medical bills. When they pointed out that there were numerous witnesses to his behavior, he dropped it."

"I hope I never see him again," Javier says.

I have a feeling that Javier wouldn't hesitate to defend me again.

"So," I say, lifting my mouth to his. Only an inch apart. "Thank you."

The door flies open. "Hey, man. You mind if I take a shower? *Estoy cubierto en arena.*"

It's Ramon again. Javier jumps away from me. Our moment, shattered. He chases after his friend.

"What's wrong with you?" Javier says, tripping over friends in the living room. "You can't even knock?"

Ramon runs into the bathroom and locks the door.

"Gotta come out sometime," Javier threatens.

Javier's right, Ramon is ridiculous. But also, it's nice to see Javier get worked up over our interrupted moment.

Javier says something to his friends in Spanish.

One of them looks at me, mumbling under his breath. "Ramon's a dead man."

"Come on," I say, lacing my fingers with Javier's, pulling him toward the living room. "Let's watch the game."

I don't know what I'm doing. Holding his hand. Leaning into him. It feels right.

Javier looks down at our hands and smiles. The only seat available is the couch corner, where Ramon left. And the soaked chair outside, getting rained on.

Javier sits down on the couch and pats his lap, a sly grin on his face.

"You want me to sit there?" I ask. Grin back.

His friends stare at me.

"Damn, dude," one says. "You need us to go?"

"No," I answer, never taking my eyes off of Javier. "We'll watch the game with you."

Javier's breathing deepens as I lower myself into his lap. My back presses against the arm of the couch and his chest.

"*Mami,*" Javier whispers into my ear. "You're so beautiful."

He kisses my shoulder. My hair hides his affection. His fingers travel up my legs. I could let this go there, where I know his mind is. I could let him touch me like this and I'd love every minute. I'd love it when he leans in to meet my lips. When his hands roam other parts of me.

"Watch the game or I'm going to sit between your friends," I say playfully.

"The hell you will," one of them says. "I don't have a death wish."

I laugh. Javier lets his hands rest on my legs.

"This isn't over," Javier whispers to me.

I can't erase my smile.

"No, it's not," I confirm.

It's only just begun.

16
Javier

Two days.

I remind myself how long I have left at the beach. White sand and crashing waves and Melissa. I need to make it count. I need to spend as much time as possible with her because I don't know what will happen when I leave.

I offended Melissa when I asked about Faith the first time she came to my room. That much was clear by her quick departure afterward. Lately, I'm trying not to make the same mistake. I'm working on pushing the thought of Diego to the outskirts of my mind when I'm with Melissa. And honestly? It's not that hard anymore.

Now that I feel her touch.

Now that she's held my hand.

Now that I've practically branded her as mine in front of my friends.

At first, I only knew the day in the water. I remembered the Melissa that was attached to Faith. I didn't think of her as separate.

I do now.

And it makes all the difference. I wonder about her stomach. I think about the way she gets a look of absolute terror anytime anyone touches her there. Like the guy I hit. I could have killed that guy. And reality is, it's not cool to touch any girl that doesn't want it, but especially not a girl that I'm starting to fall for.

I need to know what Melissa's hiding. I need to know more. I need to gain her trust. Two reasons. One, I want her to know I like her. Two, I need to ask about Faith again. The Faith part can wait a little longer. But not much longer.

"Mr. Reyes, would you like to participate in this discussion, too?" asks my summer school teacher.

Reyes, the name passed down from *mi papá*. The name that doesn't match Diego's. Good thing. MS-13 will never know we're related. Not without close inspection. Diego's *mamá* and *mi mamá* were sisters. We took our fathers' names. This difference might save my life.

"Would *you* like to participate in this discussion?" I fire back at the teacher. " 'Cause most of the time it seems like you don't wanna be here either."

I smile. It's the truth. He wants to give me a hard time for zoning out? He's not one to talk.

The teacher tenses. Hands on his desk, looking me in the eyes.

"I'm not the one failing," he says. Smiles back.

Asshole.

"And I'm not the one who has nothin' better to do with his time than sit in this boring class. At least I was ordered to take this class. What's your excuse?"

"That's it," the teacher says. "Get out. I'll be sending a message to your parents later."

Gladly. I grab my books and leave. I'm not looking forward to *mi mamá* getting that message, but it's already done. I've got something planned for today, anyway.

I jump in my truck and turn the key.

Just a few more classes, I remind myself.

And then it's over.

"Where are you taking me?" Melissa asks, hopping into my truck.

"The gas station first," I say.

She laughs. "I agree to go on a date with you and the gas station is your idea of a good time?"

"No." I grin. "I'm takin' you to the gas station because I had summer school at dawn o' clock and I didn't have time to fill the tires with air and check the oil. This is an old truck."

"Do you usually do this before every date?"

She's messing with me. I like it. "No, because I don't date."

Melissa arches a brow. "You don't date?"

"Well, depends on what you see as datin'," I reply. "Parties. Late nights at clubs. That sort of thing."

"And we're doing what?"

"Going somewhere—" I pause, trying to think of the right word. "Nicer."

I don't know what to call the place I decided on. Fun. Different. A date during the day. That's big for me.

"Got it." She smiles. "So you're taking me on a real date."

Her smile twists me up.

"Something like that," I say. "Did you bring what I asked?"

Melissa opens a purse that reminds me of a zebra, all patchwork stripes.

"This one should work." She hands me a CD. "But just in case you don't like that one, I have another."

"Mixed?" I ask.

"Yep." Her seat belt clicks. "I'm not sure what you're into."

I'm into you.

"Can you tell me again why we need a CD?" she asks.

The CD player was the one new investment that I bothered to put into this old truck.

I shift into gear. "Because you're coming on a road trip with me."

"So you needed good music to listen to?"

"Exactly."

I make a quick stop at the gas station to check the tire pressure. Add air. Check the oil. It's fine. I hop back in. Put the CD in.

"You can learn a lot 'bout a person by what type of music they listen to," I say.

And that's the point. I want to get to know Melissa better. We have two hours. There and back. No other distractions. Windows down. Radio up. We ride.

"I want to know you better," I say.

"You sure?"

The way she says it digs at me.

Why wouldn't I want to know her?

"Do you not want me to?" I ask.

"You may not want to," she mumbles.

I hear every word. Her fingers find the volume knob and turn it up like it can drown out her worries. The beat plays.

"Nice," I say.

I recognize the first song. It's in Spanish. A guy singing about how the heart has no face. Doesn't matter what you look like on the outside.

But the next song throws me off.

"Country?"

Melissa doesn't seem like the country type.

"Lyrics." Is her only response.

I listen carefully. It starts off talking about lightning across the sky. The sound. The image it creates. I picture the swollen clouds. Hear thunder in the beat.

It's saying something about a girl's daddy.

And I know. I know then that Melissa is letting me in without actually opening the door. If I want to listen. If I pay attention. There's a storm coming in this girl's life. The singer sounds like she's in pain with every word. It talks about sins.

I have sins, too.

In the song, the windows burst with the force of the wind. The wind screams at her to take cover because this thing that's coming is way bigger than she can handle alone. And this man called Daddy is the force that brought the storm.

And this girl?

She's Melissa.

I'm sure of it.

If this song is her way of letting me in, then I already know one thing: Her dad is bad news. He hurt her. I'm not sure how. Emotionally? Physically? There are so many different types of hurt. But her pinched look and clenched jaw makes me wonder if she's fighting a memory. Most likely of him. If I'm reading the song right. If I'm reading her right.

I think I am.

Before I can say anything, the next song plays. Upbeat. Not anything like the tone of the last one. And I'm lost in this song, too, because Melissa is telling me so much. If I speak, I might miss the words that tell her story.

The song says she's still into a guy.

The corners of my lips tug into a grin.

Does she mean me?

I take my eyes off the highway for a moment. Find Melissa staring directly at me. She winks. I laugh.

She's brilliant because after such a heavy song, she springs out with this and we're both smiling. Knowing, but not talking. I shouldn't have to shift for a while so I grab her hand.

When the song ends, a new one with an acoustic guitar plays. It's interesting. It talks about comparing scars. I think Melissa might know about scars in the way that I know about scars. The kind that cut you up inside and make you bleed internally and no one ever knows because you don't let them in. Those kind of scars.

Then it says something about holding hands and I look down at our fingers. Together. So different. So right.

And this here, now, this is life. How it's meant to be, I think.

I've never done this. Listened to music with a girl.

Another country song comes and a laugh slips out of my lips because I don't know any other time that I'd listen to country music. And the craziest? I think I might like it a little bit.

"Can't believe I'm listenin' to country," I say.

"You wanted to know," she replies. "Here you go."

So the songs *are* about her life.

Her other hand, the one that I'm not holding, hangs out the open window of my truck. Her head lolls back on the seat. Eyes closed. Sunglasses on. *Mi hermosa.*

The next song is summery and free. Melissa moves her hand through the air like a wave. A smile yanks on her lips. The song says that the guy looks like bad news, but she's got to have him anyway.

I can't get enough of this girl who gives me one dose of serious with three parts fun.

"She's gotta have him, huh?" I say.

She watches my grin. "Yes."

We stay like this. Driving. Sometimes holding hands. Breaking when I need to shift gears. We pull off of the highway two hours later. We listened to both CD's. And part of the first one again.

"Did every song mean something?" I ask as we drive into the parking lot.

Melissa looks around. "Yes."

"So those lyrics," I say.

"Are my life through other people's lips," she finishes.

I jump out and open Melissa's door for her.

"Will I ever know your story through your lips?"

She shrugs. "Will I ever know yours?"

"You're avoidin' the question," I point out.

"Because you already got part of me now," she replies. "I expect a CD with songs that describe *you* next time."

I smile. "Deal."

We walk to the entrance.

"The zoo?" Melissa asks. "You're taking me on a date to the zoo?"

She likes it, I can tell. Her hands get fidgety and she rocks from side to side. We approach the ticket booth.

"Not just any zoo," I say. "This zoo is ranked best in the US."

And I've never been. I don't know, I thought maybe it'd be something Melissa would like. I was right, I guess, because she wraps her arms around me and says, "Thank you."

I buy two tickets. They're feathery light in my hand like they can fly us away from our problems.

For a few hours, I believe they can.

17
melissa

Water shoots out of a manatee fountain like a rocket taking off. Everywhere I look, kids play in fountains. Some in their swimsuits, some in regular clothes. The fountains look refreshing on this baking day. I wonder if we'd be allowed in them. I wonder if Javier would have the guts to run through them with me.

I'm pretty sure he would. Because he's fearless like that. Because he doesn't seem like the type to care what people say or how they'd look at us, two teenagers making the best of a moment.

Javier grabs a map from the directory. Unfolds it. It's bent and pleated. I can already imagine using it like a fan.

"Where do you wanna start?" he asks, showing me the map.

I pull my hair into a high bun. Study the map. The zoo is huge. Primates and reptiles. Petting areas and shows. Restaurants and shops. Even a few rollercoasters.

"I have no idea," I reply.

Javier studies the map, too. "Left or right?"

"Left," I say automatically. "Wanna start there and work our way around?"

It'll take hours.

"*Sí.*"

We take off in the direction of an animal that smells like a farm. I wrinkle my nose. Pigs rolling in mud.

"Let's see the bird show," I suggest.

We're walking down a path called Zoo Boulevard. I'm struck with how normal I feel. For the first time in a while—since the diagnosis, since my best friend left—I feel normal.

Like in this moment, I don't have cancer.

Like for these hours, Javier is mine.

I don't want to share him with grief. Usually, I feel Sorrow's presence radiating off of Javier like a heat wave. Muggy and suffocating and so, so heavy. But now Javier is smiling.

"The bird show doesn't start for fifteen minutes," he says.

"We can wait," I suggest.

Something grabs my attention. A child. He's holding his mother's hand, ice cream in his other palm. But he's letting the ice cream melt because something else has captivated him.

What's more important than ice cream to a child?

I'm lost in his face, his mouth open in wonder. I follow the direction of his pointing finger. A zookeeper is walking down the path, an owl on her shoulder. The owl is bigger than her head. Colored every shade of brown. Its feathers reflect the sun like oil. The owl doesn't move, save for the blinking of its eyes. But it's there and it's real. The boy can't believe how amazing this is, says his expression.

It's heading toward us.

"Come with me," I say instinctively, taking Javier's hand.

I grab my camera.

The zookeeper stops. The bird walks down her arm. Stops

on her wrist. As long as the flash is off, the zookeeper allows people to take pictures with the owl on her hand. I wait patiently for three people in front of us to finish.

It's our turn. Javier puts an arm around me just as I lift the camera and snap a photo of us with the owl. Our first photo ever.

Memories.

I look at what I've captured. The owl, eyes open and clear. Me and three-fourths of Javier's face. The other part is cut off by the edge of the screen. It's perfect.

The zookeeper moves on to other people waiting for their chance at a photo. I wonder if it will be their first picture with the person next to them, too.

"Let's get a snow cone," I say. I've spotted the solitary cart serving flavored ice. I'm already dripping sweat.

I check out the flavor selection. It lists interesting names like Rainbow Melon, Lime Banana, Peach Apple. Things that I wouldn't have normally thought could go well together.

Like me and Javier.

"I'll have a Strawberry Coconut," I order.

Javier thinks about it a second, then says, "Lemon Grape."

With our weird flavors, we sit on a bench and wait until it's time to see the bird show. Ice melts in my mouth. Numbs my tongue. Gives me a brain freeze and red fingers. Javier's tongue is purple. I laugh. Snap a picture of him.

"Lucky yours is red," he jokingly says.

I can't eat it fast enough. Ice melts into cold, flavored water.

"You see that couple?" Javier asks.

"The ones in the big hats?" I try to figure out which couple he means. There are a lot of people here.

"No, the girl in the pink shirt and the guy with the backward hat."

I shift my gaze. Spot them. "What about them?"

Javier wraps a napkin around the bottom of his snow cone so it doesn't drip onto his clothes. "What do you think of them?"

"Am I supposed to know them?" I ask. "Do you know them?"

I don't recognize their faces, though they seem to be about our age.

"Nope," he answers. "But she's Latina and he's a *gringo*."

Like us, but backward.

I wait to see where Javier is going with this.

"What do you think about them mixing cultures?"

"Obviously," I say, running a finger down his arm, "I think it's fine."

Is Javier asking if I care that he's Latino? Because I don't.

"I think it's beautiful, even," I add.

"Some people wouldn't see it that way," Javier says.

"And some people don't like strawberry coconut snow cones either." I shrug. "People like different things. That's allowed."

"True," he replies. "But what happens when those people go further than not liking it? What happens when they discourage it?"

He leans away from my face. Glances far off.

"Then we don't make them eat strawberry coconut snow cones and they don't tell us how to live our lives." I try to make a joke out of it, but Javier is serious.

His shirt slips down his shoulder just a bit and I catch a

glimpse of his tatted up chest. Some people don't like tattoos. Some people don't like mixed cultures. I'm wondering what that has to do with us.

"Some people," Javier says, locking his eyes with mine. "Even hate it."

Does he mean someone in particular? Because it seems like there's more to his comment. It's in the way that he won't drop it. In the way that he seems bothered by these people that aren't us.

"Who hates it, Javier?"

"I don't know," he replies.

And my first thought is: He's lying.

His eyes are closed off and his hand is slack in mine.

"I don't care who sees us together," I tell him.

Maybe he needs to hear me say it. Because by this point, I know that Javier must be talking about more than that couple. What he's really talking about . . .

Is us.

It smells like rain is coming.

Bossy clouds force the sun to hide behind them. The sky changes from cobalt blue to ashen gray. I don't feel any rain, but the horizon tells me that it's imminent.

My legs are tired from walking for hours. We've seen monkeys and snakes and hippos and zebras and bears and lions and penguins and basically every animal that the zoo has to offer. I've even fed a giraffe, its long tongue like sandpaper against my skin.

My hair is soaked with sweat. I'm glad that I opted against makeup today because it would have only smeared in this heat. Even Javier is tired. His shirt is nothing but wet, sweaty cotton.

We've stopped at a garden. Taken a seat on a wooden swing. I kick my legs to make it go higher. We're working on our second snow cones. Mine is mint mango.

"Do you care about our cultural differences?" Javier asks, taking me by surprise.

His voice is normal. Indifferent. I think this is what he was hinting at earlier, when he mentioned the other couple. I think this is the question it all boiled down to.

"No," I answer honestly. "Do you?"

The swing makes my stomach flop. I reach for Javier's eyes with my own. Find truth in his stare. His face is so many things. Gorgeous. Nerve wrecking. Perfect. Terrifying. Because I could lose myself in his eyes, find myself in his mouth.

"No," he replies.

He makes my stomach flip worse than the swing.

"Good," I say. Because cultural differences don't matter to me. I don't see a separation between us. He's just Javier and I'm just Melissa and that's perfect enough for me.

"Maybe I used to care," he says. "But things changed with you. You charged in the ocean and intimidated that girl into leavin' so that you could take her place. *Recuerdas?*"

Yes, I remember. Vividly.

"You wrapped your arms around me at *la playa*," he continues.

Javier leans into me. I've suddenly lost my breath and I can't even find the energy to care because it's such a small price to pay for his nearness. The urgency to touch him is overwhelming. My hand closes over his bicep. His eyes drink me in.

"You whispered something to me," he says, voice lowered.

I remember the words I spoke right before I kissed him months back. I repeat them back to him.

"It's about damn time," I murmur.

"*Sí, hermosa.*" His voice is want. "It's 'bout damn time again, isn't it?"

And then,

and then,

and then he kisses me.

It's like I am made of every ember on earth, this moment. It's like I'm burning hotter than the sun, this moment. It's everything I've ever known thrown down ten flights of stairs, this moment, because no one has *ever* kissed me like this.

His lips, so full, so perfect, press into mine. I'm sitting on what I imagine to be the top of the world because nothing is better than this. I am a threadbare girl coming completely apart under his touch. Falling to pieces in his mouth. Dear God. This kiss.

I press harder. I'm clutching fistfuls of his shirt while his fingers close around my hips. Something wet seeps into my flip-flop and I think it must be the snow cone that I dropped when his lips crashed into mine.

Javier is beautiful. Hot breaths and warm hands and heart pounding against mine. His tongue searches mine, deliciously sweet. I taste nothing but lime and Javier and I want to

never

ever

stop.

18
javier

I've never loved someone and despised them so much at the same time. But that's exactly how I feel about *mi mamá* right now. She isn't going to make this easy on me. Not by a long shot.

I try not to stare at Melissa. Serving drinks. Hoping that she doesn't notice me, *mi mamá,* and my two youngest brothers building a sand castle down the beach. It's our last day of vacation, so *mi mamá* insisted on coming out.

"*¿Quién es ella?*" she asks me.

"What girl?" I ask. Play dumb.

Mi mamá's eyes narrow. "You know what girl. The same girl from the other day."

"No clue."

"Lies." Her eyes are hard. Angry. "Don't tell me you like her. Don't even tell me that."

No problem. I don't plan on telling her anything.

My brothers watch our interaction with interest. Antonio and Jair are five. Twins. My younger brothers mostly speak English since that's what's taught in American schools, and since that's what their friends speak. That's what's on television when they watch their favorite cartoons, too.

"Javi, you like a girl?" Antonio asks. He and Jair have been calling me Javi ever since they first learned to speak, when they couldn't pronounce my whole name.

Antonio looks disgusted.

I laugh. His expression cracks the tension.

"You'll probably like girls one day," I say, purposely not answering him.

"Will not!" he says.

"She's pretty," Jair says. He looks at *nuestra mamá* nervously, like maybe he said the wrong thing.

Antonio throws a clump of sand at Jair. "You traitor! You said girls were yucky. Remember how gross they are?"

My brothers were born in the States. It's weird to think of them as American. They have problems like whether or not they think girls are gross. Not things like whether or not they'll eat today. Not real problems like I grew up with. Not things like wondering if they'll live or die that day. I'm not sure they've ever even heard the sound of a bullet ripping through the barrel of a gun.

I hope they never do.

"But she is pretty!" Jair fires back. "Right, Javi?"

Of course, she is. But saying that in front of *mi mamá* isn't smart.

"You gonna answer him?" *mi mamá* asks.

"Nope," I say, cause I'm not walking into that trap.

"*Mi hijo,* you're smarter than that. No *gringas.*"

Mi mamá is convinced that anyone who is not Latina won't understand our heritage. But I don't understand her logic because here we are, Latinos, living in another country, learning the language and ways of a different heritage. We certainly aren't accustomed to beach adventures, full stomachs, English, good schools. But we're learning, aren't we?

If we can learn their ways, why can't someone else learn ours?

"If there's something going on, end it now," *mi mamá* demands.

I can't end things with Melissa. They've only just started.

I watch the way *mi mamá's* eyes burn with anger. I'm disgracing her at this moment. I can hear her unspoken words. That this isn't what she's raised her sons to be, people who stray from tradition. Everything she's ever done to try and give us a good life. And all she asks is that we date within our own nationality. Even though I haven't admitted to liking Melissa, it hurts that *mi mamá* would be disappointed in me. But also, I'm pissed.

I'm angry because why does it matter so much who I date? Why should that be a reason to be disappointed in me? I've never criticized her choices. I've tried my best to accept our American life. I've struggled through the shock of adaptation. And I haven't complained about it. It is what it is.

Mi mamá doesn't let up. "*¿Me escuchas?*"

"*Sí*, I hear you," I reply, annoyed. "There's nothing goin' on. I already told you."

I hate this moment, lying to her, the fact that I have to lie.

I stand up. Walk away from *mi mamá*. I stop at the water's edge, bucket in hand. It takes a few seconds for the bucket to fill with salt water for our sandcastle moat.

"Javi!" Antonio calls. "Shells!"

"And seaweed!" Jair adds.

We're building the world's best castle towers, according to them, which look more like a pile of sloppy sand. Good thing their imaginations see our creation as something else.

"I won't forget," I tell them. They need me to get shells and seaweed to decorate our castle. "But what do you say?"

"Please!" they yell.

"*En español*," I clarify.

"*¡Por favor!*"

Since my brothers prefer English, I sometimes make them answer me *en español* just to make sure they haven't forgotten how to speak it.

I take an extra minute to return. Give *mi mamá* a chance to forget about Melissa.

I try not to look at Melissa. Even though all I can think about is the way her lips were like fire on mine yesterday.

"Here," I say, placing the bucket next to Jair and Antonio. I lay a few shells and a clump of slimy seaweed on the sand.

They smile like I've given them a million bucks. And I wonder.

Was I ever this happy?

Probably not. I don't think Cuba allowed people to know happiness. Not the part I came from, at least.

"Crab!" Antonio yells.

I look down. There's a tiny crab in the seaweed. It's no big deal. I pick it out and toss it away from the kids. Doesn't matter, though. They're already worked up.

"Crab, crab, crab!" Antonio yells.

"Okay, okay," I say. "It's gone."

They don't like crabs. Antonio won't even go in the ocean because he doesn't like the creatures that live there.

His small voice carries far. Far enough to catch Melissa's attention. Now she's staring at me. Mouth twisting into the biggest grin.

My heart explodes. *Dios mío,* she's gorgeous.

I check to see if *mi mamá* caught me staring. Yep.

Here we go.

Melissa walks toward us. Face full of smiles. An empty drink tray in her hand. Her swimsuit looks ridiculously good. A tiny brown one-piece with strings lacing it up the sides. I want to untie her.

The brightness of the sun glistens off of the sweat that covers her skin. Sand sticks to her feet and calves.

"Here comes Javi's girlfriend," Antonio whispers, snickering.

Mi mamá's eyes cut into mine.

I'm hoping for a chance to fix this situation, to somehow avoid the collision that's about to happen.

But it's too late.

Everything is ready to combust and there's nothing I can do about it except hope that I still have a place to live and a girl to see. And hope that I can somehow keep them separate. Because I wouldn't put it past *mi mamá* to get angry enough to ask me to leave our home. Liking a non-Latina is the highest form of treachery. To *mi mamá*, it's like I'm spitting on our family, where we've come from and what we've been through, everything.

Melissa is close enough to catch *mi mamá's* words.

"You again," she says, staring at Melissa. "How do you know my son?"

Melissa's head tilts. Her eyes squint, looking at me strangely. I silently beg her to keep serving drinks. No luck.

"We're—" Melissa pauses like she's not sure what to call us. Then she sees me, the caution on my face.

Don't, I mouth, hoping she'll understand.

Her eyes widen. She's quiet. A couple seconds too long.

"I don't really," Melissa finally says. "I've seen him at school. I was just coming over to see if you need any drinks."

That's not why Melissa came over, but she seems to understand enough to not let on how well she knows me.

"Maybe fruit punch for the kids?" Melissa suggests. Fake smile. "Or snow cones. Too bad we don't have any of those here. Snow cones would be perfect, don't you think?" This time she directs the question right at me.

Snow cones. Our conversation about how some people don't like Latinos and Caucasians together. We had that conversation while eating snow cones.

Is she asking me what I think she is? If so, she's more observant than I thought.

"You're exactly right," I say, confirming. "Snow cones would be perfect."

Melissa's face falls.

"We don't need any snow cones or fruit punch," *mi mamá* says.

I try to catch Melissa's eye, but she won't look at me. Unlike *mi mamá.*

"Okay. Have a good day then," Melissa replies.

And leaves.

I want to go after her, but I know better. One of these days, I've got to change *mi mamá's* mind about her only-date-Latinas rule.

Or deal with the consequences of breaking it.

melissa 19

I watch the way Javier moves, kicking up sand beneath his feet like tiny dust storms. The sun glares down on the ocean, shimmering. The beach is hot as ever. One hundred degrees, according to the drink station thermostat. I wipe my forehead with the back of my arm. Keep serving alcohol as though I don't see him.

"Fuzzy navel," I say, handing the drink to an older woman with skin etched in wrinkles, looking like cracked desert land.

She hands me money. No change. Nice tip. Easy. On to the next customer. Maybe if I focus on drinks, I'll quit thinking of Javier.

He stops. Flags down Brock. I watch out of the corner of my eye as they exchange words. Javier smiles. Heads straight to a cabana in my section.

He shouldn't be here. His vacation is over, as of yesterday. *And apparently, so are we.*

I march up to Brock. "What did he say?"

I don't want to be someone that Javier hides.

Brock finishes pouring a drink for another customer. "He asked where your section is."

I set my tray down. Fill it with the next order. Blue

drinks with miniature yellow umbrellas, an orange wedge garnish. I stare at the drinks, at a loss for words. Javier asked for my section. Which probably means that he wants to talk about what happened with his mom. How could he make it seem like I mean nothing? Like I'm not even worth mentioning?

Or maybe he wants to ignore the situation altogether. Just keep touching me and kissing me and pretending it's okay that he won't admit he likes me. No big deal, right?

Wrong.

"Do you want me to run your drinks?" Brock asks.

Condensation forms on the glass, sliding down in a lazy crawl.

"I've got it."

I drop off the frilly drinks. Accept cash. Javier is in my line of sight. There are so many things I want to say to him.

Why do I matter only when your mom doesn't know about me?

Your lips, your lips, your lips, they kill me.

Why are you showing up here like everything is fine?

You look beautiful today.

Go away!

Stay.

Javier catches my eye. Studies me with intensity. I lose my train of thought. Find anger in its place. I march over to him.

"Why didn't you tell me?" I ask. Not nicely. "You should have told me at the zoo. Your mom doesn't like us together. This is your mom, Javier. That's kind of a big deal, don't you think?"

I can't see Javier's eyes through his sunglasses. I can't see anything but the sight of his naked stomach. Blue board shorts reach to his knees. Bare feet, sandals wedged in sand.

He dusts off the cabana seat. "Would you have understood?"

"I don't know, Javier," I say, a bite to my tone. "Would you have given me a chance to understand? I mean, how can I possibly understand if you don't even tell me in the first place?"

Javier reaches toward the sand. Picks up a peach shell with white lines running through it like dividers for each bumpy ridge on its back.

"How did you figure it out?" he asks.

Wasn't that hard. "Seemed obvious."

He nods. "Are you mad?"

Hell, yes. "Pretty much."

He considers that. Looks out at the ocean like maybe his answers can be found there.

"I'm sorry."

He says it quietly, eyes cast away. I wonder if he says sorry often. I think not, by the way he delivers it. Not touching me. Not looking my way. Not trying to make his apology seem real. Though, maybe it is. I wouldn't know.

"For when? The first or second time that you blew me off in front of your mom?"

He flinches. "Both."

I'm staring at his profile. I'm wondering what's going through his mind.

"I don't think this is going to work," I say.

I want it to work.

I've caught him by surprise. His face slackens. He turns to me.

"Because I wouldn't tell *mi mamá* about you?"

Because I only have this one life. Because it's already

being threatened by a beast called cancer. I don't want to lose time that I may or may not have on heartbreak, on someone who hides his feelings for me. I want to be someone that you're proud of. I want you to feel the way I do about you.

"Yes," I confirm.

Javier stands.

I don't budge.

Sunglasses move to the top of his head. I'm momentarily stunned by the passion in his eyes.

"You don't think we can work?" he asks, voice low.

I can't make myself look away.

He takes one, two, four steps toward me. Almost touching.

"Answer me," he says.

His eyes never abandon me.

I open my mouth to speak. Lose my nerve. I can't concentrate when he looks at me like this.

Javier reaches a hand to the back of my neck.

I try to fight it. I try to tell my voice to ask him to stop, but the truth is that I don't want him to stop. I'm angry with Javier for not telling his mom about us. I'm angry with him for not telling me about his mom. Even so, I don't want him to stop touching me.

"*Mami*, I think we work just fine. I think I fucked up and should have told you. I'm sorry about that. But that doesn't mean this won't work." He pulls me closer.

"You should have told me," I say. Quietly. Timidly.

Javier's body presses against mine. "Not denying that."

"I'm still not sure if—"

His lips find mine. So tenderly, so softly. His mouth is warm and wet and so inviting. He nips at me, gently, playfully. I nip him back. I feel a small smile form on his lips. And then he kisses me harder.

The tray falls from my hands like a cymbal, clattering against the side of the cabana. I don't care.

I press back. Run my tongue along the soft inside of his lips. He caresses the fleshy outside of mine. I've forgotten about my job. About the people around us.

My eyes squeezed shut, I relish the taste of Javier. Hot and breathy and *please give me more*. I run fingers up his stomach, around his back. He grunts in approval.

His lips leave mine. But only for a second. He kisses my temple, my cheek, back down to my lips.

"We," he says between breaths, "work perfectly, *muñeca*."

Javier's hands travel down my sides, careful to avoid my stomach.

He remembers. He remembers that I have parts of me that I can't discuss. He doesn't push me to explain. Maybe I shouldn't be so hard on Javier for keeping the issue with his mom from me.

I'm not sure how it would work, Javier dating me, his mom hating that her son is with someone who isn't Latina. Because that's what I've gathered so far, that she doesn't like the idea of Javier and me.

I pull away from his lips. "What about your mom?"

"Forget her," he mumbles, reaching for my mouth again.

I take a step back. "Will I always be a secret?"

I hate the way my voice trembles. I have secrets, too, sure. But I'm not sure that they'll stay a secret. I want to tell Javier why he can't touch my stomach. I want to spill my guts until there's nothing left. Then at least he can decide if he really wants me.

"I don't know," he replies.

I bite my lip. Swallow emotion. Voice what's really bothering me. "Am I just a game to you?"

Because I don't have time for that.

"No," he says. "Can't I just kiss you and watch you smile? Can't we just have fun and be together?"

"You can have fun with any girl, Javier. Any Latina girl. Why me?"

"Because I—" he stops. Chucks a shell into the ocean roughly. "Because I need you."

My eyes narrow. "You need me for me? Or for info about Faith?"

He rolls his shoulders. "Both."

And there it is. The simple, yet complicated truth. He needs me because he wants me. And because he wants to learn about what happened to his cousin.

I remember what May said. *Wouldn't you?*

Wouldn't I want to know more about my loved one? Wouldn't I need to pour concrete answers into the holes that pocket an incomplete picture? Yes.

I give in to him. It's a dangerous thing to do. But it's the right thing, I think.

"All right," I say.

Javier relaxes. Folds me into his arms. I find his lips again.

I'd like to be the only reason that Javier sticks around. Not because of unanswered questions, or Faith, or anything else other than me.

Maybe if I give Javier a path to closure, connect him to Faith, I will be.

20
javier

Picking Melissa up from her house has got me on edge. She mentioned having a few sisters and a mom. I've never met a girl's parents before. I'm breaking the rules for Melissa.

I don't usually get involved. I have fun. I play it safe with girls that I never have to call back. Create memories of good times never to be repeated. Nothing solid.

I'm taking a big risk.

I don't have any other choice. I need more info on Diego's death.

Also, I like Melissa.

"Hi," Melissa says, opening the door for me to come in. Smile on her face. I glance at her tiny shorts and loose tank top. My eyes land on her red sneakers.

She looks amazing.

"*Hola, mami,*" I say, pulling her in for a kiss.

She gives me a quick peck, even though I want more. Something smells delicious.

"You cookin' for me?" I joke. " 'Cause I only eat Cuban food. You know how to cook Cuban food?"

She looks embarrassed. "Actually, I *am* cooking. And

no, I don't have the slightest clue how to cook Cuban food, but I'm trying to. You don't have to eat it if you don't want."

I'm an ass.

"I was just joking," I say. "I eat all kinds of food."

She doesn't need to cook for me.

"I thought we were goin' to the park?" I ask.

It was Melissa's idea. Kicking the soccer ball around. She thought I'd like it, which I do.

"Yeah, but I thought maybe we could have a picnic, too?"

Food and soccer. She pretty much nailed it.

"Okay," I say, stepping inside.

The smell reminds me of home. Hot chiles and sweet fried banana. Melissa leads me to the kitchen, where one of her sisters is cooking.

"This is May," Melissa says. "She's helping me."

Four pots sit on top of burners, food inside.

"Hey," I say.

May smiles. "Javier."

"You're late," someone says from behind me.

I turn to find an uptight chick in fancy clothes staring at me. She has Melissa's face.

"What the hell," I mumble under my breath.

"I'm Megan," she says, extending a hand.

Formal. I'm the opposite of formal. This should be fun.

"Javier," I say.

I shake her hand. Her grasp is practically stronger than mine.

"Yeah, I got that," Megan says.

Melissa steps in. "Chill, Megan."

Megan grabs her purse. "Gotta run," she announces.

"Maybe next time you can not be ten minutes late? Then I can actually talk to you."

No, thanks. I'll be late every time if it gets me out of talking to you.

I immediately don't like that sister.

Megan heads out the door.

Melissa rolls her eyes. "Don't mind her. She's different."

A girl I recognize enters the kitchen.

"Concert," I say.

I've met this sister at a concert once. She got me, Diego, and a few of our friends through the front door.

She smiles. "Yeah, you remember that? I'm Monica." Monica looks like Melissa, too, only with more makeup. "How have you been, Javier?"

"Good," I reply.

My eyes slide to the living room. It's done up nicely. Modern furniture. Big TV. Huge flower vases. And lots of space. I don't know what it's like to have space. I share a room with Eduardo and Pedro. Even though they're in college, my family can't afford dorm rooms. My brothers commute to school and I get to know what it feels like to never be alone. I definitely don't have a living room with space like this.

"My mom's not here," Melissa says.

I nod. Walk to the food. May steps aside so that I can peer in. Rice in one pot, beans in another. Chicken simmers in spices. Fried bananas caramelize on low heat.

"Good job," I say, laying a hand on Melissa's back.

I kiss her. She kisses me, too, but just briefly. I watch an embarrassed grin crawl up her face. She glances at May.

May's smiling.

Melissa goes back to the stove, grin attached. I like

watching her cook. The way her eyes draw together as she concentrates on spooning food into Tupperware containers, careful to not spill it.

"We taking that with us?" I motion to the plastic containers full of food.

"If you want," she says.

I help Melissa put the food into a large paper bag. Wave good-bye to May. Monica's on the couch watching TV so I wave to her, too.

"Nice to meet you guys," I say. Open the front door.

That wasn't so bad. First time meeting a girl's family and everything went smoothly. If you don't count the uptight sister. I smile to myself. My rule of never getting serious enough to meet a girl's family? Melissa has smashed it to pieces.

And she's not even Latina.

"You have got to be kiddin' me!"

I yell at Melissa like I would a teammate. I don't hold back. She asked me not to. She said she'd prefer to be treated like an equal. She didn't want any free goals or passes. I didn't plan on it. Competitiveness flows through my veins. I couldn't play nice if I wanted to. Which is why, when Melissa scores her second goal on me, I'm frustrated.

"You lied," I say, out of breath.

She laughs. "What do you mean?"

She bats her eyes like a *princesa*, looking all innocent.

"You said you're not as good as me in soccer," I point out. "Which is a lie."

Melissa is good at soccer. She's more than good. She spins circles around me, even passing the ball through my legs once. Her kicks send the ball flying through the air, almost to be knocked away by the goal post. But she's landed a goal twice now. Both times within millimeters of the top post.

"I'm a little rusty, actually," she says.

Hate to see her when she's been practicing.

"You're crazy," I say, laughing. "You this good at all sports?"

She smiles and runs to me. "Pretty much."

She leans in for the ball. Swipes it up with one hand.

"You hungry?" Melissa asks.

"Definitely," I reply.

Wind tangles Melissa's hair around her face, wrapping her up. The smell of sulfur water is everywhere. Sprinklers go off in the distance, saturating the open fields. We find a picnic table.

"Tell me something you're not good at," I say. Mostly to make myself feel better about getting beaten by a girl.

"School," Melissa answers. "I'm not good at school. I try, but it's just not my thing. I like being outside. I like running. Playing sports. Whatever, as long as I'm not cooped up in a small room staring at books."

I know what she means.

She pulls out Tupperware containers and plastic plates. "I'm not good with stress either."

My attention is hers. "What kind of stress?"

Melissa scoops food.

"The kind that sends my best friend overseas." She hands me a plate. "The kind that leaves my stomach all wrong."

I want to ask about Faith, but I also need to know about Melissa's stomach.

"You wanna talk 'bout it this time?" I'm careful to keep

my voice even. I don't want her to freak out like the last time that I mentioned her stomach.

Melissa takes a bite of chicken. Twirls the fork in her small hand.

"Maybe."

She's not looking at me anymore.

I reach a hand to hers. Slowly. Careful to not push too far.

"What happened to—"

Melissa cuts me off with a sharp glance. Okay, so asking is off limits. I'll have to let her tell me on her own.

She withdraws her hand. Eats in silence for a minute. The food is actually really good. I want to tell her that, but I don't want to ruin the moment that Melissa has started by mentioning her stomach.

She takes a deep breath.

"I have scars, Javier," she blurts.

Her fork drops from her fingers. Rattles against the plate. Her face stills.

Scars? Plural.

From what, Melissa?

I wait for more information. But it never comes.

"I don't have a problem with scars," I tell her.

She picks her fork back up. Scoops food into her mouth. "Let's talk about something else. Like how you need to improve your soccer skills."

She attempts a weak smile.

I don't want to stop talking about Melissa's scars. But she's over talking about it, so it's done.

"Guess I *do* need to work on my skills." I shovel food into my mouth, starving. "This food is *bien*, by the way."

Her face splits into a real smile this time. "Really?"

"*Sí,*" I say, grabbing seconds. "You can cook for me anytime."

"Will you give me Cuban recipes?"

Not so easy. *Mi mamá* is the one with the recipes. And if I ask, I'll have hell to pay. She'll want to know why I need them. She'll ask who they're for.

"I can try," I say. "I'm not the one who cooks at *mi casa.*"

"Your mom cooks?"

I nod.

"Okay," is all she says.

My mom doesn't like Melissa. She doesn't even know her. It shouldn't be like that.

I pull Melissa close. "Thanks for the food."

She touches my cheek. Strokes a finger down my lips.

"You're welcome," she breathes.

I want to know what it's like to have Melissa cook for me again. I want more than a couple dates and info about Faith. I need Melissa in ways that I don't even understand yet. Like the way that I think about her when she's gone. Like how I imagine what it'd be like to touch her body in all the right places. Like how her soccer skills make me want to bring her by *mi casa* to play with my brothers, too. They'd be impressed.

Only, I can't.

I can't bring Melissa to my house because there's no way that *mi mamá* would be cool with it, and I'm not sure how Melissa would take the rejection.

"I like you, Melissa," I say, bringing her lips closer. "Even if you have scars. Even if *mi mamá* doesn't approve. Even though you're so good at soccer that it makes me crazy jealous you have that much talent." She relaxes in my arms.

I don't know how Melissa and I will work together. I'm not even sure that we will. But I want her. And that's enough for now.

She smiles. "Are you gonna talk all night, or are you gonna kiss me?"

Kiss her, of course. So I do.

melissa 21

"So, what happened at the park?" May hammers away with questions the next morning. "Did he like the food? Did you mention the thing about his mom not liking you?"

I rub my eyes. Try to wake up enough to form coherent sentences.

"What the hell, May?" I grumble. Check the clock. "It's nine in the morning."

May sits on the bed beside me. "Who cares about the time? Did he kiss you?"

I roll over. Throw a pillow over my face.

Smother the memories of my dream. Where Faith was still here and we were still friends and, God, why did so many things happen?

Like cancer.

Like Diego dying.

Like Javier becoming mine in a way I've always wished was possible.

That's the only good thing in a list of many that play through my mind.

May yanks the pillow away. "Wake up, sleepy."

"Maybe if you were home last night I could have told you," I say, yawning.

May has never badgered me about guys.

What's new this time, sister?

"I went out with Brock," May says, glancing away quickly. "Now back to you."

Nothing is easy with May and Brock, so I know there's more to her story.

"Javier ate the food. Liked it. He kissed me. His mom doesn't like me because I'm not Latina. Can I sleep now?"

"Fine," May replies. "But you're gonna have to tell me about him eventually."

Why?

"No, I won't," I mumble.

"Yes, you will," she says, a smile in her voice. "Because I know, unlike the other guys you've dated, that you really like this one."

Once again, she's right.

I'm looking at pictures of Faith. We're young. I still have braces, those horrible things. Faith is looking at me like they don't exist. Next. We're at a water park. I have one hand on my hip, another near my mouth. We're laughing. Next. Faith is sitting beside me in the cafeteria at school. Her eyes are downcast. Mine are looking far off. I don't remember who took this picture. I don't remember why. But I'm glad I have it.

I'm flipping through a photo book and wondering what happened to my best friend. I still call her that, but does she call me her best friend, too?

I'm not sure anymore.

I don't know why she won't talk to me. I'll keep trying,

of course I'll keep trying, but that doesn't make it easy. Her rejection.

Faith's refusal to answer the phone is a saw to my heart. Does she realize I'm bleeding out?

Faith's dismissal of the years we built together is a gash that I don't know how to sew together.

Faith has the needle and thread. Faith is the one who needs to make a move.

Here's a secret: Sometimes I stare at her house. At the windows, the rain that splatters against it. I watch her dad and stepmom go in and out. And then I see her little sister, Grace. Grace is a miniature Faith. Chop a little more than a decade of life away and they look identical. Forget about a broken heart, and they're the same. I stare at Grace mostly.

I can't talk to her, though. I can't because the hurt is too much and I won't show that to Grace. She deserves better.

Grace is Faith's clone. If I could go back to that age and be Faith's friend all over again, knowing how it would turn out, would I?

Yes.

It's that simple.

It's that complicated.

The person I never see come out of the house is Faith. Because it's not her house anymore, is it?

I pick up the phone. A bright screen stares back at me. It screams happy colors that feel like a lie against the truth of my mood. I'm not happy that Faith has disappeared on me.

I want my best friend back.

I punch in numbers. Each number brings me one step closer to the hope I hold that Faith will answer. And maybe, just maybe, she'll actually talk to me about something meaningful. Something that lasts more than three minutes.

Maybe even something that doesn't make me sit on my bed and fight back tears this time.

Ring.

This ring has become a horrible reminder of the friend I've lost.

Ring.

She's not going to answer.

Ring, ring.

I'll have to leave another message that she may or may not ever hear.

Ring, ring.

Forget it.

Ring.

"Hello?"

I'm so shocked that I don't answer for a second.

Then, my voice. "Faith?"

It's been almost two months since I've talked to Faith.

"Hi," she says.

Shuffling in the background. Someone's voice.

"Who's that?"

It's not really the question I want to be asking. What I really want to ask is why she left so suddenly and how did she think that made me feel and what is the reason for her elusiveness?

"No one," comes my best friend's reply.

I miss her like I miss the snow that I've only seen once but remember so much more vividly than all of Florida's sunniest days combined. Because the snow was much more beautiful. Because the snow understood the colder parts of me. Like the pain left behind by Dad leaving. I've accepted it, but I haven't forgotten it.

The cold snow is such a contrast to my warm world.

Faith is such a contrast to every other friend I've ever had.

She understands on a deeper level. She's more than the
hi, how are you, and *oh, my god, did you see blah blah,*
and *he's so cute, right,* of the girls I knew in high school.
Faith is *I'll hold you up when you're too tired to walk,* and
I understand, and *we're the same.*

"Faith, where the hell have you been?"

I want to be mad. I really, really do. But I can't because
I'm so glad she answered.

Faith sighs. "I've been here, in Nicaragua. Building
schools and, you know, stuff."

*What kind of stuff? Tell me all the stuff in your life until
minutes turn into hours because you're finally talking. I
can't believe it.*

"Are you happy?" I ask. I need to know.

"Well," Faith says. "Yeah, actually. Some things are different now and I'm really very happy."

Never mind, I'm angry.

"Good, Faith. Good for you. Glad you're happy and
didn't bother to tell me. Glad that this whole time I've
been worried about you and thinking about you and you
haven't even bothered to answer my calls."

Faith inhales sharply. "I'm sorry."

Sounds like she means it. She sounds absolutely sincere.
But how do you tell your friend that she's made you an-
grier than ever before?

I can't.

All I can do is swallow a million gallons of tears because
this, *this* is worse than finding out that she's struggling, I
think. Because while Faith's been happily ignoring my calls,
I've been diagnosed with cancer. I've had surgeries to try to
remove the cells that eat at all that's healthy in me. I've been
waiting for reoccurrence results. I've been hurting, wishing,

wanting to talk to my best friend about it more than any-thing, but I've held back because she won't answer, but also because I don't want to burden her.

She's been ignoring me on purpose. Not because of sorrow.

"I'm so sorry," Faith repeats.

Something ruptures in me. Maybe the crack in my heart has finally given way to a full-blown shattering. That's what it feels like.

"Why, Faith?" I ask. "Why all this time when you could have called, didn't you? Have you even listened to my mes-sages?"

"Yes," Faith whispers.

"Yes," I repeat, reeling. "You've heard them and you haven't called back on purpose?"

You know it hurts me to miss you? You've heard me tell you in messages? You realize that I need to talk to you?

I'm calling her out on it.

Please say no.

Please say no.

Please say no.

"Yes," she replies.

I choke back a sob. "Why?"

"I can't really say," Faith replies.

She can't say? I don't even know what that means. I don't recognize this friend that I thought I knew. Short an-swers. Like we're two people who happen to have each other's number and why did I ever bother to call her, any-way?

"Okay," I say.

It's not okay.

"How have you been?" she asks.

Do you care? I want to say.

"I've been diagnosed with cancer," I do say.

But it's not like it matters. I can't talk about it with this robot that has replaced the friend I once knew. So I hang up. Turns out after all this time of waiting to talk to Faith, I actually have nothing left to say.

22
javier

"**Y**ou make a decision?"

This is coming from the leader of the pack of four MS-13 members that I've fought with a couple times now. The one I trained my gun on in our last run-in. I've come back to their territory. I'm here for a purpose.

"*Sí,*" I reply.

I'm ready to find Wink. I'm prepared for what's to come. I know all about their powerful gang. I have no delusions that this will be easy. I know this won't be pretty.

This will be torture in the highest form.

This will be my life on the line.

I can handle it, I tell myself. Because if I don't handle it, then there's no other choice but to lie down and accept that they've killed Diego. There's no other option but to let them roam free.

I can never let that happen.

Instead, I'll be their chew toy until I've gained their trust enough to finish them.

"*Tu decisión?*"

All four of them place hands on their guns, ready.

My decision? They want to know my choice? Easy.

"*Sí,* I'll join your gang."

* * *

MS-13s are the stuff of nightmares.

They will rip you to bits. They will tear you limb from limb like a pack of hyenas hungry for every little piece. They aren't picky. They don't care where you come from, who you are, your standing in society, if you have a family, if you deserve it or not. When they receive orders, they follow through. When it's you on the receiving end of their punishments, there's no escaping unless they decide that you're allowed to live another day.

MS-13s rob people. They punish those who owe them money, who have bad-mouthed their people, who have encroached on their territory. They will pay back tenfold anyone who harms their members. They even murder.

They've been known to carry out crimes that cross national borders. They've been known to travel to find the prey they're after. They are scared of nothing but the members higher than themselves.

They are nearly fearless.

They dress how they want, act how they want, be who they want. Their colors are blue and white. Their tattoos are pictures that spell out who they are and who they belong to. They don't discriminate on which body parts to tattoo. The more easily seen, the better. That way you know who you're messing with. That way you're aware of who sent them. Head, neck, and face tattoos are the most popular, but they're found everywhere. They're proud of their *familia*.

Tattoos come in all colors and sizes. Most reflect MS-13 in an obvious way. Like tatting MS-13 boldly across the back of the skull. Or adding numbers together to equal thirteen. Or tattooing the flag of El Salvador, where MS-13s originated, with the number thirteen ingrained. And that's only the few I've seen so far.

MS-13 accepts girls, too. The girls are just as tough as the guys, sometimes more so. They pack guns and knives and fists, and know just how to use them. Like the guys, they've been shot, stabbed, bruised, and bloodied.

The members go by names like Loco (crazy), El Bestia (the beast), El Asesino (the assassin), El Tigre (the tiger). They also use English names like Wink, Psycho, Colt, and Blade.

That's what I've learned today in this little meeting that they've invited me to.

I'm staring at a group of Latinos, ones who belong to MS-13. I've followed the four gang members to a big warehouse on the outskirts of town just past a gritty neighborhood. It's surrounded by trees, so we won't be bothered.

That could be good or bad, depending on how far they want to take this.

I've told no one where I am or why I've come. There's no help waiting for me if things go wrong. I have to trust and hope that everything will be fine because I need to find Wink. That's the determination I use to fuel me.

"You wanted to meet the guy ahead of me," the member I've come to know as Loco says.

"Yes," I reply.

We walk inside. It's open in the front, a nice space with two cloth couches. They're blue. Fitting. There's a card table and fridge. Random mismatching chairs. In the back there's a series of doors leading to rooms that I can't see because the doors are shut.

I want to ask questions. I want to barge into the rooms and scope them out. I want to see exactly where Wink hides.

Is he here?

I don't have the right to ask anything. Though they asked me to join them, they won't make it easy on me. Though I'm a good fighter, I can't use my skills today, and there are too many of them for me to stand a chance.

"Sit," Loco says.

I take a seat on the couch. He walks to a door in the back. The other three that constantly flank him, Monkey, Colt, and El Toro, keep watch over me.

"What do your names mean?" I ask.

I want to get them talking. I need to know as much about them as possible.

Monkey speaks first. "Small, fast, won't see me coming."

Like a tree monkey in the forest. Won't notice him until he's right up on you. Got it.

"Mine's Colt because of this." He pulls out his gun. A Colt 45. "It's my favorite."

"My name was given to me by another member," El Toro says. "I reminded him of a bull. Fine one minute, chargin' you the next."

"And Loco?" I ask.

They grin.

"Do we really need to explain?" Monkey asks. "He's crazier than shit, that's why."

A guy with the number thirteen tattooed below his left eye comes forward.

"*Soy* El Asesino. What's your name?"

"I don't have a name," I say.

Not to them. They'll never know my real name.

He grins. "Fine. I'll think of a name for you. That's better. Leave your old life behind. You belong to us now anyway."

I'm not leaving my old life behind. I'm finding it, actually.

"Yep," I agree. Lies. "Where's the leader?"

"I'm the leader," El Asesino says.

If he's the leader, where is Wink? I can't just throw his name out there. I can't just ask where he is. So I grit my teeth and accept that Wink is higher up than I thought, and I'll have to go through quite a few members to get to him.

It'll be worth it.

"Is there a problem?" El Asesino asks, face hard.

"Nope," I say, relaxing a little.

Four more Latinos walk through the warehouse door. There are nine now.

"Think I'll call you Peón," El Asesino says. "Our pawn, doing our bidding."

Nothing they ever call me will matter because I'm not here for names and friendship. I'll answer to what they want just long enough to get what I need.

"Do we need to explain how this works?" El Asesino asks.

"No," I say, because I already know how the initiation process works.

I'll be jumped in. No fighting back allowed. They get to beat me while they slowly count to thirteen, or until I pass out. Whichever comes first. And truthfully, sometimes they continue to throw blows even after a new initiate passes out. It's just the way things are.

"But let me explain something to you," I say, standing. "I'm here because your boys want me here and because why not, you know?"

I act like I don't care. Like I have nothing better to do.

"So here's the thing, you can hit me all you want, but not in the face."

El Asesino laughs. It's a darkly twisted sound. "You don't tell us how things go," he spits. Lands one solid punch to my mouth.

I balance the impact and smile back at him as blood drips down my lip.

"That's the only one you get," I warn.

This trips him up. Or pleases him. Or something because he grins and looks at Loco.

"Is he serious?" he asks Loco.

Loco nods.

"Is he worth it?" El Asesino asks.

"Yes," Loco answers.

Apparently pulling a gun on him that night only gained his respect.

El Asesino turns back to me. "Fine, we'll play by your rules. But since we can't hit your face, we'll add these."

He reaches in his pocket. Pulls out a pair of brass knuckles. I'm not expecting this. But I have no choice, now do I?

"We doin' this or what?" I ask.

Get this over with.

They push the table out of the way. Circle me.

Here goes nothing.

The first punch isn't so bad. The second, fourth, and tenth, either. But that's where things start to change. That's where the boys get into it. Adrenaline makes an appearance in their grins and faster movements. They all take turns kicking and punching. The brass knuckles are especially brutal. I won't complain. I won't stop them. I'm on a mission.

They've counted to seven. I'm grunting in pain. By the time they get to ten, I swear a rib has cracked. It's hard to breathe. The ground sways. I'm gonna go down soon, I can feel it. I hear El Asesino say something in Spanish about me being a strong one.

Doce, they say, one number away from the end, and I drop to the ground. Standing isn't an option anymore. They've respected my wishes to stay away from my face. There's no way to hide something like that from *mi familia*. Bruises under clothes will be easier to disguise. But staying away from my face doesn't make the blows to the rest of my body any less severe.

I think one name over and over again as they beat me relentlessly.

Diego.

I focus on the revenge that I can practically taste.

Thirteen.

Finally.

I'm coughing and huffing in pain. My world is spinning and dipping and I'm gonna vomit. So I do. But I don't pass out. I make it to thirteen.

"Welcome to MS-13," someone says.

I can't tell who. There's too much pain. I need to sleep for a little while. Maybe days. Someone says that I'm one of the few who have stayed awake. I'm already earning my place in their ranks. They have respect for me.

If I could laugh, I would.

Respect?

Not even close.

What I have is your attention.

And next I'll take your leader.

23
melissa

"**M**elissa."

No one has ever said my name like Javier says my name. It's darkness with a hint of light. It's deeply seductive and completely terrifying. It's right, never wrong.

"Melissa," he repeats, his mouth inches from mine. "You look incredible."

I've done something very daring today. I've done something that I might regret, but the look on Javier's face makes it all worth it if only for a moment.

My toes are boiling in beach sand. Sun slaps my back over and over again, making me feel like I'm burning alive.

"You don't wear bikinis," he points out.

I don't, no, not normally. I don't own the nerve, courage, bravery.

"You're wearing a bikini today," Javier says, eyeing my suit.

I've changed out of my normal one-piece. Slipped on a white bikini splattered with black spots like a Dalmatian. Vintage in style so the bottom comes up high over my hips. They stop above my belly button. My scars are hidden. Even though Javier already knows about them, he can't see them. I don't have to tell him what they're from.

I don't have to tell him what they're from. I don't have to tell him what they're from.

I say this over and over again in my head because if I don't, I'll chicken out. I'll run away and change back into my one-piece and I'll pretend that I never had courage in the first place.

I'm off work as of ten minutes ago, so it doesn't matter if I feel uncomfortable because I can always tell Javier that I need to go. I can make something up and leave. I'm hoping that doesn't happen. I'm hoping that I can breathe in and out and focus on the delicious grin that spreads across Javier's face.

"*Chula,* you weren't wearin' this earlier."

He's right. I was wearing my work one-piece. When he called yesterday and said he wanted to hang out after I got off work, I decided to pack the extra suit. I changed into it for him. I changed for myself, too. I'm testing my boundaries. I'm wondering if I can handle showing a little more than normal. Not my scars, of course. I'll need to start small.

I've been jittery all day, aching to see his face again. It's been a couple weeks since I've seen Javier. His torso is covered in fading bruises that he doesn't comment on. He claims that he had to finish up summer school. He was busy. Phone calls have been our means of communication.

"What happened to you?" I ask.

He glances down at his stomach, ribs, chest. "Got in a fight. But I don't wanna talk 'bout it."

I do want to talk about it.

I want to know who would beat him like this and why. But I also understand that Javier will tell me when he's ready. Just like I'll tell him about my scars when the time is right. So I forget about the bruises for now.

"You wanna go in the water?" I ask.

My face is drenched in red from the attention of his stare, from the way he licks his lips, from the intensity in his eyes.

"Sure," he says.

I walk away first. Butterflies smash against the inside of my stomach. My feet hit the water and it feels like the warmth of summer rain. It's body temperature. It's perfect and inviting. Javier is next to me. He's taking big steps.

"It's stingray season," I warn.

He looks at me funny.

"You need to shuffle your feet in the sand. It scares them away. Someone got stung here just yesterday because they didn't shuffle," I continue.

He laughs. "I never knew that."

He shuffles his feet this time. We're waist deep. I don't expect him to pull me against his hard stomach, but he does. I don't expect his eyes to grow heavy with my closeness. My breath is weighty because he didn't even warn me that I'd be so close to his lips.

"Get on my back," Javier says. "Then you won't have to worry 'bout being stung."

I obey. Wrap my arms around his chest and my legs around his hips. My stomach presses against his back. Even my scars. But it doesn't count because he's not touching them with his fingers, because the fabric of my bathing suit is a barrier.

We're shoulder deep now. Javier spins me around so that I'm attached to his chest this time. My stomach presses against his stomach. Our hearts race in sync. Javier is much taller than me. I couldn't touch the bottom even if I wanted to, so I stay attached to him.

"Melissa," he whispers. "You told me about your scars and now you're wearing a bikini. Are they related?"

Don't talk about that, please.

He strokes my hip underneath the water. Kids splash down the way, farther in. Endless ocean and rafts and other people all around us, but here, in this little speck of the monstrous sea, it's only Javier and me.

"It's okay," he says. "You can tell me things."

He kisses me slowly, torturously. Sucking on my bottom lip. Pressing so very, very gently.

"Tell me," he says.

I'm drifting with the sea. I'm wrapped around this guy who's prying open my life. With his lips, with his touch. I let him in just the tiniest bit.

"Yes, Javier," I say, staring at his lips. "They're related. I wore this suit because you know about the scars."

I'm completely vulnerable. He could eat me alive right now. He could tell me to show him what they look like. He could ask why, where, how? I'm begging him with my eyes to please not say anything more because I just might tell him if he asks and I'm not, not, not ready.

"One more question," he says.

I begin to clamp shut. But Javier, once again, calms me.

"You can trust me," he says.

I feel his lips again. He moves them along my jaw. My fingernails dig into his back. He's so close, too close to be kissing me like this. I want to shove him underwater where no one can see, and do things to the body that he presses against mine.

"You play dirty," I say in little whimpers.

Javier's sly grin says that he knows exactly what he does to me. It says *I will ravish you,* and *you're beautiful,* and *I have the power to destroy you, but I won't.*

He delivers the blow.

"How long have you had scars?"

I've been trying to hold on for nearly six months. I've been tossing my cancer diagnosis around in my mind, trying to find a way to make it fit in my life, but it just doesn't belong. It's a sore spot. It's a stain on a beautiful painting. It's wrong, wrong, never right.

"Five months," I say, voice hoarse.

Javier closes the distance.

"No more questions 'bout scars," he says.

Good, wonderful, thank you.

"Do you have any idea what you do to me, Melissa?" he asks.

Is it the same thing you do to me? Is it sweaty palms and heart bashing and please, please, please kiss me? Is it you're amazing and give me more and never, never, never go?

"No," I whisper.

I study his face thoroughly. I see small pores where he's shaved recently. I see a spot below his bottom lip, his labret, where he lets a small patch of hair grow.

Javier looks at me like I'm the sun and the moon and the stars.

"You make me—" he pauses. Tightens his fingers around my ribs. "You somehow make me—"

Yes?

"More," he says.

I make him more? More alive, more happy, more anything, everything, what?

He doesn't elaborate. But his look seems to tell me that whatever I make him, it's something good.

So I kiss him this time. Javier is breaking into my soul. How dare he? I never gave him permission.

Please don't stop.

"I want you all to myself," he says.

"I already belong to you," I reply.

Because it's true. Because I've belonged to him since the moment he earned my trust.

"You know what that means though, right?" I say with a smile. "You're mine, too."

He chuckles. "That a promise?"

24
javier

I ache from the wounds inflicted by MS-13. I'm bruised from chest to feet, but I don't care. It's done. I'm a part of their gang. Falsely.

Maybe to them I'm a member. Maybe in their eyes I've earned my place. I'm someone that they will call on soon to start discussing my job amongst so many criminals. Believe it or not, I'm lucky. Some members have to carry out horrific acts, like murdering innocent people, to show that they have what it takes to be a part of the MS-13 family.

I got off easy. A beating that could have killed me, but didn't. Loco says he respects the members who get jumped in more than the ones who commit a crime because the ones who are jumped in put their own lives at risk, while the ones who commit crimes only put other people at risk.

I've accepted that I'll have to be a part of this to get close to the inner workings of MS-13. I haven't decided what to do when I find Wink. But I will find him, that's for sure.

Mi mamá doesn't notice the bruises that splotch my torso and thighs. I've covered them with a brown shirt that comes up to my neck and jeans that fall to my ankles.

A couple fading yellow marks on my forearm don't suggest foul play.

Mi mamá will never know.

"Javier!" she yells from the front door. "You did it, *mi hijo!*"

She's gone to get the mail. Come back with a white sheet of paper and a manila envelope. She holds up the paper with letters too small for me to read from this far away.

Mi mamá stops in front of the couch where Eduardo, Pedro, and *mi papá* are sitting with me, watching a game.

"I'm so proud of you. Stand up."

I do what she asks, trying to get a closer look at the paper.

"What'd he do, *mamá?*" Antonio asks, momentarily forgetting about his play trucks on the floor.

"Your brother graduated high school, just like you will one day," *mi mamá* says.

Mi papá smiles. "Good job, *mi hijo.*"

Mi mamá wraps me in a tight hug that crushes my injuries. I try not to grunt in pain.

"I knew you could," *mi mamá* says. "Come on, let's celebrate."

She goes to the phone and dials *mi tío's* number. Invites him to dinner. She and the girls are going to cook something big. She sends Eduardo to the store to get beer. I've made her proud. She worried that I wouldn't make it. That I wouldn't graduate and fulfill the plans she has for me to be something better than she ever was. To go to nice American schools and have a sheet of paper that says I'm worth something, if you buy into that sort of thing. She wants me to be able to apply to good colleges, graduate from there, too. Get a wonderful job that pays enough so that my kids never have to share a room. I don't tell her that I like sharing a room. I don't mind it like some people do. I don't see what the big deal is with large houses and so much space. None of that can fit into a grave. You can't take it with you when you're gone. All that work for something that's left standing long after you.

It's not what matters to me.

Mi mamá is thrilled that I've checked one thing off of my life to-do list. I'll go places with this graduation, she believes. I'll have a nice life now, she promises. I don't have to worry, she says.

And I wonder, will I ever make her this proud again? Will she look at me like this, so happy, if I tell her I'm hunting Wink, if I tell her that I'm falling for a girl who isn't Latina?

Not likely.

Love should be unconditional. Is it, though, really?

Tío Adolfo makes it to the house in twenty minutes.

"Congrats," he says to me.

His English is getting better. I'm dying inside, listening to him and looking at him, because everything about him reminds me of Diego.

Does he miss Diego to the point of thinking about him daily?

Does he ever wonder what his son's murderer looks like?

Can he tell me how he's not a mess when Diego is gone?

What's your secret to being okay, is what I want to ask him.

"Thanks," I say instead.

He grabs a beer. Plops down next to me on the couch.

"She's right, you know," he says, nodding toward *mi mamá*.

She's in the kitchen, talking about my accomplishment.

"About what?" I ask.

"About you graduatin'," he replies. "It's a good thing. You should be proud."

I don't feel proud.

Mi tío hands me a beer. I glance to the kitchen where *mi mamá* is cooking, a smile on her face. She doesn't see the beer in my hand.

"I can't drink this with her here, she'll flip," I say.

He laughs. "Nah, she's too proud of you right now. Just don't take it too far, you know? One or two and she won't mind."

I look at him like he's handing me a bundle of lies that I'd like to believe.

"I'll take the fall, if she asks," he offers.

Good enough for me. I twist off the top. Down half the beer. It's bubbly and cold on its way down my throat. Maybe if I have a few, it can dull the throb of healing wounds inflicted by MS-13.

"How have things been?" *mi tío* asks.

Not great. Horrible. Miserable. Except for Melissa.

"Fine," I reply.

Mi tío sips his beer. Looks at me like he doesn't buy my lies.

"Fine?" he asks. "You sure?"

I finish off the beer and reach for another. *Mi tío's* eyes narrow.

"What? You said I could have it," I say.

"And you can," he replies. He keeps staring at me. "Anything you want to tell me?"

Nope. Smile. "I have another construction job lined up

in a few days. I'll be gone on the other coast for a week. Should bring in good money."

It's true. I'm not sure what he's hinting at, but that's pretty much all I can tell him. Well, maybe besides Melissa.

I glance back to the kitchen. *Mi mamá* is busy at the stove.

"Let's go outside," I say to *mi tío*.

That way we're not around other people. That way I can mention Melissa without *mi mamá* freaking out.

Mi tío closes the sliding glass door, blocking out prying ears.

"There's this girl," I say, once we're outside.

Mi tío smiles. "A lot of stories have started with those same words, Javier. And most of them mean trouble."

I laugh. "She's not Latina."

Might as well say it. Get it out there.

"And Ria doesn't like that?"

No, Ria, *mi mamá,* doesn't like it.

"Not at all," I reply.

He knows how *mi mamá* is.

"Is the girl worth the trouble she will cause you, that's the first thing to ask yourself," he says.

I don't hesitate. "Yes."

"Is she strong enough to handle an angry Latina?"

Is she? "Maybe."

Mi tío's eyes lock on mine. "Here's the thing, Javier. One day you will leave home. One day you will have to be happy on your own and you need to consider what that really means. Is happiness what your *mamá* says it is? Maybe it is for her. But what is happiness to you?"

Happiness is Melissa's laugh. Finding Wink. Knowing

that Diego is in a better place, though I miss him. Happiness is Melissa's touch and soccer and Cuban food.

"Thanks," I say, because I think I understand what he means.

"Your *mamá* means well, she really does, but being Latina doesn't decide whether a woman is worthy or not. Look at that girl Diego loves. Faith, she's not Latina but she's somethin' else. She changed my boy for the better. That's what you need, Javier. A girl who'll make you a better person than the day she met you."

He said *loves*. Not *loved*. Loves. He still thinks of Diego present tense, which tells me that he hasn't completely let go either.

This is comforting in a torturous way.

"She's worth it, I think." I imagine Melissa's scars, what she must have been through. I imagine her lips and smiles and laugh. She's worth it, definitely.

"Are you gonna tell me about the bruises?" *mi tío* says, taking me by surprise.

Silence.

"Be careful when you lean to grab things like, say, a beer." He eyes my covered torso. "Your shirt stretched. I saw the marks on your side. What happened?"

He's not happy about the bruises says his tone.

"Nothing." Can't get him involved.

"Whatever it is, Javier, walk away."

Not that easy.

"Are you in trouble?"

Maybe. "No."

"Do you need money?" he asks.

"What? No, nothin' like that."

He sips his beer, eyes cast away at the watery blue sky. "Is it about Diego?"

I work to stay calm. "Diego's gone. Nothing I can do now."

Well, that's not true, now is it?

That's the thing about lies.

I tell them well.

25
melissa

One, *two, five rings.*
My best friend is calling. Across states and borders and thousands of miles, she reaches out.

Six, seven, ten seconds that I still don't have an answer because it hurts too much.

This isn't how I wanted to tell Faith about my cancer. I didn't want to say it over the phone, angry, as I hang up on her. I wanted to act more mature, reasonable, calm. But Faith has a part of my heart. Faith is twisted so deeply into my emotions that she's no longer removable.

She will always have a part of me.

I wasn't collected enough to hold my emotions together the last time we talked. I spilled my secret like a toppled glass. I'm not ready to clean up my mess.

I'm not ready for all of Faith's questions.

"You gonna answer that?" Javier asks.

I've been trying not to.

"Probably not," I say, glancing down at the phone.

His eyes narrow. "Who is it?"

"No one," I say.

Javier is at my house again. Everyone is gone. No interruptions. Except for my phone.

Javier is sitting at my kitchen table because I've attempted to make Cuban food again from an on-line recipe. I'm not sure if he really likes it, or if he's just being nice by not complaining. I'm not sure if it matters either way because he's eating it and we're together and I'm the luckiest girl because I can call Javier mine.

He asked me to be his. He wants me to be his. Well, he didn't actually ask. But the result is the same. He's mine.

Mine.

The phone stops ringing. I turn it to silent and set it facedown on the table.

Javier doesn't like that I haven't answered him.

"Is it a guy?" he asks.

I'm not expecting this. I laugh. Take another bite of food.

"Why? Jealous?" I tease.

I would be jealous if a girl called him and he didn't want me to know about it, so I get where he's coming from.

Before he can answer I say, "It was a girl, actually. So, no."

I don't want him getting the wrong idea.

"Good," he says, and pulls my chair close for a kiss.

I'm absolutely ready to give him one, but my phone starts vibrating on the table. She's calling again, I bet.

Javier pulls back. Flips my phone over.

My mouth drops open. I'm surprised he has the nerve. I'm also stuck in a bad place because he sees the name on the screen. Emotions flare in his stare.

Pain.

Wonder.

Pain again.

"It's Faith," he breathes. "Answer it."

He needs to talk to her, I see in his look. He needs to know, I see in his tense position.

"I'm mad at her," I say.

Ring, ring, ring.

I'm also very selfish because if I cared about Javier, I would answer and let him speak to Faith. I would let him have his closure. I wouldn't keep that from him.

I can't keep that from him.

"Hello?" I say, picking up.

Javier watches me.

"Melissa," Faith says. "Is what you told me true?"

Do you have cancer?

"Yes," I reply.

"God," she says. Silence. "Melissa, I'm so sorry."

"I can't deal with this," I say. "I only answered because someone is here who wants to talk to you. Just answer his questions, and I'll talk to you later."

It's the best I can do.

"You'll answer again sometime? You promise?" she asks.

"Yes." Anything to get her to talk to Javier. "Will you talk to him?"

She doesn't ask who. She doesn't press me for more.

"Okay," she agrees.

I see then that even though Faith's ignored me for whatever reason, she's still partially the same friend I knew.

I extend the phone to Javier. He looks at me like I've saved his life. *Thank you*, he mouths. The phone goes to his ear.

"Hi, Faith. It's Javier." Pause. "Yeah, Melissa and I are hanging out now."

I can't hear what Faith is saying. I don't like not know-

ing what's going on. It's not really any of my business. I
push the chair out to walk away, but Javier grabs my hand.
He wants me to stay. He wants me to be a part of this moment. My heart constricts.

"Yeah, we're together," he says. "Funny how that happened, right?"

He winks at me. Then his face goes serious. His attention is Faith's.

"Listen, I know this might be hard for you," he says.
"But I really need to know what happened to Diego that
night." He clears his throat. "You know, his last night."

A battle takes place in Javier's eyes.

"I need to know everything. I can't stop thinking
about him."

Ten seconds.

"Please, Faith," he whispers.

She must agree because Javier goes silent. His eyes find
the ceiling and his throat swallows one, two, three times.
Javier's face falls. Twenty seconds. His muscles clench.
One minute. His grits his teeth.

"Fuck!" he yells, startling me. He bangs a hand on the
table. Gets up and paces the kitchen with the phone to his ear.

"I'll kill them," he says.

I don't know what to do. I don't know how to comfort
him. I don't know if there is ever really a way to comfort
someone who has lost something so important.

Javier stops in front of the window. Turns his back to me.

"Can you describe their faces?" he asks Faith.

His knuckles are white from clenching the phone.

"Anything you can remember will help."

I wait a few minutes, so long, an eternity, it seems for
him to finally hang up. Javier turns back to me. Places the

phone in my hand. His eyes are terrifying, brutal, fero-
cious.

"I have to go now," he says to me.

Half of his food is uneaten. I don't argue, though.

"Thank you, Melissa."

He kisses me roughly and leaves.

26
Javier

I will find them. I will find every single gang member that ever tormented Diego and I'll torment them right back with my bare hands. Thanks to Faith's description, I now have an idea of what the cartel members look like. Lot of good that does me since they're in Cuba. But the gang is here. I have access to MS-13. I need to use this to my advantage.

I hop in my truck. Gun it to the warehouse.

I will ruin them. I will be a sleeper cell in their powerful army. I will detonate and they will burn.

They didn't have the right to take Diego away.

They didn't do their homework well enough. They didn't bother to look up his family. They don't know what killing Diego has left behind. They should always consider the aftermath of carnage. That would have been smart of them, to know what they're up against. To know just who they've pissed off by ending a life. But they didn't assess the damage done.

This is my advantage.

I pull up to the warehouse. Notice the gang members hanging out by the door. Young and strong. Tattooed and packing heat. I recognize Monkey and Colt right away.

Colt with his shaved head and pudgy face and Monkey with his lean, short body. I've never seen the other one standing next to them.

"You must be the new guy," the one I don't recognize says, a cigarette dangling from his mouth. He laughs likes he's made a joke.

"Yep," I say.

I step up to the door but he blocks it. He already knows about me, so he should know that I'm a part of the gang now. This looks like a guy who's intimidated by the newest member. Does he think that he needs to show me how tough he is?

"Goin' somewhere?" he asks.

I'll take that as a yes.

"Yeah, inside. *Muévete de mi camino.*"

He really shouldn't mess with me right now.

"Lay off," Monkey says. "He's new, yeah. You're not, got it. We done with this?"

Monkey's trying to talk him off the ledge, but I'm kind of hoping he doesn't move. Because my conversation with Faith left me angry, and Wink isn't here to take my anger out on. This guy is the next best thing. He's still a gang member. Maybe not one that ever messed with Diego, but a member all the same. An enemy just as well.

"He wants to walk right in like he owns the place. Not even sayin' a word to us. He needs to show respect," dude says.

He wants to teach me about respect? Pitiful.

"He didn't pass out during initiation, Jewels," Monkey says to him. "Careful."

Jewels is taken by surprise, but only for a moment before his face returns to stone.

"Should that scare me?" he asks.

He wants me to say sorry, probably. Never happening. There's only one way to solve this.

I step forward. He reaches for his gun. I quickly bend his wrist backwards. He screams in agony. I don't stop there. I grab his gun and toss it aside.

"You will move out of my way next time," I say as I bend his wrist more.

He tries to punch me with his other fist, but I dodge it easily.

I take note of Monkey and Colt. Make sure they're not gonna make me fight them, too. They aren't. Colt is smiling and Monkey is saying, "I warned you, Jewels. Always have to be the big guy. Shouldn't have been a prick."

They're on my side.

Too bad I'm not on theirs.

"On the count of three your wrist will break. I want you to think 'bout that next time you consider pullin' a gun on me."

There's something animalistic about telling your prey exactly how you plan to hurt them. He needs to know that he can't just pull a gun on me if he feels like it. I need to have the upper hand from the beginning. I can't afford to fall behind.

"One," I say, bending his wrist farther.

"Don't," he pleads, but it falls on deaf ears.

"Two," I say.

I hate this part. I hate that I enjoy this. That the need for revenge is so strong that I have to release it.

"Three," I say.

Snap.

His wrist breaks underneath my fingertips. I let him go. He falls to his knees, clutching his hand. He throws a million curses out at me in Spanish.

I smile, though I feel dead inside.

"I will go inside when I want to," I say, making eye contact. "I earned it."

A million hits from your gang decided so.

More curse words from him.

I step past. Open the door. Take a seat on the couch.

"Did you really have to break it?" Monkey asks, sitting next to me.

Colt stops behind us. Makes a call. He says something about what I've done. I don't know who he's talking to.

"He was ready to pull a gun, Monkey. Did I have much of a choice?"

Monkey laughs. "I knew from the moment *you* pulled a gun on us in the parking lot the second night we saw you that you were needed here. We have too many guys like Jewels back there. All talk and intimidation. Don't get me wrong, he'll do damage if necessary, but mostly he runs his mouth. You don't. You get your point across. You don't need many words to do it, either. That's what MS-13 needs."

What they need is to show me Wink.

"What you did back there was crazy. All slow and methodical. You never even hit him," Monkey says. "If you can use that sort of power towards our enemies, you'll be a good asset."

Monkey pulls out a cigarette. Lights it.

"You gotta keep it together, though. Save it for our enemies, not members. We can't have loose screws."

"He's right," El Asesino says, coming into view. "So my question is, are you a loose piece?"

Yes. "No."

He smiles. "Let's hope not."

"Jewels brought it on himself," Monkey says, sticking up for me.

Maybe Monkey and I could be friends in another life. He has the instant devotion of a real friend. Doesn't matter that he's known Jewels longer. We clicked for some reason. But we can't be friends. Not ever. He belongs to MS-13 in a real way. He helped deliver the blows that gained me acceptance. He answers to the one that I'm tracking down. There's no changing that.

El Asesino nods. "Okay. But don't break any other brothers."

This, he directs at me. An order.

I won't agree.

"Let's talk about your job," El Asesino says. "I want you to stick close to these guys for now." He motions to Colt and Monkey. "They'll show you around. You need a few weeks to learn our territory, our enemies, our profits. Got it?"

"Yep," I reply.

He has just given me my timeframe.

"I got something to do next week," I tell him, remembering the construction job I have lined up. "I can start right afterward."

He throws a wad of cash at Monkey. "Take care of the jobs I gave you this week. Peón will join you next week."

It's settled. I have a month before they'll make me go on real runs. I need to find Wink before then. I won't hurt people for MS-13.

Which also means that Wink has a month. Four weeks to accidentally show himself to me.

Unless I find him first.

melissa 27

Three days.
Two missed phone calls.
One burning question.
Where is Javier?
I've tried his cell. I've waited for a return call. I've heard nothing.
Maybe Faith didn't give Javier closure. Maybe what he got instead was more pain. Or maybe he just needs time.
Time is all I seem to have lately.
Waiting, waiting, waiting.
The doctor said it would take six months to know if the cancer has come back. Six months to find out if the cells metastasized and spread to other areas, namely my lymph nodes, where they would be hard to fight. I would need more than surgeries then. I would need chemotherapy. I would maybe need radiation. I would be sick for months and years and it's not something I like to think about.
"Melissa, are you hearing me?"
Yes, a thousand times yes. I can't hear anything but the doctor's words over and over again.
"The cancer might come back. . . ."
I look at the doctor. Glasses and long nose. He's been

telling people for years about cancer. Every week he walks into this office and announces whether a person can go on living freely, or whether they have to be hooked up to IV's and medicines and live in hospitals. He must have a hard life, too. He must hate having to deliver this news to me. He, with his many years on me, has seen a lot of life.

I don't know if I ever will.

I will wait. I will wonder. I will doubt.

"I'll see you in six months for more blood work," he says.

He smiles like he wants me to accept that this is the way things are.

"We'll fight it together," he says, taking my hand. His fingers are freezing. "I'll do everything I can to help you."

I believe that he means it.

He's removed my cancerous cervix. Ovaries, tubes, and uterus, too, just to be safe.

I can never have children. I don't even know if I ever wanted them, but now that choice has been taken from me before I had a chance to decide.

The doctor lets go of my hand.

"Stay strong," he says.

And wait, *I tell myself.*

Six months.

It's been five.

This last month is both dragging on and going too fast. I want to know already. But then again, I don't want to know. Not if it's bad. I'm a mess either way.

Three days of not talking to Javier may not seem long, but when I only have a month left before the world could potentially crash around me, it feels like forever.

I wonder . . . if I told Javier about my cancer, would he run away?

Or stay?

Too bad I'm not brave enough to find out.

He's here.

No call. No text. At least I don't think so. I double-check my phone. I'm right. Javier hasn't sent me any warning that he planned to see me today. But here he is, parking his truck, and walking up my driveway.

I know because I'm sitting down to dinner with my sisters and Mom. Mom actually has time to eat dinner with us before going back to work the night shift.

I wasn't expecting Javier. Black shirt and rugged jeans, baggy around his legs. His hands tucked into his pockets. His hair blowing around his face in the nighttime breeze.

I like the look of him. Dark, Cuban skin and full lips. Warm brown eyes and square jaw. Tattoos hidden, but I see them in my mind anyway.

I want to run to him. I want to kiss him. This is the effect he has on me. Strong and pulling. Dragging me toward his presence.

My sisters look at me. Out the window. Back to me.

"What?" Mom asks, not realizing why the table has fallen silent.

"Melissa's boyfriend is here," Megan says to Mom. Turns to me. "You didn't tell us he was coming."

"I didn't know."

Megan makes a sour face. "Rude. So he just shows up without being invited? Not to mention that he was late last time."

I break away from the sight of Javier. Stare at Megan.

"If it's 'not to mention' then why mention it?" I ask.

"Because," Megan says, taking a sip of water. "Shouldn't he at least be on time?"

"What is it with you?" I sigh, exasperated. "Why are you so uptight all the time?"

The doorbell rings. Mom silently watches the interaction between me and Megan.

"I'll get it," Megan says, beginning to stand.

"You will not," I say. I don't bother to say it nicely. "I don't know what's gotten into you lately, but give it a break, okay?"

Megan backs down. "I'm just worried about you. You've been sick and now this new boy comes along. How well do we really know him? Is this the right time to have a boyfriend?"

Megan acts more like the mom than Mom does. I wish she would relax.

"I'm fine, Megan." That might not be true. "I like him a lot. Don't ruin this for me." Definitely true.

The doorbell rings again. I get up to answer. Nerves follow me every step of the way.

"Hi," I say, pulling the door open.

Javier grins. *"Hola, mami."*

I step outside and close the door behind me so that we can talk on the porch. In private.

"Bad time?" he asks.

A little. "We're just eating."

Javier's hands move out of his pockets. Reach for me. They stop on my lower back. Pale moonlight kisses my skin, wraps around Javier's jaw.

"Sorry about the other day," he says. "I came here in person instead of callin' 'cause I figured I owed you an apology face to face. I shouldn't have left you hangin' like that, especially after you let me talk to Faith. It was just . . ." Javier works to keep his tone normal. "It was just horrible. To hear 'bout it. I thought that I prepared myself for Faith's words. I had been waitin' so long to hear them. But when they came, I don't know." His jaw twitches, tightens. "I couldn't deal."

I'm pretty sure that this is Javier's way of telling me that he needed time. That it wasn't me. He needed space.

I'm glad he's back.

"It's fine," I say. It really is. "Wanna go somewhere?"

I would invite him in, but I miss him and I don't feel like sharing. Also, I don't want Javier to have to deal with Megan and her overprotectiveness.

"*Sí*, where to?"

I shrug. Hadn't thought about it. Just not here.

"There's this pond down the road," he says. "You have to walk the trail a little bit, but it's private. No one will bother us."

"One second," I say.

I run inside. Grab my purse.

"Be back later," I say, not waiting for replies.

I shut the door and hop in Javier's truck.

"I've missed you," Javier says.

Quietly is how he says it. Looking out the window.

A mad blush sweeps over my entire body. It's only three words, but they melt my insides.

28
javier

Melissa's mouth curls into a smile the minute we hit the trail. She's wearing flat shoes, jean shorts, and a thin white tank top. I can see the outline of her bra when the moon shines just right.

I want to touch her. I want to lay her down in the leaves and kiss her mouth, her neck, her shoulders. I want to feel her fingers on me.

Does she understand what she does to me?

I reach for her. Grab her hand. Lamp posts light our path. Branches spread toward us. A cover of shadowed leaves. Hooting in the distance.

"This place is incredible," Melissa says.

The path splits off into other paths. Technically, we're in a local park, but it doesn't have specific hours, so I figure we can't get in trouble. Plus, no one comes out here at night. I've been a few times on my own. Trying to figure things out. Trying to get over Diego's death. It hasn't worked so far, but the park is nice anyway.

"How did you find it?" she asks.

"I worked on a job in the neighborhood across the street," I explain. "Came over on my lunch break one day."

I've already told Melissa that I work on houses. The

contractor who hired me has taught me enough that I swear I could build my own house. Everything from tiling floors, to installing drain pipes to wiring electricity. The money is good, when it comes. Jobs aren't always lined up, though, so sometimes I go weeks without a paycheck.

We reach the pond. It's lit by a watery beam of reflecting moonlight. I take a seat on the bench. Splinters snag my jeans. The bench is old, with iron legs. Melissa sits next to me. Runs a finger around the outside of a bruise on my forearm. Left over from my initiation.

"Why did you get in a fight that day?" she asks.

Not telling. "No reason."

"Some reason." Her eyes find mine.

She holds my stare. Doesn't let up.

What's the deal with your scars?

"Are we sharing stories now?" I ask. It's a low blow. The only fair way.

The thing is, I know she won't tell me where her scars came from. Melissa has built a barrier one million feet long and equally as high.

Melissa's face changes to stone. Her eyes to ice. Her palms flatten against the bench.

No, she won't utter a word, I'm sure. Her reaction at the mere allusion to scars, though I haven't said the actual word, is answer enough.

Melissa understands what I'm implying. She gets where this conversation is going and she wants nothing to do with it. I couldn't pry it from her tight lips, even if I wanted to. And until she tells me, I'm safe to hide my bruises behind non answers.

Neither of us can really be mad because we're both liars. We both act like they're no big deal, our scars.

They are.

"We're not talking about that," she says.

That's settled. I break our stare. Look out at the water.

"I'll tell you something different, though," Melissa says. "Something about me, not my scars."

I didn't actually expect her to open up about anything.

"My dad was a great man," she says to the ground. "Had a respectable job. Loved his family. At least that's what I always heard other people say."

I'm frozen solid. I hang on every word. The song from our ride to the zoo plays in my mind. Something about there not being enough rain to wash the sins away. Melissa is telling me about the person who made that song mean something to her. Which, as it turns out, is not a good thing.

"He was great with me and my sisters, they said." Melissa looks at me then. "They were liars."

If he's the one who gave Melissa her scars, I'll kill him.

"My dad was *not* a good man. People assume that because he led what seemed to be a normal life, that he must be this great guy. They were wrong. He was not nice. He yelled a lot. If I spilled my juice, if I stained my clothes, if I made a sound. He didn't stop with yelling. He pushed Mom around. He slammed the doors and shattered whatever was within his reach. My mom used to tell us to go into our rooms and shut the door because our rooms were on the second floor and he was always on the first. On the couch, specifically, with the television volume high, watching whatever game was on. I think Mom thought that sending us to our rooms would save us from hearing his screams. He used to say so many things. That no one would want a woman with four kids, that me and my sisters ruined his life, that he could have played ball but he had to raise a kid instead because my mom wouldn't get rid of 'it' after high school. He used to complain about having five mouths to feed."

I grit my teeth. Stomp on the need to get up and pace.

"He never actually hit us. Didn't need to. We were too scared to breathe around him, let alone disobey. Whenever I did something wrong, like the time I accidentally broke his coffee mug, Mom took the blame. She claimed it slipped while she was doing dishes. I was too scared to ever tell Dad the truth even though I knew that he yelled at Mom, made her cry, left bruises where he grabbed her too hard, all because of a mug that she didn't even break."

Melissa picks at her nails. Somehow finds courage to speak.

"It was just a mug. We were just kids," she says. "I didn't understand his constant anger. I don't think—" A tear slips down. "I don't think he ever really wanted a family."

She's whispering now. Peeling pink paint off of her fingernails.

"I don't remember him ever hugging me, reading me a bedtime story, taking me anywhere." She laughs bitterly. "So he left us. Packed his stuff and left. Some other childless woman welcomed him into her home, which worked perfectly for him."

I've always had *mi papá y mi mamá*. I know what it's like to starve, fight, run, fear. But I don't know what it's like to be abandoned.

"I haven't talked to him since."

I should tell her how much I want to kill this guy that I've never met. How much it *disgusts* me that he wasn't man enough to take care of the family he helped create. How she deserves so much better.

"Why are you telling me this?" I say instead.

She wipes away one solitary tear.

"Because," she replies.

Nothing else. No explanation that makes much sense, but I'll take it.

Because she wants to trust me, is what I think this means.

Because the story behind her scars is off limits, but she can give me this story for now, is what it seems.

"Come here," I say, pulling Melissa closer.

She's beautiful in this moment. Hair pulled back so that I can see her face. Eyes shining in the moonlight. Tiny dark freckles sprayed across her cheeks.

"Your dad is an asshole. It doesn't matter that you still had your mom; you didn't have him and that's not right. I don't know that kind of pain," I admit. "But I know other things. So I get it, Melissa."

One, two, three breaths.

"I get what it's like to hurt over things," I finish.

I won't tell her that it'll be all right. People naturally want to believe that things will get better. But sometimes, they just don't.

29 melissa

I told Javier about my dad.
It's real, it's real, it's real.
I've let someone else in besides Faith and my sisters. I've let a *guy* in. I've trusted him with the second biggest secret of my life. And he's trusted me with his pain, too, the truth about Diego. Though, honestly, I already knew most of it from Faith. Still, we're connected by these events that rip, pull, shred our hearts.
I trust him.
Trust isn't easy. I've tried to choke my insecurities. I aim my arrow at forgetting the past and miss every time.
Javier has a piece of me.
I won't ask for it back.

"How was your date?" Mom asks.
I help her put the dishes away. It's nice to not worry if one slips and breaks. Now we clean it up and shrug, knowing that it's not the end of the world. Knowing that Dad won't punish her for small things that shouldn't matter. Not anymore.
"It was good." *Really good.*
Mom is much happier with Dad gone. She doesn't date,

though. I don't push the topic because I get how it could be hard to ever trust a man again.

"Tell me about him," she says.

Mom's smile is contagious. Brightening her whole face. Wrinkles crumple together in the corners of her eyes. Blond hair falls across her cheek every time she reaches for a dish.

"He's," *perfect, sexy, amazing,* "nice."

Mom laughs. "Nice, huh?"

More than nice.

"I had a nice boyfriend once," she says.

I didn't know this. All I've ever heard was that Dad swept Mom off her feet their senior year of high school. He was actually sweet to her then, she claims. But that all changed with an unexpected pregnancy and the realization of Dad's shattered dreams. He became bitter, angry, resentful. It only got worse as the years passed. It was all Mom's fault, according to Dad, because she didn't just take care of the problem.

Mom never saw any of her kids as a *problem.*

"He wasn't as good looking as your dad, but he was sweet. He liked me a lot."

Mom reaches for the last dish. Puts it away and dries her hands on the kitchen towel.

"I left him for your dad," she says.

Wonder if she regrets it. Knowing Mom, probably not. She says everything happens for a reason, that suffering brings freedom. Without meeting Dad she wouldn't have had us, she's said before. So it couldn't have been a mistake that she stayed with him all those years.

I feel bad for what she could have had with someone else. Maybe her happily ever after. She sure never got it with Dad.

"So this guy of yours," Mom says. "You going to tell him?"

About the cancer, she must mean. "I haven't decided." I'm not really sure how.

"If he leaves you because of it, you'll know," she says.

"Know what?"

"If he was ever really worth it."

I watch Mom. Years of grief and suffering. Years of trying to hold a family together. Picking up what was left after Dad drove off. That's what Mom's done. Wiping our tears and telling us a million and one times that we are not worthless, though that's how Dad's abandonment made us feel. That's what Mom has done.

So, I believe her. I trust Mom when she tells me that letting Javier in on my diagnosis may make or break us. That with one big confession, I'll know if he's worth it.

And even more, if I'm worth it.

To him.

"Thanks," I say, wrapping my arms around Mom's secure body.

These are the arms that tucked me in every childhood night. The arms that carried me. The arms that have, when the time was right, let me go, too.

"I love you," I tell her.

I tell her every day.

"You need to answer Faith's calls," Mom says, shocking me.

How does she know?

"How did you . . . I don't understand. . . ."

Mom's blue eyes pin me down. "She called the house. You told her about your cancer and left her hanging, Melissa."

"She left me hanging," I say, defensive. "She's my best friend and it's been months since I've had a normal conversation with her."

"She must have had her reasons," Mom says, ever positive.

"Her reasons?" I ask, exasperated. "Her reasons were because she didn't want to answer. She admitted that, Mom. She heard my voice mails and never called back. On purpose."

I can't keep the pain from my voice.

"Do you trust her?" Mom asks.

"I used to."

"And now?"

"And now—" *Do I trust Faith now?* "I don't know. Maybe. It's hard."

Mom laughs. I'm caught off guard by the genuineness of it.

"Nothing that's truly good is ever easy. You of all people should know that."

Nothing that's truly good is ever easy.

"Just answer her call. Give her a chance," Mom says. "I have a good feeling about Faith. Always have. Friendships take work."

Work is not something I want to have to do. I want it to be natural. I want the Faith I've always known. I want the friend who stuck up for me when girls bullied me in school. I want the friend who let me talk about my dad without judgment. I want the friend who grew into a person who learned how to take risks and go after what she wanted.

I'm not sure if any of that person is left.

30
javier

Today is the day I'll learn the streets for the first time. I'll see through the eyes of MS-13. They'll show me hot spots—what roads, allies, and blocks belong to MS-13; where rivals can be found.

I won't tell *mi mamá*. I'll look her in the eyes and spit lies because I'm good at that. I'll fill her mind with what I think she wants to hear and hope for the best.

Because anything could go wrong. It does all the time. Rival gangs carry just as many weapons as MS-13. They shoot and stab and murder, too. I could be hurt. Or worse. I try not to think about what it would do to *mi familia* if they ever got the news that something bad had happened to me. Not now that I've made *mi mamá* happy by graduating high school. I'm doing better, she thinks. I'm finally getting over Diego's death and moving forward, she thinks.

I never said that.

I'm just learning how to lie better. I'm learning to keep my voice firm and my body relaxed and everyone believes because that's what they want to hear, anyway.

From them ...

How are you: Fine.

What's new: Not much.

How's work: Good when it comes.

Congrats on the diploma: Thanks.

You gonna get a real job now, they always want to know.

You gonna mind your own business? I never ask.

No one knows the difference. Except *mi tío*.

Mi tío knew something was wrong. Saw the bruises. Never told a soul.

"Where you going?" Antonio asks, crayons in his little hand.

He's coloring a picture. It looks something like a dragon.

"Out with friends," I say, sitting next to him for a moment. I grab an orange crayon. "Can I show you something?"

He nods his head eagerly.

"If you outline like this," I press the crayon into the paper to make the outline of the dragon bold, "and then color it in lighter, it stands out more. And then you'll stay in the lines."

He's been working on staying in the lines.

Antonio smiles hugely. "Thanks!"

He begins outlining everything like I showed him. The clouds, the sun, the grass. I like seeing him this happy. I sometimes wonder what it's like to be as happy as Antonio.

"Later, kid," I say, getting up.

Mi mamá smiles and pats me on the cheek, like I've done something good. She doesn't doubt me. She doesn't question further. She lets me go.

"Have fun," she says.

Not likely.

*   *   *

The street sounds like music if you listen closely. A knocked-over garbage can rattling in the wind is the cymbal. The pounding of footsteps on concrete are the drums. And all these voices speaking—drug deals, people hustling, businessmen and women stopping for drinks at a dive bar—are the singers.

I don't know where to look. There's so much all at once. Sensory overload. Small stores and packed sidewalks and a million things competing for attention.

"See the barbeque joint?" Loco asks.

I don't spot it at first. We're on a busy boulevard. I have to scan every store until my eyes come to the end of a long line of shops, restaurants, and bars.

"Yeah, I see it," I say.

"It's run by MS-13," Loco informs me.

A barbeque joint?

"Wanna tell me how an all American barbeque place became a home for MS-13?" I ask. Because I have to know. Because I don't understand at all.

"Would you suspect it?" Loco walks beside me, weaving through people.

"No."

He laughs. "Exactly. Who would ever think that it could be run by a Latino gang?"

"Nadie."

"Which is why it's the perfect cover," he replies.

We stop at the barbeque joint. Only six booths fit inside. I can see clear through the narrow restaurant. Out the glass back doors where more tables crowd the patio.

It's packed.

The front has one long counter for ordering. A few menu selections sit on display. The customer ordering points to one of them. The employee rings him up.

"Follow me," Loco says.

Me, Loco, Monkey, and Colt all slip through a side door. End up in the middle of a bustling kitchen that feels hotter than hell. I look around.

Now it makes sense.

The guys back here are Latino. Cooking, running back and forth to get orders together.

"*Necesito pollo con maíz para llevar. ¡Rápido!*"

The guy closest to us is yelling for food to go. A customer is waiting on it. Everyone ignores us for the most part. Too busy to care. Only one guy stops when he notices. He nods for us to follow him into a cramped room. I guess it's the office. At least it has a fan.

"Who's he?" the guy asks, staring at me, shutting the door.

"One of the best members we have. Don't ask questions," Loco answers.

The guy scowls. "I only deal with you and these two." He points to Monkey and Colt. "No one said anythin' 'bout a new guy."

Loco places a hand on his gun. Not subtly.

"Are we gonna have a problem?" Loco looks the Latino directly in his eyes.

He doesn't need to say more. The guy turns a knob on a safe. Reaches inside. Pulls out a bag.

"Tuesday at four. Everythin' is inside," he says, standing. Meeting's over.

"Nice doin' business with you," Loco says, grin cocky.

We leave. If I blinked, I might have missed the entire exchange. I'm not sure if that was a run. Thought I wouldn't go on those for a while. Maybe we were just picking up something. Like to-go food. In and out.

I have no clue what's in the bag that Loco has tucked underneath his shirt.

"Let's split," Loco says, leading the way back to the car.

He and Colt get lost in a mass of bodies ahead of me and Monkey.

"What's in the bag?" I ask Monkey.

I don't know if I'm allowed to ask these things, but now is as good a time as ever to find out.

Monkey keeps his voice low. "Gun and cash."

I work over the possibilities in my head.

"So," I say, "the guy back there delivers info and things that MS-13 needs."

Monkey nods.

"Is he in the gang?"

"He's a middleman," Monkey clarifies. "He has connections to someone higher up. Someone who doesn't go to the warehouse."

"El Asesino gets orders sometimes, too, right?"

We reach the end of the sidewalk. Start making our way across the street to the parking lot.

"Sí," Monkey replies. "We mostly get orders from El Asesino and Jorge back there. Higher leaders like to stay private. They mostly reach us through other members. We carry out their plans. They deal in bigger things."

I need to know these bigger things.

"Like?"

"Like major shipments of goods. Like million-dollar transactions. That sort of thing."

We're almost to the car.

"That's all for now." Monkey's face is neutral. Like he didn't just share info with me. Which makes me think that maybe he wasn't supposed to.

"Thanks," I whisper.

Loco's already in the car, engine running. I hop in the back of the El Camino with Monkey since Colt and Loco are up front.

"One more thing," Monkey says as we ride.

Loud music. No one to hear him but me.

"Watch out for Loco, okay?" Monkey glances at the front of the car. Loco and Colt are laughing about something. "He'll smile in your face."

Monkey's next words send a chill down my spine.

"And shoot you in the back."

melissa 31

Working at the beach is much more distracting with Javier here. He watches me walk to my tables. His face is limestone. I wouldn't know that he's grinning if it weren't for the tiniest lift of his lips. A lopsided smile that doesn't even look like a smile. That mostly looks like he's caught in deep thought.

But I know better.

"What's funny?" I ask.

I pass by him between running drinks. Javier grins his almost smile.

"What are you not telling me?"

A secret joke that I have no part in.

"Nada, mami."

I don't believe Javier. I think he showed up right as my shift is ending for a reason. I think he knows exactly what's going on. And I think that Brock knows, too.

I glance at Brock. He is not nearly as good at hiding his smile. He is passing out drinks and constantly looking over at me.

I walk away from Javier. Approach Brock.

"Spill," I say.

Because he knows what's going on. It's written in his face.

"No way," he says, smiling wider. "And your shift is over."

"Since when have you rushed me out of here?"

Brock normally appreciates any extra time I put in. I'm one of his best servers.

"Since now," he says. "So go."

I eye him a moment longer. "Fine."

I walk back to the bar. Wipe it down and stack the drink trays. Clock out. Javier finds me.

"How were tips today?" he asks.

"A little less than normal," I reply.

Some days are good. Some are average. None are exceptionally bad. The perks of having a good job.

Javier's sunglasses rest lazily on his head. He peers out at the water.

"You ready?" he asks.

"For what?"

"To come with me."

Even though I have no idea what's going on, I take his outstretched hand. And suddenly I'm being shocked with pleasure. Skin to skin. My eyes on his. The rough pads of his fingers touching me. I want to stop in the middle of the sand. I want to kiss his lips. I wish we were people sketched onto a drawing board because I'd erase everyone else around us. It would be me and Javier and not one other soul. For this time. For these moments.

Javier drags me along. My sandaled feet burn where hot sand flicks up onto my toes. He stops at a small boat that's lodged in sand. Normal for this part of the beach. People park them here and drag them out to the water when they're ready to go for a ride.

Which is exactly what Javier is doing now. Pushing the boat toward the sea. I almost don't even notice when Brock joins him.

"You remember what I showed you, right?" Brock asks.

But he's not talking to me.

"Yeah," Javier answers.

They push until the boat reaches the shore. Until the bottom is soaked in water. It bobs a little there.

"Have fun," Brock says, wiping his hands on his shorts.

I walk to Javier, because I get it now, but I still don't believe it.

"You're taking me on a boat ride?" I ask.

Finally, Javier smiles. *"Sí, vamonos."*

It's been years since I've ridden in a boat. So long that I barely remember what it feels like.

I turn around to ask Brock where he got the boat, but he's gone.

I want to ask a million questions. I want to know how it works. Where I'm supposed to get on and where I stand once I do. Or do I sit? I'm not sure. Do I have to wear a life vest? How do you drive this thing?

I don't say a word. I sew shut my lips and decide that I'm going to have fun with Javier, because why not?

I take off my sandals. Carry them in my hand. Wade into the water, grateful to be wearing my bathing suit. I'm up to my hips by the time I reach the boat, which is now being dragged by the current.

"Climb the ladder," Javier says.

I'm not sure where the ladder is so I walk around the boat until I find it attached to the side. I throw my sandals over the lip. They land with a *flop* on the floor. The ladder is easy enough and I'm in the boat with only four steps up. Javier stays in the water.

"You coming?" I ask.

He pushes the boat out farther. It's easier for him to do in the water.

"In a sec," he replies.

We're deeper now. Javier isn't standing on the sea bottom anymore. His feet kick behind him in the small ocean swells. We're finally deep enough for him to climb the ladder, too.

He hops in. Wet and gorgeous. He goes straight to the wheel. Presses a button on the dash and turns the key. The motor flares to life. I watch the way Javier's muscles move, sure and practiced, his back taut. Sweat and water glisten off his muscles like oil. I have an urge to touch him there. Just the thought of it makes my cheeks warm.

He catches me looking and grins.

I try not to be embarrassed. To not blush. I fail horribly.

I channel my attention into the boat's interior instead. White floors that feel like plastic beneath my bare feet. Red seats that conform to me as soon as I sit on them. Hand rails that stretch around the boat—ten feet maybe. I grab on to one as Javier drives into deeper waters.

Javier doesn't say anything. I take the opportunity to watch him again. His eyes are on the water and wind in his hair. Striking, beautiful, delicious. My hair lashes out at me with each gust of briny air. It smells like fish and salt and seaweed.

And I love it.

The way the wind roars in my ears and salt stings my skin. Steady, even, perfect, we glide across the surface, motor chopping the water. A wake follows us wherever we go.

I love the way the sun punches my skin with its intense rays and the way birds fly ahead and the way pelicans dive into the water. I watch boats in the distance. Other things bob on the water also, too distant to make out. Perhaps a bird or a fishing net.

I don't remember ever feeling this alive. I wonder if I've ever told Florida thank you for the beauty that it surrounds me with. Fish and sea and hot, hot, hot. I want to jump into the water and smile at the sun and hold on to this feeling forever.

The wind begins to die down. I almost like this more. Cruising slowly until we reach a stop. My hair is a tangled mess. We haven't come that far at all, I realize, as I glance back to the shore.

Javier cuts the engine. The key stays in the ignition. He throws an anchor down. The boat tugs as soon as the anchor hits bottom. Which is only moments after he drops it. How can that be?

I peer at the water again. Understanding dawns on me. We're at a sandbar. The ocean is shallow here, unlike the water we rode through to get to this point. Here fish swim just below the boat in clear water. Shells collect in troves.

"It's beautiful," I say.

I spot a jellyfish. The outline of something, maybe a stingray, buried beneath the sand. The sandbar itself only has inches of water above it. Shallow enough that people are standing on it, fishing, farther down.

Javier takes my hand. "Come with me."

I'll go with him anywhere.

He hops off the boat. Helps me down. My feet sink into sand, leaving imprints.

"Brock says that sharks hang out by sandbars," Javier informs me.

This is not comforting. I eye the boat. Maybe it's safer to stay out of the water. Javier sees my expression and laughs.

"Don't worry. They won't come this close," he says. But I'm still not sure. "They're too busy lookin' for food around the sandbar."

We walk a little down the sandbar. The boat stays anchored and waiting. Javier's hand finds my lower back and rests there. I'm wearing a one-piece again, but the back is cut out so I feel his skin against mine.

I want to drown in Javier. I want to sink into the way his mouth moves and the feel of him on me and the way his eyes swallow me whole.

"I thought we could look for shark teeth," he says.

What a normal thing to do.

It's so normal that it feels abnormal. Like everything in my world is backwards and now Javier's flipping it right side up.

"I've always wanted to," he says.

He's trying to be normal, too, I realize. With everything Javier has told me about Cuba—running away, hunger, violence—I get why he'd want a slice of average.

We walk the sandbar, searching for shark teeth. Javier takes time to tell me more about his family. Three sisters. Eight brothers. A laid-back dad. An overbearing mom. A small house. Big love. I picture it all. I imagine bunk beds and shared space and Cuban food. I imagine soccer in the backyard and brothers fighting over who's the best player.

It reminds me of me and my sisters. Growing up together. Sharing a room with May. Playing sports. Always competitive. I tell Javier about them, too. It's a good part of me. It's a truth that I'm willing to share.

It takes nearly an hour to walk the whole sandbar. Twice. A few times I think I've found a shark tooth, but it turns out to be a rock or chips of shells. Finally, Javier picks up something. Small, black, and sharp. Shark's tooth.

"Good job," I say.

I still haven't found one, but that's okay. For this time—water surrounding us, on our own island of sorts—I'm free.

Javier allows himself a small smile, and tucks the tooth into his pocket. We make our way back to the boat, sandbar to ourselves now. The fishermen have left. The sun will leave soon, too. It slowly descends, sliding down clouds and blue sky. Preparing to paint a beautiful sunset.

Javier helps me up the boat ladder before hopping on. He goes to a compartment and pulls out two granola bars. Hands one to me. He doesn't say a word as he eats it, eyes cast away. I sit on the red seats across from him and watch his face.

Javier watches the sky. His eyes are full of something that I want to be a part of. I remember the first time that I kissed his lips in the water. The time that he nearly kissed me in the hotel room—if it weren't for Ramon's interruption. I think about our kiss at the zoo, and about how he fits perfectly with me. How we're made from this mold that's so different but that we both, shapes of our own, fit into this space rightly. I watch as he finishes the granola bar. As he drinks water and offers me some. I drink it, too.

And suddenly . . .

I can't take it anymore.

I set the bottle down. Walk to Javier. He turns to me, a little off guard. I sit next to him, almost in his lap, and lean toward his face. I don't have to lean much because Javier is hungry for me, too.

"*Mami,*" he breathes.

He kisses me deeply. Reaches into my soul and caresses it softly.

His fingers are on my neck, trailing lightly. Making me shiver.

I touch him back. I feel his bare stomach, his chest, his lips. And then, with his body pressed against mine, I feel other parts of him. Parts that confirm how much he needs me, too.

Javier touches me like he never wants to stop. Which is good.

Because I don't want him to.

32

Javier

When Melissa presses her body against mine, I lose it. I kiss her back. Hard. I reach for pieces of her, all of her. Lips and thighs and hips. Stomach and ribs and that spot on her lower back.

Necesito mas.

"*Mami,*" I breathe into her.

She rakes fingers through my hair. Pauses at the base of my neck.

I don't want her explorations to stop, but I take her pause as a chance to fold out the bench seats. Melissa stands. Watches me. Only takes a second for our seats to become a makeshift bed, all joined together. The cushions are low enough that no one will see us.

I pull Melissa against me. Lower her to the cushions. Blond hair slides off of her shoulders and lands on the improvised bed.

Mi preciosa.

"Are you okay with this?" I ask.

I might die if she says no.

"Yes."

She assures me with kisses. Scalding lips and grinding

hips. I reach for the string that ties around her neck, holding her suit in place.

She lets me undo the tie. Her breaths become heavy. I watch her face. I'm controlled by her eyes and this need.

There's something else, too. An undercurrent of emotion. I'm afraid to name it because I'm afraid of what it means. That I might actually like Melissa in a very real way. I've kept myself locked up. I've known that liking a girl leads to a relationship and that's just not my style.

Melissa has destroyed my style, not caring that I have this pain because she understands pain, too. She describes her life through songs. She kisses me and makes me forget that this world hasn't been very kind. I lose myself in Melissa. Strings undone, but bathing suit still covering.

I like this girl too much.

I'm too far gone to stop now.

I pull the straps down farther.

I suck in a breath at the sight of her bare chest. Small breasts. Goosebumps across her tanned skin. I can't see any farther than her ribs because that's where I stopped. Where my hands abandoned the straps and landed on her flesh instead.

"Melissa," I rasp.

I kiss her like I'm disappearing. Like this will be the last time.

This can never be the last time. I want to stare at every inch of her body one hundred thousand times.

"Javier," she answers back.

Melissa's hands are whispers traveling across my stomach. Landing just above my board shorts. She pauses, deciding. And then slips her hand inside.

I groan.

Now she knows just what she does to me. Every kiss

and teasing flick of her tongue against mine. I'm glad she knows. I love the way she's touching me.

I yank her suit down lower. Kiss along her ribs. I'm falling apart.

"I need you, *mami.*"

It's the biggest truth I have. More solid than the shaky ground I normally stand on. More complete than this life that's left me not totally whole. Melissa is the best thing I know.

She needs me, too. Say her deep kisses. Say her movements against me.

I reach into her suit. Ready to feel more.

I don't get the chance.

Melissa yanks my hand out and pushes me away with sobering force.

"What are you doing?" she asks, voice shocked.

I can't understand what's happening. One second I'm kissing her, the next second Melissa's done, putting distance between us.

"What?" I ask, confused.

"You touched my stomach," she says. Not nicely.

I reattach the Velcro on my board shorts so that they sit low on my hips again. Rake a hand roughly through my hair.

"Yeah, Melissa," I say. "That's normally what people do when they want each other."

I'm wound up too tightly. Her lips and kisses and I thought . . . I thought . . .

"What just happened?" Might as well come out and say it.

"My stomach, Javier." Melissa looks like she's ready to cry. "You touched my stomach. You almost t-t-touched my s-s-cars."

I thought Melissa needed me like I needed her. There was only one way to make that happen.

"How else was I supposed to touch you further?"

"I don't know," Melissa says. "You can't touch my scars. You know that. You just . . . never mind. Can we go?"

I don't want to go. "If you want."

Even though I'm frustrated and she's angry, I'm still staring at her chest. I want to kiss her again. I wish there were a way for her to block out the scars and whatever put them there. They're controlling our moment. I want her to be with me. I want her concentration to be on me, not her past.

Melissa readjusts her bathing suit. Ties it in a bow again. My chance, gone.

It could have been something more. It would have been pieces of me shared with her. It would have been me and Melissa leaving our problems behind and being together freely.

I turn the key in the ignition and head back to shore. Melissa stares blankly out at the coast. No life in her eyes.

We're left with no words. Motor running. Water lapping. Gulls screeching.

This isn't how I was expecting things to go.

Life doesn't give a shit about what I want.

33
melissa

I don't know what I'm doing. Driving back home from the beach. Wondering where things went wrong. No, that's not true. I know exactly where things went wrong. It's just hard to accept.

I messed up.

Javier was touching me, wanting me. Just an hour ago, I had Javier's lips against mine. All the privacy we needed, and I ruined things.

I couldn't help it.

My scars and their story are insecurities that wreck my life. I couldn't let Javier see. There's no way he could touch them. Then he'd feel my brokenness. It'd become too real.

Javier didn't seem to mind the idea of the scars, but that's only because he doesn't know them for what they really are.

A reminder.

A forever.

Jagged.

Broken.

Ugly.

Coming by your house in 30 minutes.

I reread the text three times just to be sure. It's ten in the morning on a Saturday. I have to be at work by noon.

Javier is on his way.

I'm worried. He's not breaking up with me, is he?

I hate the thought.

Maybe he wants to talk. Maybe what happened yesterday on the boat is still bothering him. Wouldn't blame him. I don't know how to make it right. The fact that I denied him. The way I left him.

I wonder why Javier even wants to still talk to me at all. I wonder at the fingers attached to these hands that touched him so intimately. I wonder at the fluttering, fluttering, fluttering of a million wings in this churning, nervous stomach of mine. I close my eyes and relish the taste of him. Needy and delicious.

No, I can't lose Javier.

I jump out of bed. Covers attach to me like cobwebs, ensnaring me. I nearly fall, flustered.

I throw on green shorts and a white top over the one-piece that I'm wearing to work. Slip my feet into flip-flops. Make my way to the bathroom to brush my teeth and hair. I don't bother with putting on makeup.

Fresh faced, I grab a banana and a yogurt for breakfast. Scarf them down. My eyes are on the window. On the driveway, specifically.

Javier arrives early.

I'm quick to grab my purse and meet him outside so he doesn't have to knock. It's a hasty move. Eager, and he probably knows it. I don't care. I need to make things right between us.

I open his truck door. It protests my pull with a small metal groan. My body sits on seats that are worn down to the springs, ripped in some places. The truck smells like dampness mixed with cologne. I roll down the window. Let fresh, humid air blow across my face.

I'm not sure if Javier wants to talk right here in his truck. In my driveway. But I don't want to have this conversation inside where my sisters can hear. I wonder if this is all right, me coming out here and sitting in his truck like I belong here.

Can he hear my galloping heart?

Nerves taunt me, eating at my stomach with a sharp bite.

I risk a glance at Javier. He's clean shaven. White shirt and ratty jeans. Sunglasses in place. His usual grin gone.

"Wanna have breakfast with me before work today?" he asks as he stares at the windshield.

I regret already eating. I won't tell Javier that.

"Sure," I reply.

With the truck in gear, he drives a few short minutes to a family diner. Silence sits between us, making the ride nearly unbearable. I want to know . . .

Are you mad about yesterday?

Will we talk about it?

Is this your way of letting me down easy, over eggs and toast?

What, exactly, are you thinking about, Javier?

He cuts the engine. Invites silence to walk beside him into the diner. A girl in a red apron welcomes us and asks if we need a booth. Javier says yes because I can say nothing. Because I'm tongue-tied, needing to see his eyes. Maybe then I can read him.

Javier stands in front of the booth with me. Waits for me to pick a side. I choose the right, not caring. But then Javier surprises me. He scoots in close to me. On the same side. Our thighs are touching.

I've forgotten how to breathe.

He takes off his glasses. "I'm sorry."

His words are firm. He looks me in the eyes like he wants me to see truth.

"I didn't mean to push you yesterday," he continues.

I watch the way his lips move. Close to my own.

"I got a little carried away. Obviously, it's hard for me not to touch you."

I should say that I'm sorry, too. I should tell him it's no big deal and we'll figure it out next time because please let there be a next time.

I watch his mouth and say nothing. My mind is molded to the thought of Javier. I can practically feel his breath against my insides. I can practically feel his tongue dancing with mine. I remember the way he touched me, needed me. I remember my brave hand. I allowed that hand to explore parts of him.

"I won't touch near your scars again," he whispers. "I'll be careful."

And his lips are so perfect that I might need to taste them.

He's not angry. He's sorry. He's apologizing for my insecurities. He's letting me deal with my issues how and when I want to, and he's respecting me. I'm not sure if my anxiety about the scars is warranted or reasonable or normal, but they're *my* feelings and Javier is okay with that.

A piece of me breaks then. Not a huge break, more like a sliver. A crack that releases part of my anxiousness.

"Thank you," I murmur.

He nods. Opens his mouth like he has something more to say, but the server interrupts us. She asks for our drink order and if we know what we want. I haven't looked at the menu, but I say water and eggs. They must have something with eggs. The server names a meal and asks if that's the one I mean. *Sure,* I tell her. Sounds good. Javier knows I haven't opened the menu. He hasn't either, but he says that he'll have the same. I don't care what we eat as long as Javier keeps looking at me with those brown eyes. As long as he keeps touching me with his stare and making me remember with the presence of his lips.

"*Mami,*" he says, close to my face. "I don't know what happened to you. I don't know what the scars are from. But if someone hurt you—" He grits his teeth. "If someone hurt you and you want me to take care of it, I will."

That might possibly be the nicest thing anyone has ever said to me.

Also, I can't help but smile. Because something is different about this conversation. Javier still brought up my scars. But this time I didn't flinch.

It makes the smallest difference in my heart, that Javier would offer to take care of it for me. That he cares enough.

It's the tiniest thing—me not flinching at his offer—like the first snowflake falling at the start of winter, seemingly lost amongst the rest freefalling from the sky.

But I see it. The first one. The start of something better. Something that might cover the ground of my heart and freeze all the poison that has grown there lately.

Javier is my start.

These moments are my something new.

34
javier

"Time to go on a run. You're comin' with us."

Loco interrupts our poker game. Which is a shame because I'm winning. Monkey smiles. He doesn't like losing, so this works perfectly for him. The other two MS-13 members playing don't seem to mind either. Their pockets aren't deep. I'd want to hang onto my money, too, if I were them.

"We're leavin' in five," Loco announces.

Time's up. My construction job is finished. I have no excuses for not going on a run with them. I'm still not sure if the barbeque joint pickup is considered a run, or if this will be the real deal. But when Loco tells me I have to come with, I need to go. I'm a chameleon. I'll blend in and follow orders and not complain about it because that's what they expect of me. I'll change every color of the rainbow if they'll just lead me to Wink.

It hasn't happened yet.

But it will.

"One sec," I say.

I lay my cards down. Collect the money I've already earned. Fifty bucks. Not bad. This is the third time I've taken someone's money. It's a nice way to earn extra cash. And it passes time in the warehouse when we don't have streets to prowl and runs to take care of.

Business doesn't always happen for MS-13s, I realize. Some days, they collect debts. Raid the streets. Pay back rivals who have wronged them. But some days are slow. Those are card days. Those are days that the boys, sometimes girls, smoke and drink and chill at the warehouse.

The warehouse is a second home to most of the members in this area. Some walk in and go right back to one of the rooms. Some relax in the open. There's about twenty MS-13s that own these streets. More in other districts. This warehouse belongs only to the members who are assigned to our district. This is what I've learned.

Four districts make up Orlando, I've also learned. MS-13 is everywhere. Like toxic mold.

"Listo?" Loco asks.

Not really. "Sure."

I don't want to go on their runs. What I want is to hang out at this warehouse until Wink walks through the doors, and then hope that he doesn't recognize me. That's always a possibility, that I do all of this and Wink remembers my face. But I don't think it'll happen. He only saw me once. In the dark. When all of his attention belonged to Diego, anyway.

Wink hasn't showed up yet. I'm getting worried that he won't. That he's moved to another city. That he's one of the high members that meet at some other location.

I wouldn't know because I can't say his name. Too suspicious.

I need to wait for someone to slip and mention him, or for Wink to show his face.

Until then, I'll go on runs. Maybe I'll see Wink on the streets. Somewhere in the slum of this dirty city.

It's worth a shot.

"Who are we lookin' for?" I ask.

We're riding in Loco's old El Camino. The paint job makes it stick out, which is maybe the point. That way people know who they're dealing with when he pulls up. Long blue, metallic flames lick up the hood. One shade darker than the rest of the car.

I've taken the passenger seat. Monkey and Colt lounge in the back, which looks like a truck bed—open to the outside.

"Guy who owes us," Loco says. Deep drag of his cigarette. "*Hombre* was supposed to sell some of our stuff. Wasted it on himself instead."

A drug deal.

"We need our money from the product that he sniffed away," he says. "Dude says he'll come up with the money, but that was a week ago. He hasn't showed up yet. It's our turn to find him."

We're on our way to collect money from a user, who probably doesn't have the money since he used it instead of selling it.

We pull up to a house. Boards on the windows. Graffiti on the concrete walls. Lawn overgrown. Weeds choking the cracks in the sidewalk leading up to the front door. We take the sidewalk. Knock on the poor excuse for a door.

No one answers. Not surprising. Wouldn't want to answer if the money is gone.

"Figures," Monkey mumbles, trying the knob.

It's locked. Monkey motions for us to back up. One

swift kick, and he breaks the door open. Splinters fall to the ground. I step on them and make my way inside.

The stench is what hits me first. Like dirty toilets mixed with something dead. The boys notice, too, because their noses scrunch and we're all suddenly breathing through our mouths.

"Shit, that stinks," Loco mumbles.

A dirty rug covers the broken hardwood floor in the living room. The kitchen, to the left, is nothing but a wasted space. No table. Old takeout boxes litter the counter tops.

Life was bad in Cuba, for sure, but at least the families there tried to make something of the little spaces they had. This place is a disaster. I'm not sure that it's even safe to walk through.

We make our way down the small hall to the only bedroom in the back. Colt draws his gun. Puts a finger to his lips. The door creaks like old man bones. Colt rushes in, gun drawn.

But it's useless. No one's home. I try not to let my relief show. I didn't want to run into anyone. I didn't want to help inflict whatever punishment MS-13 thought the guy deserved. And maybe he did deserve it. He stole from them, after all. But maybe he doesn't deserve their wrath. Maybe he's just a guy on hard times with a dangerous addiction.

I'm glad that this time I didn't have to be a part of whatever they planned.

A nagging voice reminds me:

Eventually, you will.

35
melissa

My car won't start, which figures because I have to be at work in twenty minutes. I try again and again. No use. I storm back inside.

"Megan!" I call upstairs. "Can you give me a ride?"

Monica doesn't have a car. May is out somewhere. Mom's working, like always. So that leaves Megan.

Megan walks down the stairs swiftly. Like she's not wearing six-inch heels. Though she is. Have no idea how she manages to wear them all day.

"If by 'ride' you mean to *my* work, then yes."

Obviously, that's not what I mean. "To my work, Megan."

"Then, no."

She applies an extra coat of red lipstick and smacks her lips together loudly.

"Please, I'm gonna be late."

"So will I if I take you to work," Megan replies. "Try a cab."

She opens the fridge for a soda. Uncaps it and drinks. Careful to not spill any on her perfect outfit.

"Really?" I say, frustrated. "You want me to take a cab when you have a car and are on your way out, anyway?"

Megan opens the front door. Totally serious about the ride situation.

"I don't have time, Lissa, or else I would. This is a brand new job. I cannot be late. I'm sorry."

She doesn't sound sorry. But I kind of understand. She loves this job. She went to school for years to get this job. I don't want to mess that up for her.

"Forget it."

Megan walks down the driveway, hollering over her shoulder, "Call your boyfriend to get you."

I could try Javier. I don't like to ask non-family for favors, but maybe he wouldn't mind. If he's not busy.

I dial his number.

"Hola, mami," he answers. Sounding good enough to eat.

"Would you mind doing me a favor?" Cut right to the chase. "I have to be at work in"—I check the clock— "thirteen minutes and my car broke. Are you busy?"

Guess I could call a tow truck. Wait for them to get here. Pay lots of money. Lose out on tips from work. No thanks.

"I'm leaving now."

He hangs up. That was easy. But by the time Javier makes it to my house, I'm already five minutes late and we haven't even driven the twenty minutes to the beach.

"You a fan of speeding?" I say by way of a greeting.

"I've been known to go a little over the limit." He grins.

"Wonderful," I say, hopping in. "Let's go."

Today is decorated with a gorgeous, glassy blue sky. Scraps of clouds that play with the sun. A slight breeze, lazy in its pull. A perfect day for the beach. A perfect day for tips.

Javier is true to his word. He does ten over and takes the highway. Shaves six minutes off our drive.

"What happened to your car?" Javier asks.

"Have no idea," I say. "I know nothing about cars. Except that mine won't start."

"Did it make a clicking noise when you tried to start it?" he asks.

I shrug. Don't know.

"Do you remember anything about it?"

"I remember that it doesn't work," I say.

Javier reaches out and grabs my hand. Rubs my pointer finger softly. Brings my palm to his mouth to kiss, eyes on the road. It's intimate, his little gestures in the middle of my rush to get to work.

"Sorry," I say, feeling bad for rushing. "I just hate being late."

"No prob, *mami*." He sets my hand back down. "Call me when your shift is over. I'll come get you. I can look at your car afterward."

Perfect. "Thank you."

We pull up to the beach. Javier leans in and kisses me softly. I swallow the taste of him. Move my hands to his face. Pull him in harder.

"Mmm," he says, grinning against my mouth. "Hate to say it, but you better go. Unless you wanna be even more late."

I kiss him again.

"Or we could just leave," he says. "I'm game for that."

With him, I'd love to. "Can't. Thanks again for the ride."

I break the kiss and reach to the floorboard for my purse.

That's when it happens. I pull out something that is definitely not my purse.

"What is this?" I ask. Horrified.

Please don't be what it looks like.

"Nothin'." Javier tries to grab it, but I pull back.

I unfold the tan shirt with red splotches. My eyes narrow.

"This is blood."

Silence.

"Javier, why do you have a shirt stuffed by the seat that's covered in blood?"

He looks away. "Like I said, it's nothin'."

Anger edges its way into my tone. "At least look at me when you lie to me."

He faces me then. Expression fierce. Muscles coiled.

"Let it go."

The conversation or the shirt?

I gladly drop the shirt, disgusted, but won't drop the conversation. Not until he tells me what this means.

That's when I see the gun and bandana lying next to my purse.

"Oh, my God."

Javier looks down. Curses. Reaches across the console to grab his gun and bandana. Stuffs them in the glove box like hidden truths. Like if they're gone, out of sight, then what I saw must not have happened, right?

"What the hell, Javier?" My voice rises. A fever pitch. "A bloody shirt? A bandana? A gun? Are you kidding me?"

Javier won't admit anything, though he's caught.

"Just answer this for me," I say, trying to keep it together. "Are those things yours?"

"Technically," he says through clenched teeth, "yes."

I try to not let Javier see how much this bothers me. I try desperately, but I'm no good at hiding. My eyes well with tears.

"Did you hurt someone?" I need to know.

"No," he replies. "The blood is mine."

My hands shake as I grab my purse. Slide it to my shoulder.

"You know what this looks like, right?"

He nods. Sun glints off his hair, and brightens his always tan skin.

So much blood. All from him.

"You've been lying to me. You have a bloodied shirt and a gun and a bandana with gang colors, Javier. Are you going to try to deny it?"

This is where he tells me that I've misunderstood.

Do it, Javier. Contradict me. Prove me wrong.

Please.

"I'm not denying it," he says to the window, not looking at me.

"Damn it, Javier!" I yell.

How could he?

Javier makes a move to touch me but I'm too fast, mad, upset.

"Don't," I say, a tear slipping out. "You can't just be a part of something like that and not tell me."

"Melissa I—"

"Stop," I say. "You've lied enough."

It hurts, but I throw open the door.

And slam it shut on the one who has my heart.

36

javier

She saw my gun. Not only my gun. My bandana and shirt, too.

I should have known something like this would happen. I forgot about the shirt and bandana. And my gun never leaves my truck, except for when I have it on me.

Slipups. This shouldn't have happened.

I didn't think Melissa would ever have a reason to look under my seat. I never imagined that she'd reach down for her purse and grab evidence instead.

I check my watch. Ten p.m. Melissa hasn't called. She's supposed to be off now, unless she had to work late, closing the bar.

I hop in my truck. Drive to the beach anyway. I have a sinking feeling in my gut the moment my feet hit sand. I find Brock. Melissa is nowhere in sight. Maybe she's in the back. Maybe she went to the bathroom. Maybe, maybe, maybe. Not.

"Where's Melissa?" I ask him.

He looks up from pouring a beer. "Gone."

That's what I thought. "Who'd she go with?"

Brock looks away. Not a good sign.

"I don't wanna get in the middle of it, man," he says. Slides a beer down to someone at the bar.

"Guy or girl?" I know I'm asking too much, but I need to hear.

"Like I said, not getting in the middle."

A guy then. Why else wouldn't he answer?

"How long ago?"

I like Brock, but if he doesn't answer me I'm gonna jump over this bar.

"A few minutes."

I take off. My feet hit the sand, not stopping until I've reached my truck.

Melissa left a few minutes ago. I could have passed her in the parking lot. I decide to take the highway. It pays off in the worst way. I pull up at Melissa's house and cut the lights just as an unfamiliar car parks by the curb.

I walk right up to it. Melissa opens the passenger door. Says something to the guy driving. Some dude with short blond hair and board shorts. Surfer type.

"Who the hell is he?" I ask, not bothering to keep my voice down. I want him to hear me.

She shuts the door and walks past me. She's still angry, understandably. I'm angry, too. I don't ride in cars with other *chicas*. Not since Melissa.

Part of me wants to run back up to the car before it has time to take off. Yank open the door and demand to know what's going on. But if I do that, Melissa will go inside. I'll miss my chance with her.

I catch Melissa by the waist and spin her around. "Who was that guy?"

She pushes me away. "None of your business."

I recognize anger in her eyes. Hurt, too.

"I'm sorry, Melissa," I say.

About everything.

I didn't want her to learn about the gang. I didn't want to involve her in my demons.

"It's too late for sorry," she fires back.

I can't believe she rode with another dude instead of calling me.

"Why'd you go with him? You should have called me."

"And you should have told me the truth!"

I step toward her. She steps away. All I want to do is hold her and erase time from the moment she found out until now.

"Was everything a lie, Javier? All of it? Have you belonged to them from the start? Have I been in danger every time I was with you?"

"I would never put you in danger." Not willingly. "And, no. This is a new thing."

"Great," she says, arms crossed. "So you joined a gang after you told me that you wanted me to be yours."

"Shh," I warn. Look around. No one in sight. "Someone might hear you."

She grunts in frustration. "I need you to leave."

"I don't want to leave."

"I don't care," she says.

But I can tell by the tears in her eyes that she does.

"We're done, okay?" Her voice wobbles. "I'm done. I can't be with someone like you. Someone who deliberately decides to throw away his life and lies to me about it."

I have no idea how to change her mind. I might not be able to.

"I just need you to go please," she whispers.

I should just go. But I can't. I care about her too much.

"I need to fix your car," I say, out of options. "I won't bother you. But I promised to fix it, so I will."

I can tell she wants to argue, so I say the only thing I can. "I'll be by in the morning at ten. See you then."

I have to see her then.

I'm not ready to let her go without a fight.

melissa 37

Javier shows up at ten the next morning. As promised.

"I don't need you to fix my car," I say. "That's the only reason why I'm out here. To tell you to go."

Because if I didn't meet him outside, he'd knock on the door. And then what? And then I'd have to tell my family that I don't want him here. They'll ask why. I'll never betray Javier's story. Though I'm angry with him for not telling me, for letting me find out the way I did.

He could have lied, a small voice tells me. *At least he told the truth when you asked.*

"You don't belong here," I say.

I stare at the ground. Picture the green shirt that hugs his torso. The jeans that hang low on his hips. I think about where my hands have explored. Though I'm mad, I'm not immune to him.

"I belong wherever you are, *chula,*" he says.

I look up then. His hair is mussed. Like he didn't bother to brush it this morning. Like he hopped out of bed and came straight here. His eyes are trained on me. He takes a step toward me. Grabs the keys from my hands. Snaps me out of my trance. But it's too late. He has the keys now.

He's walking away from me. He's unlocking the driver's side door of my candy apple red Camaro.

I'm standing with my arms crossed over my chest, glaring at him.

"It shouldn't take me long. Luis works at an auto body shop," Javier says. "I'll see what's wrong and get the parts for you. Piece of cake."

I watch his lips move. Hating that what he says makes sense.

"I'll pay for parts," I offer, relenting.

Doesn't erase the fact that Javier is in a gang. That Javier carries a gun.

"I'm not makin' you pay," Javier says, popping the hood. "So you can stop with that."

I'll slip the money in his pocket when he's not looking. Or his truck, or somewhere so that I don't feel guilty about him buying. It's my problem to take care of. He's already saving me money by working on the car.

Javier bends over the car. Blocks my view of the engine. His arms reach for something, stretching the thin cotton of his shirt over his lean muscles. The sun says hello from its perch in the sky, already heating things up to ninety-something degrees.

"When's the last time you had a tune-up?" Javier asks.

His voice is muffled. Head under the hood.

"I don't know," I answer.

"You need one," he replies. "Won't get the car running, but it's a start."

Javier's shirt rises, revealing a strip of tanned skin along his back. I have an urge to touch him. I won't.

I lean against a flowerbed surrounded by concrete block. Take a seat on the driveway. Wait for Javier to finish.

For a moment, I pretend I'm not in a world where Javier is in a gang, where I'm in remission, where the two of us will never work out. Instead, I remember the feel of his lips and the way his fingers know how to touch me just right.

I let my eyes rake his body. From his feet to the back of his head. He turns around. Catches me staring. I try not to look away. Even though his stare has me nervous and wanting and, and, and . . .

"Do you have a towel?"

I glance at his oiled hands. Open the garage door and grab a rag. He catches it midair.

"Thanks."

He goes back to work. A few minutes more and he's by my side.

"I need to run to Luis's shop. I can be back in an hour," Javier says.

"I have to go to work," I reply.

His eyes narrow. "How will you get to work if your car isn't runnin'?"

I don't miss the way his muscles coil, the way his jaw goes rigid.

"Someone is taking me," I reply.

He doesn't like this answer. Well, too bad.

"That guy from yesterday?"

"None of your business. We're not together anymore, remember?"

I have to keep saying it to make it real. Truth is, I don't want the other guy who drove me home. He's a server at the beach. We have nothing going on.

Javier looks away. Works to stay cool.

"Yeah, I remember," he says. "Doesn't mean that I like it. You should let me drive you."

"No way. The lies, the way things have gone down—your mom not approving of me, finding the gun and gang bandana, the bloody shirt."

He can't talk his way out of this one.

"Fine," he says. "I'll see you tomorrow. Same time. I'll fix it then."

"This doesn't change anything," I whisper.

He's too close. My lungs can't find air. My pulse thrashes inside of me, begging for his attention. I am a girl made up of bones and blood and this treacherous heart that gives away the fact that Javier still affects me.

And he knows it.

"Never said it did. See you tomorrow."

"Tomorrow," I say, giving in.

"Maybe then you'll stop pushin' me away and see that I made a mistake. Doesn't erase how I feel about you."

I am a frozen block of ice. Chilled by his words. He's not giving up on me. He thinks I'll forgive him and be okay with his gang status.

I don't know how to be okay with the fact that he's clearly more dangerous than I thought. I can't find it in me to accept his standing in the gang.

If only I could get Javier and my heart to believe me.

38
javier

Melissa doesn't bother to look at me. I bend under the hood of her car, hands full of new oil and spark plugs. What my hands don't hold is the one thing her car needs.

A new battery.

It's that simple. I won't tell Melissa, though. I can clearly see that nothing else is wrong with the car—besides badly needing a tune-up—but I'll tell her what I need to until she forgives me.

I concentrate on the car. Try not to stare at Melissa sitting on the driveway in cute little pajamas. Looking at her phone. Intent on paying me no attention.

"It looks complicated," I say. "Might take a few days to fix."

It's a dirty lie, I know that. But if I say it'll take time to fix, Melissa will have to see me for the next few days. In the meantime, I'll change the spark plugs, rotate the tires, put fresh oil in. Try to talk to Melissa.

"Fine," she says, still not looking up.

She'll probably never know the difference. She's worse than my sisters with cars, and that's saying something.

She'll think I'm doing work.

I'll actually be spending time with her.

Win, win.

Hopefully I've bought myself enough time to get her back.

I turn into Melissa's neighborhood at nine like planned. The sun is nowhere to be found. Pushed away by a cloudy, dark night. It's been five days of coming over. Three, four, five, not enough days of me trying to get Melissa back and her refusing to talk to me, though I secretly think she wants to.

The wait for Melissa to get off of work is a million years long. Or at least that's how it seems. I try not to be jealous of the fact that some other dude is driving her. Every time I think about it, I want to hit something. He shouldn't be anywhere near my girl. Just because her car doesn't work doesn't mean that he gets a shot with her. Just because I messed up, doesn't mean that I'm out of the picture.

Even if Melissa says I am.

Anger is alive, raging in me. I try not to think about the fact that he might be touching my girl. Maybe they're just friends and he's only being nice, but even that nearly sends me over the edge because it should be me driving her. If she would just forgive me.

I turn onto Melissa's street. Park my truck in front of her house. Tonight is different because I'm met with an angry glare from Melissa and her car running in the driveway.

"It was the battery, Javier. A simple battery," Melissa says, as I hop out of my truck.

"I know." I look around. No other cars home. "Are you the only one here?" I like the possibility.

"Yes, but that's not the point," she huffs. "Why did you lie? Again."

"To have more time with you," I admit. "And because you needed a tune-up."

"You can do a tune-up in an hour, Javier."

I go to her Camaro. Pull the keys from the ignition. Have no idea who told her the truth about the battery. But it doesn't matter. She knows now.

"Right." No point in denying. "But that wasn't enough time to convince you to forgive me."

I don't give her a chance to object. I walk closer. Make sure that her breathing still trips over itself with my nearness. That her heart slams against her chest. That her voice quivers when she speaks to me.

I need to know that I still affect her. That she still cares. And she does. It's obvious.

"I don't regret it," I say.

Maybe she wants me to. I refuse.

I unhook her arms. They fall to her sides, lifeless. But Melissa's arms lie because her fingers move toward me, only to be caught by her at the last second.

"You still care, *mami,*" I say so close to her lips. Heat radiates off her. Off me. Off us both. "Don't you?"

She doesn't like my question. Presses her lips together.

"Dare you to admit it," I challenge. "Or are you scared of what it'll mean? That you *know* what I'm a part of, you know that *mi mamá* doesn't approve, and you know that I pack heat and still you want me? Does that scare you?"

Admit it, Melissa.

"Tell me that you don't still want me," I say. It's getting hard to be this close and not touch her. "Tell me that I disgust you and you want nothin' to do with me."

She refuses to answer. Which is answer enough.

I lean in. Inhale the scent of sunscreen and sweat that lingers on her. I dare to kiss her. I'm not gentle about it. I miss tasting her lips. I'm hungry for her. Nipping her mouth with my teeth. Teasing open her lips with my tongue. Being rewarded with a small moan from Melissa.

I pull back. "Are you seeing that other guy who drove you home?"

"No," she answers.

Thank God.

"Because you still want me?" I ask.

No answer.

"Say it," I demand. "Say that you don't want me. That you don't need me to pick you up and carry you inside right now."

Her eyes slowly go half-lidded. She licks her lips.

"Tell me that you don't want me to show you how sorry I am, because I am sorry, *mami.*"

I wish she would believe me.

"Tell me to walk away, Melissa."

I won't promise to listen unless she means it.

She doesn't speak. She swallows five times and says nothing. She opens her mouth but no words come out. She stares at my lips and breathes irregularly. But she doesn't tell me to stop.

"Say it," I request.

I touch her hip, her thigh, her face.

"You're playing dirty again," she whispers.

"Do you like it?" I ask.

"Yes," she whimpers.

I collect her body in my arms. Throw open the front door.

"Which room is yours, *muñeca?*"

melissa 39

There's no denying it. I do want Javier to touch me. Because I miss him. Want him. Need him. I don't know how to say no when he kisses me. Runs his fingers down my face. Down my neck. Over my breasts.

Javier opens the front door. Brings us inside and closes it. Never lets me out of his arms. I'm staring into his eyes. So brown. Like his hair. Like his skin that I need to see more of.

Javier is right about me and I don't know what that means. I do still like him, despite the fact that he belongs to a gang and carries a weapon and loves a family that will never accept me.

I still desperately need him. Staring at his body bent over my hood for almost a week, and not being able to touch him, has been the purest form of torture.

And then here he is, telling me to say that I don't want him.
I do.
Telling me to deny my attraction to him.
I can't.
Daring me to tell him to leave.
I won't.

I don't want to let Javier go, despite what I said. Despite telling him that it's over.

We're not over. He's always known it. Maybe I have, too.

"Mami?" he says, a question in his look.

"Yeah?" barely a breath on my lips.

"Where's your room?"

His voice sounds like he's swallowed a thousand rocks and they're scraping against his throat. His chest rises and falls alongside mine. Slowly. Heart pounding.

"Second on right," I say.

I could tell him to put me down, but I don't want him to. What I want is more of his lips. The way he presses them against mine. Sucking on my bottom lip and then the top.

I try not to think about my surgery. Will being with him hurt? Will he notice my scars? But then Javier kisses me and I don't care about anything but him.

Javier makes it up the stairs faster than it takes me to blink. And suddenly, he's laying me down on my bed. Dropping onto the sheets with me.

And he's everywhere.

Kissing my lips. My shoulders. Every freckle and inch of my neck. He's pushing a hand through my hair, up the back of my head. Pressing my lips harder into his.

"Javier," I groan.

I don't even own lips anymore. They belong to him. I want to kiss every speck of him.

"Melissa," he says. Voice and eyes and body desperate for me.

Javier slips a hand under my shirt. One, two, ten fingers grab my ribs. I see only half of his body, framed in moonlight. The rest is dark. The room. These sheets. I don't know how much of me he sees.

I'm comforted by the dark. The dark will hide my secrets.

Shadows will storm in and cover my scars. They won't ever show them to anyone. I trust the darkness. And so all of this is okay.

The way Javier slowly lifts my shirt over my head.

The way I gather a thousand pounds of confidence and lift his shirt, too.

I drop it somewhere on the floor. Both of us lie on our sides, facing each other. If the lights were on . . .

But they're not. So he can't see my scars. Or ask questions like *why*.

It's my turn now. To kiss Javier's chest, every tattoo there. Run my fingers along the inside of his hips. Earn a groan from somewhere deep in him. My fingers find the button on his jeans.

Pause.

This is where things change. This is where I let someone in. Where I have to block out *everything*.

"Melissa," Javier says, sensing that I'm shutting down.

I glance at his face. Watch his mouth open to form words. Barely a whisper. More like a plea.

"Tócame."

I'm undone. I'm unbuttoning his pants and he's unclasping my bra.

"You chose me," he says, sounding surprised. "I thought you'd shut down. I thought with the scars—"

He thought I'd run into the part of my mind that remembers, always remembers. That I wouldn't unbutton his pants and kiss his lips and want, need, hunger for more.

"I never stopped choosing you," I say.

Because it's the truth. Even when I told him that it's over between us. I didn't mean it, as much as I wanted to. I still don't like the gang, or the gun, or the fact that his family hates me. But Javier is so much more than that.

His lips crash into mine. He drops kisses down my throat like warm rain.

"Mami," Javier groans. "I need you bad."

I'm on the verge of diving into him. Of letting him have every piece of me.

"Don't t-touch—" I trip over my words. "Don't touch my s-scars."

There. It's out. The ugly truth. I want him to fill every part of me with kisses and caresses and more, more, more. But not the scars.

"I won't," he promises.

One, two, three seconds and the rest of my clothes are on the floor.

Six, seven, eight seconds and so are his.

I feel every bit of Javier on me.

He takes my hands and presses kisses to my palms, down my arms. Down my stomach. Stops just in time.

He pauses. Grabs a condom. Drinks in the look of me against him.

"I need you to be mine, *chula*," he says.

He's absolutely drugging me with his stare. He's kissing me and not stopping. Wanting me and not stopping. I need him, too. His lips and fingers and, and, and . . .

his heart.

40
javier

I replay last night in my mind as I get ready to pick up Melissa.

Holding her afterward.

Telling her she's beautiful, because she is.

Asking her to please do something for me.

"Do what?" she asks.

"Come with me somewhere tomorrow," I reply.

"Where?"

"My house."

I have to prepare Melissa for *mi mamá*. How can I possibly explain that *mi mamá* will not accept her? That the best chance we have is to stick together and for Melissa to stay strong.

I throw on a shirt, pants, and shoes. Don't mention to anyone that I'm picking her up.

Melissa is perfect for me. *Mi mamá* will never see it that way. But *mi mamá* isn't one to insult people. Chances are, she'll simply tell Melissa to leave. She'll make it clear that *gringas* aren't welcome in our home.

I think about our differences, Melissa and me. Her: blond hair, blue eyes, skin tanned by the sun, American. Me: not.

Melissa doesn't know the ways of Cuban people. She's

technically not one of us. She hasn't spent hours in the kitchen with a Cuban *mamá* who can teach her how to cook our food. Though, to be honest, from what I've tasted, Melissa cooks just fine.

I want to explain to *mi mamá* that these things can be learned.

Melissa can't speak Spanish. Which isn't really that important, I don't think, because we all speak English. Even though some of us speak it with a broken tongue, it's still a way to talk to each other.

I want to tell *mi mamá* that other languages matter, too.

It's the fact that Melissa will never, no matter how much I tell her, understand what it's truly like to grow up in Cuba. Starving and fighting and struggling to survive.

But maybe that's a good thing.

No one wants to live that way.

Mi mamá isn't easy to talk to. She doesn't see things outside of herself. I'm not sure that I can change her mind. In fact, I'm almost certain I can't.

But I have to try.

I picture Melissa's face. I remember what it felt like to kiss every bit of her.

Soft skin and scars that I promised not to touch.

Breaths and whimpers and so much more.

Melissa is mine again. I don't think we were ever really apart. But I'm glad she's not mad anymore.

I hop in my truck and maneuver around the cars crowding my driveway. The party is nearly full. So many people. Melissa will meet them all. I trust her to stay by my side, strong. I trust her to not mention anything about the gang.

I think of MS-13. I need to find Wink soon. Then I'll leave the gang. I'll never return to their streets. They don't know the real me—not my name, address, anything. I'm hoping that I can disappear from their radar. After all, where would they even look for me? Or maybe I'll move, see what other states have to offer. Haven't decided yet.

What I do know is that Melissa deserves better than a *novio* who belongs to a gang. I want to be someone that she's proud of. She shouldn't worry about me. And I don't want MS-13 to find out about her.

If everything goes well, they won't.

"Do you get what I'm sayin'?" I ask.

Melissa is riding in the passenger seat of my truck. Looking at the dash like it can give her confidence.

"You've got to be strong. Don't worry about what *mi mamá* says. She'll get mad either way."

I don't want to lie to Melissa. Not anymore.

"Can you do it?" I want Melissa to say yes. I think she will.

She offers a small nod.

"Good," I say.

We stop at a light. I check out her sexy dress.

"I'm not gonna be able to keep my hands off of you in this," I tease. Run a finger up her thigh.

She laughs. Playfully smacks my fingers away.

"What if she really wants us to leave, Javier?"

Well, she really will. No doubt.

"We'll stay anyway," I say.

"But what if she yells?"

Already anticipating that.

Shrug. "Then she yells."

Melissa is brave to deal with it. I couldn't ask for a better girl. I wish I didn't have to ask her to do this at all. I wish it were easy.

But life isn't.

"And if the rest of the family doesn't want me there either?"

"Not all of them are like *mi mamá*," I say. "Actually, most aren't."

"Will she ever like me?" Melissa asks in a shaky voice.

Moment of truth.

"Will you leave me if she doesn't?"

She meets my eyes. "No."

I grin. Relieved. "Then it doesn't really matter, does it?"

Because that's the way some people are. Stubborn. So stubborn that they refuse to see the world beyond their fingertips. *Mi mamá* is one of those people. I've never stood up to *mi mamá*. Haven't had a reason to.

But now?

I will.

41
melissa

I think about the wonderful night I spent with Javier as we pull up to his house. I imagine the way his hands touched me, how I let go for once. I finally trusted someone after my surgery. Makes me wonder if I can trust him with even more. Like the truth about me. What I've been through recently.

"Let's do this," Javier says.

I have to pick my courage up off the floor. I have to gather enough strength to put one foot in front of the other and march up his driveway. Up his front porch. Stop by the door that leads to it all.

I hear voices inside. Music, too. Spanish words that have meaning. But not to me, because I don't understand them. Maybe one day, I will.

He's staring at me. Javier lets me soak in this environment. He's giving me time to adjust to the fact that it's been exactly one day since he suggested that I come to his house, to the *fiesta* his *familia* is having. Something about how they do this once a month. Something else about how I need to prepare myself.

For reality. His mom doesn't know that I'm coming.

None of his family has any idea that I'll be walking through this door.

Javier has planned it so that I haven't had enough time to back out, to let nerves destroy my bravery. He's made sure that I've said yes to coming. He's kissed me and assured me that this will be difficult, but that he needs them to know that we're together. And it's important that his family accepts me, he says.

Which might be pretty hard for them to do since our relationship will be forced down their throats tonight.

"You good?" Javier asks, one finger against my cheek.

"This is not subtle," I comment.

Nothing about the situation is.

"The Reyes family doesn't do subtle." He grins. "There's no talking them into things. You just got to make them see it quick and real."

I like the way Javier's grin fits his face lopsidedly.

"So none of them know about me?" I double-check.

"Diego's dad knows." Javier surprises me. "*Tío* Adolfo is chill. He's good with it."

Speaking of.

"Why do you and Diego have different last names?" I ask. "His wasn't Reyes."

"Our mothers were sisters," Javier explains. "So I got the last name of *mi papá*. And Diego got the last name of his."

Javier takes my hand. Studies my eyes. His palms are rough and right. His touch calms me.

"*Vamonos, mami*. We got to do this now. Walk in and let them see what we have."

Javier grabs the doorknob. I take a shaky breath.

"Mírame," Javier says. I look at him. "I won't let them hurt you."

I trust him.

Javier pushes the door open. I expect fifty eyes to be glued to us, but surprisingly nothing happens at first. His family is everywhere. Some in the kitchen. Some in the living room. A lot outside in the small backyard.

We walk into a party already in bloom. But not a party that I would expect. This is more of a family thing. Some beers, some music. A lot of food. I notice people our age. I notice older adults, too. I watch little kids run around in the yard. A group of them kick a soccer ball. One kid has on gloves, acting as the goalkeeper. The goal is marked off by two small orange cones. There's no net. But they don't care. They play anyway.

Javier's house is simple. A Cuban flag hangs from a shelf along the living room wall. Soccer balls sit on the shelves next to the flag post. Pictures in frames clutter every surface. The kitchen is decorated with one island. Every speck of the counter is covered with platters of food that smell like heaven. Coolers lounge on the ground here and there, full of drinks.

"Hey," Javier says into my ear.

I realize that I'm frozen with nerves. I cannot move an inch.

No one has noticed us. No one has looked our way at all. This seems too easy. I thought people would stare. People would get angry and I would have to sew on ten thousand pounds of thick skin. Act like it doesn't bother me. Because Javier wants me here. That's enough to make me stay.

"Relax, *preciosa*." Javier's voice pours into my ear, salt on my frozen nerves, melting them away.

"You got this," he says, a last-second encouragement.

We walk into the room.

Time hiccups.

Heads swivel toward us.

I look down at my soft gray dress. Deeply interested in the way it fits me just right. In the way the spaghetti straps leave my shoulders almost bare. In the way it stops a few inches above my knees. My heels pop out. Cardinal red. They match my purse. There's no way for me to go unnoticed.

"Javier!" someone yells in friendly greeting.

I dare to look up.

Meet the eyes of his shocked family. I recognize Pedro. Smile. A friendly face. Pedro smiles, too. Gets up from the couch and wraps me in a hug.

"I don't know what you've done to *mi hermano*," he says. "But whatever it is, don't stop."

I'm not sure if Pedro meant to say anything else, but there's no way to know because I'm being yanked away from him by Javier. And just then, I fit perfectly against Javier. My back to his chest. He places a kiss on the top of my head. His arms wind around my waist protectively.

"Why are you touchin' my girl?" Javier asks.

He called me his girl. I chew back a smile.

Pedro laughs. "I'm just sayin' congrats." His eyes are on me. "Good to see that you're not correctin' him this time."

I *am* Javier's girl this time around.

"Hi!" a little kid yells over the music.

I look down to find a boy grabbing the hem of my dress

with dirty hands. He leaves a stain once his fingers are gone.

"You're Javi's girlfriend, right?"

The little boy speaks good English.

"Jair, didn't anyone ever tell you to wash your hands before you touch girls?" Javier says teasingly.

Jair looks embarrassed. "No."

"You left a stain," Javier says, throwing me an apologetic look.

"I didn't know!" Jair says. "I've never had a girlfriend."

I laugh and bend down to Jair's level.

"I don't mind the stain," I say, staring into his big brown eyes. "I'm Melissa."

"I'm Jair," he says. "Javi's brother."

Just then another boy runs up.

"You touched a girl!" the boy yells. "That's sooo gross!"

"Antonio," Javier says, laughing. "Did you just call my girl gross?"

"Yes," Antonio says, crossing his arms over his chest. Which looks ridiculous and cute because he can't be more than five years old. "Girls are gross and they smell funny."

"Like what?" I ask, amused.

"Like ice cream and sprinkles," Antonio says, looking at me.

Everyone watches. I don't care right now because Javier's brothers are adorable.

"You don't like ice cream?" I ask.

"I like ice cream," Jair says. "And I love sprinkles, too."

"You shouldn't touch her! You'll smell like a girl," Antonio warns.

"Guess what, Antonio," Javier says. "Melissa knows

how to play soccer. She even beat me and I tried really hard."

Antonio's eyes go big. "You play soccer?"

" 'Course," I reply. "Bet I could beat you."

Antonio is already like Javier, not wanting to back down from a challenge.

"I've been practicing," he brags. "I'm really good now."

"Maybe you can play later," Javier says. "Right now I need to introduce Melissa to people, okay?"

Antonio nods. "Will you play too, Javi?"

"Sure," he says, pulling me back up to his side.

The tension in the room is a tightrope, and I'm walking the center. Javier's mom approaches me.

"Go play outside," she tells Antonio and Jair.

Javier's arms stay around me, protective. His mom turns to us.

"*¿De verdad la trajiste a mi casa?*" She says something in Spanish that I don't understand.

"Yes, I'm bringing Melissa into our house," Javier says, letting me know what she's saying.

"*Me mentiste.*" She says something else I don't understand, eyes hard.

I stare at her blue apron. I like the small yellow birds on it. I would tell her, but I don't think she'll appreciate the fact that I like her apron, or that I think her house is beautiful, or that I'm in love with her son.

"I lied to you because you won't accept anyone who isn't Latina into our family." Javier continues to answer his mom in English. For my sake.

"I knew it," his mom says. "Why, *mi hijo?*"

"Because we're good together and I want her to meet the family."

I'm scared to death that his mom will tell me to leave. That all of this will be for nothing. That I'll never fit into his world.

"*¿La amas?*" his mom asks, a bite to her voice.

"I'm not answering that here," Javier says, tightening his grip on me.

"You need to leave," his mom says in English, this time talking to me.

She carves me up with her stare while she tells me to leave her house, and how can I say no to that? So I turn to go.

Javier stops me.

"No," he says, firm. "She is not leaving. We are not leaving."

His face is resolved, like he knew this would happen.

"Melissa is my girl. That's not gonna change anytime soon," he says. "I love you, *mamá*, but you can't make me choose between you."

She stares into his eyes. Hands on her hips. She's not any taller than me.

"I'm not gonna be like Pedro," he says. "You're not gonna run her out like you did his girl. If you make me choose, I'm gonna pick what I think is right and I'm tellin' you now that I think you're wrong."

Javier swallows three times. The room is silent except for the music. People watch their interaction with interest.

"Javier, take her home," his mom says.

"I care about her, *mamá*. And if you care about me, you'll try to understand that. You'll let me like who I want."

"She's leaving," Javier's mom says. "Now."

"No, she's not," comes a voice, but it's not Javier's.

A man steps next to Javier's mom, towering over her. I don't know who he is, but Javier does and he's smiling.

"You can stay," the man says to me. "You are welcome whenever you'd like."

"She is not welco—" Javier's mom begins, but her words are cut off by the man's stern voice.

"Our son likes this girl and you are causin' a scene. She's done nothin' wrong." He turns to Javier. "Maybe you can go outside for a bit. I'll handle this."

Javier nods and leads me outside, a grin on his face.

"So that's your dad?" I ask.

"Yep," Javier says. "And he doesn't stand up to *mi mamá* often, so when he does, and he's serious, it sticks."

My belly is suddenly filled with a million lightning bugs. Fluttering around. Giving me hope.

"Your mom still doesn't like me," I point out.

"She'll come around," Javier says.

People pile outside. Taking seats around us.

"Good job," a man says.

"Thanks." Javier greets him with a handshake.

He introduces us.

"*Tío* Adolfo, this is Melissa. Melissa, *Tío* Adolfo, Diego's dad."

"Nice to meet you," I say. Shake his hand. See the similarities between him and Diego.

I watch the way people talk to Javier. Happy that he stood up to his mom. Like his words have shifted the world they live in. Like what he's done here—by bringing me and having me stay—has somehow disrupted the way they know things. In the best way.

"I should have done the same thing," Pedro says, next to me. "I brought a *gringa* home one day and *mi mamá* told her to leave. I argued some, but not enough. I didn't stand up strong like Javier did. I let *mi mamá* win."

I listen to Pedro's story with one hundred ounces of interest.

"Javier wants it more, though." He sips his beer. "I see why."

I'm waiting for him to explain why. I'm waiting for Pedro to tell me what the difference is between me and his ex.

Pedro meets my stare.

"Javier loves you more than I loved her."

42
javier

I don't know what Pedro has said to Melissa, but her mouth is hanging open like a broken hinge.

"What happened?" I ask, studying my brother and my girl.

"Nothin'," Pedro replies and winks at Melissa.

"Don't wink at her," I say.

Melissa closes her mouth and grins.

"Really," she says. "It's nothing."

Liars.

"Hmm," I say, grabbing a Coke. "You sure?"

"Positive," Pedro says, not even hiding his grin.

I don't believe him for one second, but there's nothing I can do to force the information from them.

I lean in to Melissa's ear and whisper, "Do you have any idea what I want to do to you in this dress?"

Her cheeks flood with pink blush. She glances at Pedro, embarrassed. He can't hear me, but the look on his face says that he knows what I'm up to.

"Can you at least wait until I'm gone for that?" Pedro asks.

I kiss Melissa's neck. "Depends. How long you gonna be standin' there?"

Melissa playfully smacks my arm. Her smile drops when my sister approaches with an angry scowl.

"Can I talk to you?" my sister Maria asks.

I'm not in the mood for this. I make sure my tone lets her know. "Can it wait?"

Though she's just barely turned fifteen, she's exactly like *mi mamá*. Taught by her. Made by her. Acting like her.

Maria sends a sharp look Melissa's way. "No."

"Then talk," I say.

Here it goes.

"Alone," Maria amends.

"Nope." Not going there. Not giving her a chance to diss my girl.

"Fine," she says. Looks at Melissa. "You shouldn't have brought her here. Mom's upset. It's not a pretty picture inside."

I get that.

But.

"Melissa goes where I go." I make sure to drill my seriousness into the tone of my voice.

Melissa looks uncomfortable. Heel tapping on the ground.

"Is it worth what this is doing to our family?" Maria asks. "Mom inside, upset. Dad standing up for you, though I don't know why. The family split over this."

I don't even hesitate. "Yep."

I sip my Coke. Wait for Maria to finally understand that nothing she says will change my mind.

Maria is too old for her age. The first girl. The one who is most like *mi mamá*. The one who holds our family together when *mi mamá* can't. Like when *mi mamá* is sick, Maria cooks and cleans and keeps things normal.

Maria sees that this is going nowhere, so she simply leaves. Walks back inside. A bitter trail drags behind her.

"Sorry, *muñeca*," I say to Melissa, an apologetic look. My girl is strong to deal with all this and not crack.

She shrugs. "Win some, lose some."

Pedro and I both smile.

"Got a good one here," Pedro comments. "A fighter."

Melissa is a good one. The best one. One day, maybe, the rest of my family will see that, too.

I take Melissa home, though I don't want to. I want her with me. Me beside her. Where I belong.

That much is clear.

Especially after tonight. Especially after I saw the way Melissa held her ground and dealt with *mi mamá*, though she deserves so much better.

Three cars sit in Melissa's driveway. I cut the lights and kill the engine.

"What you did tonight—" I begin.

She cuts me off with a kiss. I'm not expecting it.

"I'd do it again," she whispers against my lips.

Distant glow from a streetlight lets me see Melissa's face, happy.

I pull Melissa closer. Fit her against me.

The cold landscape of my past pops into my mind. I think about the warmth I have now. Melissa. Her blue eyes stare at me. Her mouth reaches for mine once again. Her fingers lock behind my neck. Our lips drive toward each other. A collision course that tastes so good.

She needs to go inside before I get too worked up.

"*Mami*," I groan.

She smiles a little. Backs up enough to look into my eyes. Sees the desire there.

"Either you gotta go, or I'm kidnappin' you for the night," I say playfully. Maybe a little serious.

She chews her lip like she's considering going away with me for the night.

"You're killin' me," I say.

A cute smile. "Good night, Javier."

"Night." I kiss her once more.

I think about the crack in me. The one that's allowing Melissa to slip through and invade my thoughts, my choices. Like tonight. Standing up to *mi mamá*.

And I want to thank her.

Because I like the change she's made in me.

43
melissa

The beach burns bright with yellow. The sand. The sun. My bathing suit. Two layers of sunscreen aren't enough to keep my skin from browning under the sky's stare. Nearly every day I see the same scenery. The same blue sea spilling into the same lighter blue horizon and I think:
perfect
endless
beauty.

I wonder about the sun. The sun never gets any time off. It burns day after day. Never a moment's break. Even when we see darkness, it works a double shift on the other side of the world, bringing them light. I wonder if the sun ever gets tired. I think about how exhausted it must be.

Like me.

I think about how I work constantly just to make a dent in the hospital bills. I think about how it could be worse. I could have no job. I could be drowning in debt with no way out. At least I have these drinks to serve endlessly.

I try to be positive.

I would like to think that one day soon I can pay off my medical debt. I can maybe save for college and live long enough to enjoy it. I picture classrooms. I think about all the studying I'll do. I wonder if I'll make better grades in college than I did in high school.

I think I might.

Because it means more to me now. I look forward to hitting the books and groaning about finals and practically sleepwalking because there will be so much to do and so little time to do it. People to meet and homework to complete and reports to write. I think about the gallons of coffee I'll drink with a laptop open and books spread out.

I see it all.

Gone.

Because of cancer.

I concentrate on the drinks in front of me. My tray is heavy with them. I stop at a cabana of girls, the same girls who made me think of college, complaining about some test coming up that they're sure they're going to fail, but whatever, because they want to enjoy this day on the beach, they say. Let's not waste it on studying, they say.

You have no idea how much I'd like to take your place, I want to say. *Study for you, be able to complain about tests*, I don't say.

"Here you go," I say instead, smile. It feels forced.

"Thanks," one chimes. Hands me money, a decent tip.

On to the next cabana, the next customer. His head tilts up. My face breaks in half with a real smile this time.

"Javier," I say, surprised.

He pulls me down to sit next to him on the green-and-white striped cabana cushion.

"Why do you look sad?" he asks.

Never misses a beat.

"It's nothing," I say.

How could I possibly explain without spilling my guts?

"Something," he says.

Lays a peck on my lips. I want more. So I lean into him. He pulls back.

"Not until you tell me what," Javier stipulates.

I sigh. "Those girls were complaining about college," I say. He doesn't understand. I don't expect him to.

"And?"

He wants to know. Okay, fine.

"They have no idea how much I'd like to go to college," I explain. "I wish I had enough money for classes and books and everything. I wish I could be stressed about exams instead of—"

I pause. Almost said too much.

"Instead of wishing that I could go to college," I finish.

Javier's eyes narrow. "You don't have enough money for that?"

"No," I reply. "My high school grades weren't good enough for a scholarship."

"What about money from working here?" he asks.

He's getting too close to the truth. Time to shut down.

"I have some debt to pay," I say dismissively. "Anyway, you have the day off?"

Off of work? Away from the gang?

We don't really talk about it. We should.

"My next contract job is in two days. It's a short job. Maybe a week. And it's local," Javier says.

I take a breath. Gather courage.

"And the gang?" I ask.

I haven't said a word since we got back together. But I've wanted to. I've contemplated the right way to bring it up. To somehow convince Javier that there has to be another way.

He needs to leave the gang.

"Let's not," he says.

But it needs to be said.

"I want you to quit."

I've forgiven Javier for lying to me, but that doesn't change the fact that I want him out of the gang.

"Not that easy," he says, jaw taut.

"Why not?"

He shakes his head like this is the end of our conversation, but it can't be the end. I need to know more.

"Tell me about it, Javier. Help me understand."

"No." Firm.

"Please," I say. Kiss him. Beg him with my lips to let me in. I gently pry open his mouth. Taste his need. "Just tell me why."

He groans, a mix of pleasure and frustration. Looks around. No one near.

"Take ten and we'll talk."

It's all he offers, but I'll take it.

I run back to Brock. Tell him that I need a break for a few. He covers for me.

"Want to walk?" I ask Javier.

Javier nods toward an alley between two hotels. "We can go there."

I walk with Javier to the alley. Take a seat on a wooden post. Javier sits beside me.

Deep breath. He begins.

"Revenge," says Javier, "is a dangerous thing."

He cracks his knuckles. Rests the back of his head against the side of a building. His words find me, but I don't believe them. Not at first.

"It's not what you think. I didn't join a gang just to join. You have to know that somewhere deep down. I'm not a guy who joins gangs, Melissa. I have a family. I have support. I'm not like most members who need someone, who have no one so they join a family of sorts. Believe it or not, I actually have little brothers that look up to me. I don't want to set a bad example. But this—" Grinds his teeth. Face hard. "This is different. This is retribution, Melissa. This is the purest form of retaliation."

For what? I wonder. Then it hits me.

"Diego," I say.

"Yes," he confirms. "MS-13, the gang I joined, is the same gang that got Diego killed. And the member who set it all up? He got away. He never had to pay for anything. For stabbing *mi primo*, for gettin' him shot. Diego never got justice. I'm gonna make sure he does."

He looks at me. Eyes pained. Twisted with something like agony.

"Please understand," he requests. "I gotta do this. I need to make Wink pay."

He wants me to understand. I do. And I don't.

"But he's gone," I whisper. It hurts to say it. "Diego is gone, Javier. He can't be brought back. How does finding this guy, Wink, change things?"

His fists ball. "Yeah, he's gone. That's my point. Diego's fucking gone and the guy who arranged his death is walking free!"

He's being loud now. Doesn't matter. There's no one to hear us.

"Javier," I say, trying to talk reason into him. "You have to let him go. Please reconsider. Do they know where you live? Does MS-13 know who you really are?"

"No," he replies, to my relief. "But it's done, Melissa. I'm doing this."

Conviction in his voice tells me there's no talking him out of it.

"You won't reconsider?" I ask.

But I already know.

"Don't ask me to do that." Deadly calm.

Something snaps in me. "I have cancer."

I can't believe, I can't believe, I can't believe . . .

"I have cervical cancer," I whisper. An echo.

I've said it. Out loud. I've let my secret slip through the fissure in my lips. It rolls into the space between us.

"You—" Pause. Incredulous look. "You what?"

Javier's voice is weighed down by five hundred pounds of concern and disbelief.

"You heard me."

Realization mars his face. "The scars are from cancer."

I can't look at him. I let my fingers trail down the sole of my flip-flop. Bumping over the ridges.

"So please," I say, but there's not much left to my voice. I'm trying not to cry. "Please reconsider. You have this life, this amazing life. You can't spend it this way, in a gang. I don't know how much time I have left."

This part is especially hard to say. I swallow my shame, remorse, anxiety.

"I want to spend the time I do have with you, Javier. I want you to be here with me. Not in a gang."

Javier's fingers find my chin. Tilt it up so that I have to look at him. I desperately hope that my unshed tears won't fall.

"I will spend all the time I can with you," he says. "But I have to do this. I'm too close. I just—" He runs a hand roughly through his hair. "I have to, okay?"

"No," I say. "It's not okay, Javier. It's really not." I stand. Done. Can't believe that I told Javier about me, about my cancer, and he still chooses the gang.

He stands, too. Reaches for me. But I'm already steps ahead of him.

"I can't watch you destroy yourself," I say. "I need some time away."

From everything.

I hate to leave him standing there, holding my heart prisoner, but I have to break free of the panic clutching me.

The gang is Javier's top priority.

I need to leave, and I know just where I want to go. I quickly walk away from Javier. He's too stunned to follow.

I run down the beach until I'm back at the cabanas. There, I tell Brock that I need to go home. He lets me off early, no questions asked.

Once in my car, I dial Faith.

Ring, ring, ring.

"Hello?"

One word. Two syllables. Three seconds.

Then.

"Faith," I say, ready to talk this time.

"Melissa! You called."

"And you answered," I reply.

Time to bury pain under a mountain of forgiveness. I want to see my best friend again because maybe, just maybe, there will be a time when I can't.

"Where are you working now?" I ask.

While Faith tells me about the village she's working in, I grab a pen to jot down the name of the city. That way later, I can look up her location. A last-minute flight has its cost, but I'm willing to pay.

"Faith," I say. "I want to visit."

See your face. Hear your voice in person.

"I'd love that," Faith says.

I need to get away. Nicaragua will be my escape.

* * *

Two days later, I've taken up residence in a car that is somewhat like an SUV, and nothing like an SUV. There are no doors, no windows, no top above me. There is an engine. Big tires. There are seats for me and the driver. Rails that connect to the side of the vehicle. I hold on to them with a death grip.

The driver looks over at me. Says something in Spanish. Because that's what they speak in Nicaragua, where I am. I have no idea what he's saying so I have no idea how to answer him. The car jolts forward, dipping where the ground is uneven. We roll over the bump. Go up another one steeply.

The landscape is a challenge.

I would hold on tighter if I could, but my hand is already clamped to the rail. My seat belt is the only thing holding me in place. I would maybe fall out without it. I look at the driver—older, gray peppering his hair—and wonder if he feels nauseous from the ride, too. Probably not. He's most likely used to it.

"Better soon," he says. The first English I've heard him speak.

He must see my discomfort. I look around—green everywhere—and wonder if there's no other possible way to get to Faith. I knew she was working in a remote village. She mentioned on the phone before I came that they're building a school for children who have never sat in a real classroom because they've never been fortunate enough to have people who care about their education.

Faith wants to change that. Faith has set out to change the world.

All I see are leaves and bushes and thick vegetation like walls closing in around me. It's a wonder that this vehicle fits through here at all. Soon as I think it, the man cuts the engine. Hops out. Offers me a hand to help me down. I don't want to give him my hand because it's sweaty. My fingers are cramped, my bones practically glued in a death grip. I give him my hand anyway. Jump down onto dirt.

I don't know what we're doing. There's no village here.

"*Camina,*" the driver says.

I remember enough of Spanish to know that he just told me to walk. Apparently, the village is farther in, where the car cannot go. I'm having a hard time imagining Faith in a place like this. Mosquitos everywhere and bugs buzzing. The sun wants to shine, but the trees block its path to the forest floor.

I follow the driver along a path that I couldn't remember my way back through to save my life. The trees become thicker, allowing almost no visibility past my face. It takes some time, but finally I spot brown things that look like homes. Mud buildings, perhaps.

The driver leads me out of the thick trees into the village, which is still green with vegetation, but not as dense as the forest. He says something to a villager in Spanish. I wish I could ask what's going on. In the time it takes for me to wait, I decide that learning Spanish is a top priority for me as soon as I get back to the States.

I'm busy staring at a crowd of children who have gathered to watch me. One reaches a hand to my hair. Rubs it between her fingertips.

And then Faith approaches.

"Sorry, they don't see too many people with hair as blond as yours," she says.

I smile at the sound of her voice. Hug her by instinct. It's been so long. Too long.

"Missed you," she whispers.

"Me, too." I pull back.

Faith looks different. She smiles easier. Her hair is lighter. I'm guessing, from the sun. I look down at her hand.

It's there, the friendship ring that matches mine. Bought four years ago. Faith kept it all this time. Faith kept a piece of me with her.

Faith sees me watching. Knows just what to say.

"Forever."

Unanswered calls and missed voice mails mean nothing now because I'm here. And Faith never forgot me either.

Faith thanks the driver in Spanish. Offers him money. He takes it and smiles.

Some of the children step forward. The shy hide behind the brave ones.

"This is Melissa," she says. Turns to me. "I'm teaching them English."

"Hi." I offer a wave.

Another girl touches my hair. "Pretty," she says.

"Thank you."

Her hair is as dark as charred wood. Her skin, too.

"I'm going to take Melissa to her room," Faith says.

The children watch us leave. We pass a pile of cement blocks.

"Drivers make several trips into the village with cement mix," Faith explains. "We have molds that we pour the cement into. They come out as blocks. We build the school with them. It will also serve as a safe place if the village ever gets hit by a bad storm."

Faith leads me to a nondescript brown structure that looks as though it's made of the same materials as the other homes.

"We'll be staying here tonight, you and me," Faith says in the doorway.

I look at our arrangement. Two blankets on the floor. One pillow each. Nothing else. I feel like we've gone on a camping trip. This is how some of the people live their whole lives.

"We'll be finishing the school tomorrow. Just the last pile of blocks that you saw and we're done," Faith says.

I nod, trying to take it all in. There's such a divergence between this life and the one I'm used to. Maybe that's a good thing.

"You okay with this?" she asks.

I realize that I haven't said much. "Sorry, it's just so—" I try to think of the right word.

Faith nods. "Different, I know. I get it. We'll go back to my place, a village an hour east of here, the day after to-morrow. You'll be more comfortable there." She checks her watch. "Twenty minutes until sundown. Let's get you something to eat."

Light meals on the flight over didn't stanch my hunger. My stomach twists at the thought of something more sub-stantial.

"Faith, what you're doing here"—I motion to the vil-lage—"is beautiful. I'm proud of you."

I always knew she'd break free.

44

javier

I'm standing in the warehouse with Monkey, Colt, and Loco. Something big is going down tonight, is all I know. I feel the tremble of excitement in my veins. From what I've overheard, we're going to see a guy who's higher up in the gang. Need to drop off a package. I don't know what's in the package. Don't care. What I want to know is the name of the member we're going to see. But names aren't passed out around here easily. They're on a need to know basis. Apparently, I don't need to know.

If it's Wink, I'll know by his face.

I do my best to relax. Quiet the thrum of anticipation. I'm good at disguises. Look at me now. Wearing one. Face neutral. Chilling on the couch like I could care less.

You don't know the inner workings of my mind.

Every day with MS-13 is Halloween. I wear a mask each time.

Dedicated member, they see.

Worst nightmare, I hide.

I try not to think about Melissa. The way she took off to visit Faith. How she said she needed time away. Mostly how she told me about her cancer.

Cancer.

I can't stand the thought. What she must have gone through. What she might still be going through. I couldn't hear the details because if I did, I might have changed my mind. Thrown away all that I've worked so hard for, every moment spent getting closer to Wink, to be with her. I was ready to kill whoever put those scars on Melissa. I can't do anything about cancer, though. I can't kill it. I can't stop it.

Helpless, that's how I feel.

I miss Melissa like crazy. I might have messed things up by refusing to leave the gang. But how could I leave when I'm so close to finding Wink?

Loco talks in shaved sentences on his phone. I'm not close enough to hear him. He hangs up and turns to us.

"Ready?" he asks.

He looks like he means business. Like this is a serious run. Which is good news for me.

"Same place as before?" I ask.

I hope not. I want to be meeting somewhere different, someone higher in command.

"What's it matter?" Loco snaps.

I'm not used to him being short with me. His tone is aggressive, like I asked the wrong thing. Like I have no business questioning him. He's pretty much right.

"Forget it," I say dismissively. Like it's no big deal. I don't want him to suspect.

Monkey bounces his leg on the couch. Always ready to go somewhere. Always anxious for the next move. I swear he can't sit still.

"Let's go," Loco says, smile nowhere in sight.

This is a serious side of Loco. I remember Monkey's words.

He'll smile in your face.

And shoot you in the back.

The ride to the meet-up point is only ten minutes.

Wink could have been ten minutes away this whole time. Holed up in a club that I've passed a hundred times but never entered. What are the odds?

I don't think I'm that lucky. I hope I'm that lucky.

Loco steps out of the car, briefcase in hand. He looks wrong. Baggy clothes. Ripped jeans. A nice expensive-looking briefcase with a gold handle. Doesn't fit.

I play the part. Walk into the club after Loco. My eyes flick around to the bouncing lights and dancing bodies. Act like I belong. No, not like I belong—like I own the place, following Loco's lead.

He keeps close to the wall, careful not to mix with the crowd under the strobe lights. Careful not to mix with the crowd gathered around the bar. This is business.

We carve a path through the crowd. I eye the spot where we've stopped. Nothing special about it. Just a plain door.

Hopefully leading to Wink.

A man in front of the door exchanges words with Loco. Music plays too loud for me to hear anything but lyrics and a beat vibrating the walls.

Whatever Loco said works because now the plain door is opening and we're entering a hallway that's split like a T, doors on either side. End of the hall, a black door. One, two knocks. It opens. The other side is decked out in luxury. A chandelier hangs from the ceiling, sparking light. Two brown leather sofas sit against the back wall, a couple of guys lounging on them. Purple wallpaper that looks fuzzy to the touch covers three walls. A mirror spans the fourth. The room reminds me of a hotel suite with its kitchen area and living room. Like I've just stepped into someone's house.

I don't know where to look. Five guys inside. I'm not

sure which one is the leader—one of the two on the couch, or maybe one of the two seated at a thick cherrywood table made for six. Probably not the security standing guard on the inside of the door, closing it behind us. I do know one thing.

None of them is Wink.

"You got it?" one guy asks, flicking cigarette dust into an ashtray. He's sitting at the table. Thirty-something. Dark hair. Latino accent.

Loco holds up the briefcase.

"All one hundred g's," Loco replies.

We've been carrying around one hundred thousand dollars? No wonder Loco was uptight. That's a lot of money to be responsible for.

"Bring it over," the guy says. It's a demand. I have a feeling this guy doesn't ask for anything. I have the impression that he says something and it gets done.

He's MS-13, for sure. The tattoo of a thirteen with blades running through it on the inside of his left forearm is proof. My guess is that they all belong to MS-13.

Loco walks the money over to him while Monkey, Colt, and I remain standing in the middle of the room. We haven't been invited to sit. It would be a bad assumption on our part to think that these members are our friends. That we can just relax with them, even if we do belong to the same people. Well, not me.

The man who demanded the briefcase has Loco set it on the table, and open it up. He begins counting bills. This could take awhile.

"Have a seat," one of the guys on the couch says.

I don't like the situation. Caged and staged. I don't want to sit. I have to sit.

Colt, Monkey, and I take a seat on the unoccupied couch.

"Drink?" the guy with no name offers.

"I'm good," I say, not trusting them with a drink. Who knows what they'll put in it.

Colt and Monkey decline, too. On the same page. Or maybe not thirsty.

"You got a bathroom around here?" I ask.

I've needed to go since we left, but Loco seemed like he was in a hurry.

"Yeah, right over—"

The guy on the couch is cut off by his buddy next to him. "He needs to use the one outside."

"What's the big deal?" first guy asks.

"We haven't cleaned up yet," second guy replies.

Do they think I care about a dirty bathroom? I don't.

"It's not like he's never seen blood before," first guy says.

"*Cállate,*" the second hisses.

It clicks. The bathroom isn't dirty. The bathroom is a place where something went down. Something that left someone bloody. Evidence. They don't want me to see it.

"Where's the other bathroom?" I ask, not wanting to start anything.

The tension is nearly suffocating.

"Out the door. Down the hall. Hook a right and it's the last door on the right," second guy says.

I take that as my cue to go. The security guard lets me out of the room. It's not until I'm down the hall, turning right, that I realize something.

There's more than one door.

There's more than one room.

Who knows what the others hold. Maybe more of the same. Guys collecting debts and running an illegal system. Maybe not.

Maybe Wink.

I look around. Check for security. There isn't any. Besides the guard on the outside door that leads back into the club, and the one on the inside of the room I came from. There could be more inside other rooms. A big risk. I could act like I forgot where the bathroom is. It's not like I'm not allowed back here. I can explain that I'm MS-13, too.

They could shoot me before I get the chance.

I risk it anyway. Turn the knob of the first door. It's locked. I swallow my frustration. Try the next door. It's locked, too. I curse. Twist the knob of the third door. I'm not met with resistance this time. I hold my breath. Hope the door doesn't squeak. It doesn't, but the bed in the room does. Two people are tangled in sheets, a hot embrace, not realizing that I'm at the door, seeing them through the crack. The man's face comes into view. Not Wink. I close the door before they realize that I've opened it.

I'm running out of options. Two doors left before the bathroom. I try the fourth. Unlocked. And empty. Similar to the one where I left my crew. I slip inside anyway. Do a quick check.

I go through scenarios in my head. Maybe the lights are off because Wink is sleeping. Or maybe he's not here, but there will be evidence of him. I check the room. Dare to flip a light on. There's nothing. I close the door quietly.

Last one.

I try the knob. It gives way to a room with one couch, two tables, and two men.

"Quién demonios eres tu?" one asks.

Who the hell are you? he wants to know.

"*Sólo estoy buscando el baño,*" I say.

Just looking for the bathroom, I lie.

They stand.

"*Soy parte de MS-13,*" I explain. "*La última puerta en el pasillo.*"

The moment I mention the last door down the hall, where I came from, they halt. Faces change. Expressions full of . . . fear. I'm guessing that the men we're handing the money over to are not men they want to anger.

"*La siguiente puerta,*" one says.

He's telling me that the bathroom is the next door. I've got the wrong door. Of course, I already knew that.

I shut the door on the men. And on my hopes. Wink isn't here.

I find the bathroom exactly where I knew it would be. I open the door. Loud music bangs against the walls. Stale bathroom air slips into my lungs. I feel like it might be my last breath.

I halt.

Stunned.

Then gather the pieces of my shock. Slap them together with the force of revenge and breathe. One, two, three breaths.

A guy is stepping out of a stall. Going to the sink. Water turns on. I'm out of sight, cast in shadow. Not in the reflection of the mirror that hangs above the only sink, and directly behind . . .

Wink.

He's alone—of all places—in the bathroom. I don't talk. I don't give any warning at all. Wink doesn't know I'm here. He doesn't see me. Yet.

But I see him. It's the face of my nightmares. And my dreams. I dream of dealing him the same fate he dealt Diego.

I creep along the wall to the bathroom door, grateful for the dim lighting. Think about how lucky I am that there's a lock. I make sure it's secure before I glide closer to Wink, taking care to keep my reflection out of the mirror. The sound of sink water punctuates the air. Music continues to thump outside the bathroom walls. Disguising my breaths. Disguising any noise I might make.

I don't waste another second. I slip a hand into my waistband. Draw out my gun.

And pull the trigger.

45
melissa

Two days of finishing the school. Two days of stacking blocks, painting walls, and watching children run into their new school with huge eyes, smiles that light up their faces.

I can say I've been a part of something life changing. I know, no matter what happens, that I helped children who wouldn't have otherwise had a chance. I know that I've made a difference.

I get it now, why Faith hasn't bothered to come home yet, though she only originally planned to be gone six months. There's something real about what she's doing here. It's work that rips your heart right out of your chest and molds it into something more compassionate, giving, authentic.

I don't really want to leave either. But my flight is in two days.

It's been two days of Faith and me hanging out and helping villagers and being so tired by the end of the night that we fall asleep as soon as our heads hit the pillows. I've been wanting to talk to Faith about her life here, about my life back home, but there hasn't been time.

"Ready?" Faith asks.

I'm standing in front of a small bungalow.

Faith's house.

"Yes."

Faith looks around. I try to see what she's looking for, but there's nothing.

She unlocks the door. Welcomes me in. She lives in the cutest button of a home. Wooden walls. A loveseat. Television on a stand. Galley kitchen and one bedroom. It's perfect.

"Wow," I say, impressed.

Faith's place is more beautiful than I'd imagined. A palace compared to where we slept the last two nights. It's huge, spacious, amazing compared to the hut we stayed in. It's smaller than a New York city apartment.

"My home," Faith says with a shy smile.

Like she's proud of it, but doesn't know what I'll think.

I run my fingers through a row of beads that separates the bedroom from the living room.

"The couch folds out into a bed," Faith says. "You can sleep there, or in my bed, or wherever you're comfortable."

"I'll take the couch," I say.

After sleeping on a floor the last couple days, I'm grateful for anything with a cushion.

"I'll let you get settled," Faith says. "The shower is all yours. I have to run somewhere for a few. Be back soon."

I eye the shower. There weren't any showers in the last village. I'm desperate to scrub twenty layers of dirt off my skin.

"Sounds good," I reply. "And really, Faith, this place is wonderful. Thanks for letting me come."

I set my duffel bag on the floor. Rummage through it for my toothbrush. Put that in the bathroom. The front door closes just as I step into the shower. Hot water pounds onto my skin, a refreshing burn.

I stand under a waterfall of steam and think about absolutely nothing. A million drops fall into my hair, slide down my back, turn the liquid under my toes to a muted brown. Dirt swirls down the drain. I'm so happy for a shower that I don't bother to move for a full two minutes. When the water turns clear, I open the shampoo. It smells like strawberries.

I still smell like strawberries after my shower. Hair wet and leaving water marks on my pink tank top. Faith walks back in.

"Feel better?" she asks.

"Much." I smile. Sit on the couch.

"My turn," Faith says and goes straight to the bathroom.

I flip on the television and wait for Faith to finish. When I don't find anything on, I look in the cupboards for something to eat. I find beans and rice. In the fridge I spot a block of cheese, a tomato, and a couple jalapenos. I get to work cooking enough beans and rice for Faith and me. By the time I'm finished, I have two bowls of steaming white rice and black beans topped with diced tomatoes, chopped jalapenos, and shredded cheese.

"Hungry?" I offer when Faith returns.

"Very." She eyes the bowls in my hands. "Smells good."

"Hope you don't mind that I helped myself."

She plops down on the couch and pats the spot next to her for me to join. " 'Course not."

The Faith I used to know was controlled by the fear that she had to be perfect for everyone else. The Faith I've seen over the last few days isn't the same person. She's more relaxed. She's living on her own terms.

Faith takes the bowl I offer.

"So," Faith begins. "Do you want to talk about things?"

Yes. "I don't know."

I take a bite. It burns my tongue.

"Why didn't you tell me about your cancer?" she asks.

"Why didn't you answer my calls?"

It's a conversation that's sitting on the tip of my tongue. Waiting for Faith to open up. Tell me why she was happy and never bothered to call. Maybe if she had, she would know my story already.

"I didn't answer because I was upset about everything that had happened," Faith says.

"But you're happy now. How can you be happy?" I ask, confused. "I mean, I'm glad you're doing well, but the last I saw, you were devastated. Diego was gone and you needed to get away. You came here and stopped answering my calls. I'm trying to understand," I say. "I really am, but I don't get it."

"What if," Faith says, eyes on the ceiling, "you lost the best thing that ever happened to you? Would you be answering calls?"

Probably not.

"I needed you," I whisper, almost ashamed.

I needed my best friend. I wanted Faith to tell me that my diagnosis was okay and that I'd get through it and that everything would be all right. I would have believed her.

Faith winces. "If I had known . . ."

But she didn't. It's done.

"From now on," I begin.

"I'll always answer," she finishes.

Bygones.

"I was diagnosed with cervical cancer six months ago," I tell her. "They took out everything. I can't have kids. I have to take hormone pills to regulate my body. I'm a shell of what I used to be." I swallow. Beg my heart to slow down. "They took pieces of me, Faith. I'll never be whole again."

I finally say the words aloud. I've thought them no less than a million times, but I've never—not once—admitted how hollow I truly feel.

"Melissa," she says. Sets her bowl down on the coffee table next to mine. "You are still here. I know what it's like to lose pieces of yourself. I nearly lost *all* of myself, would have if it weren't for you. You told me to break free. It's your turn."

Free, free, free.

"How?" I whisper.

"By being happy," Faith says. "What makes you happy?"

Family.

Life.

Javier.

"Did I tell you that I'm with Javier?"

A smile inches up Faith's face. "Javier might have mentioned that."

"He's amazing," I say. "I think I love him."

I know I do.

Faith wraps her hair in a bun. Legs crisscross on the couch.

"Why do you say that with a frown?" she asks.

Am I frowning? Probably. Because Javier's in a gang. Because his future is too bright to be weighed down with violence and drugs and weapons. I thought that was why he left Cuba.

"Because," I say, giving in. "He's messing up."

I play with the string on my pajama pants. Decide that I want to trust someone.

"You know how that gang kept hassling Diego? The one that set him up in the end?"

Faith sucks in a breath. "You know about that?"

"Yeah." I let it out. "Javier joined the gang to find the guy who set up Diego."

"Shit," Faith says.

"Exactly. And he won't quit looking for this guy, Wink. I tried to get him to back out."

Memories of Javier kissing me, touching me, introducing me to his family.

"I don't want to see him go down like that. I'm worried," I admit. "And he won't stop."

I need to say the next part. I don't want to say the next part.

"I'm terrified that he'll end up like Diego." I try to breathe. "He's lying to them. Making MS-13 think he's one of them. What happens when they find out that he's lying? That he wants one of their members dead? What then?"

Faith curses some more. Paces the room.

"There's really only one way to fix this," she says.

"How?"

I'll do anything. I'll pull down the sun and stop time from turning and give myself infinite moments to figure out an answer.

"With the truth," Faith says.

She looks guilty and frustrated and what is the truth?

"Which truth, Faith?"

I'm impatient to hear her answer.

"The truth that there is no reason for Javier to get revenge. He's putting his life, *his life*, at risk. Does he understand how dangerous they are? I saw them smile when Diego was shot.

Wink was *happy* to watch Diego bleed. And Javier wants to find him? No. He can't. He just can't," she says. "It's all for nothing."

She pauses. Finally stops pacing. Looks me in the eyes and whispers words that slice me right in half.

"Because Diego isn't dead."

46
javier

A roar rattles the wall. Pain and shock and total confusion in his expression.

Wink falls to the ground, another agonized cry rolling off his lips. Hands clutching his thigh where I've shot him. Blood. So much blood.

"Pendejo estúpido," he hisses.

I catch his curses with my ears and smile.

A real, finally-found-you smile.

Wink reaches for his gun.

Did you really think that would work?

I'm too quick for his labored movements. I snatch his gun and slide it across the floor to the other side of the bathroom. Punch him in the face. Watch his head snap back. Take a hit from his left hook. But I'm faster. I whip Wink's hands behind his back. Tie them together with my bandana. Pause at the irony of it. The colors of my fake affiliation are securing my enemy in place.

I stand up and look at the damage I've done.

Wink, sprawled out on the floor, wincing in pain. Shot. Dark stains pooling beneath him.

"Who the hell are you?" Wink spits.

I wonder if Diego's blood pooled like that, too. I wonder if he was able to speak after being shot. Rage rushes through me.

"You don't remember?"

Wink clutches his injured leg, jeans ripped.

"Or maybe," I say, "this will refresh your memory."

I step closer. One word out of my lips.

"Diego."

Wink's face changes. Something like a memory. He takes a moment to process it. "I shot you."

He means outside of the club the night me and Diego fought Wink and his gang.

Now we're even.

"Yeah, you shot me," I say. "And you got my cousin killed."

The last words are bitter. Clogging my throat with pain and anger.

Wink has the nerve to smile. Looks down at his leg. Mocks me. "I would say I got the better end of the deal."

Because he's not dead. Because he hasn't been shot through the heart.

"I can change that," I snap. I pull my gun back out and aim it at his chest.

His smile slips. Turns into a scowl. "If you're gonna kill me, do it already."

My biggest wish.

"That would be nice," I reply. "But too good for you."

What I want to do and what I'm going to do race for first place.

"No," I continue. "I'm not givin' you an easy way out. You'll pay for Diego's death."

I'm running out of time. My absence for this long won't go unnoticed. With my gun focused on Wink, I unlock the window. Push it open for an escape. I can't go back to the room now. MS-13 won't be happy that I've shot one of their leaders. I'm wondering if anyone's noticed Wink's absence. I'm wondering if gunshots can be heard over the pounding music.

"We'll see how well you do in prison," I say. "One tip to the police, and you're there. You're a wanted man. Maybe now that arrest warrant will actually mean somethin'."

I know there's a warrant out for Wink, but the police didn't bother to invest their time in a worthless gang member who got a former cartel member killed. They figured Wink would turn up somewhere eventually, and then they'd lock him up.

I'll make sure that he turns up today.

The cops don't care that Diego is dead. They don't realize that he was a good person with a hard life. How can they possibly understand that he made the best of what Cuba handed him?

They can't.

So they've never found Wink. They haven't cared enough to look.

I think back to the word *justice*.

Justice, I reason, is what will happen to Wink after this moment.

I pull out my phone. Dial. Listen as the police answer. Watch Wink's face turn murderous. I keep my gun on him. I cannot afford to slip for even one second. Wink will take any opportunity to run. Any opportunity to grab my gun.

I let Wink hear my every word, the tip I call in. The part about how there's a gang meeting in the back of the club. The other part about how one of them is tied up in the bathroom. I leave out the part about how I am one of them. Because, truthfully, I'm not. The police don't have to know that I'm involved. I could be anyone. A person at the club who overheard something, who saw the gang, anything. Safer that way.

It's a strange feeling. Knowing that I've finally found Wink. Knowing that he will suffer many years in prison. I shouldn't like the feeling coursing through me. I shouldn't, I shouldn't, I shouldn't.

I do.

The darker parts of me like knowing that he will suffer. That Wink will be bossed around. Told when to shower. Served food he doesn't pick out. Left chained and waiting, wasting his life away.

I hope the wait drives him crazy. I hope that looking at the same enclosing walls will never be comfortable for him. I hope that Wink's future is as bleak as my cousin's.

He deserves no mercy.

Forgiveness is a word that I don't know the meaning of.

His home will be a cell.

It's still better than being six feet under.

I try not to think about that. I hang up the phone. Flash Wink a cruel grin.

"I hope you rot, *puto*." My words feel good. My job here is done.

I think of Diego.

For you, I tell him.

Para tí.

My time is up. There's a knock at the door. Knob jiggling. Another knock. Someone calls for Wink. The butt of my gun comes down over Wink's head before he can answer. Knocked out.

The person on the other end of the door knows that something is wrong. They're banging on the door now. Pushing against it to open it.

I hoist myself onto the window ledge. Look back at an unconscious Wink.

Someone shoots the lock.

Uno, dos, tres.

Jump.

The fall isn't far. I hear the sounds of whooshing wind in my ears, and I'm off. Running. Hoping to get lost in the streets. Dark alleys. Midnight wraps a cloaking hand around me, creating the perfect disguise.

I look back only once. See a face in the window. Hear yelling. I've been spotted.

Guys jump out of the window. I'm not prepared for pursuit. I was hoping they wouldn't see me. Too late.

I pick up my pace. Buildings blur past. There's chipping concrete and innocent bystanders and too much open space. I slip into a tight alley. Hop over trash bags and around homeless people. I navigate through constricted walkways.

Pop, pop, pop.

Someone is too close. Firing bullets. Missing me by mere inches. I'm full of luck and hope. Just a little bit farther. A bullet strikes the brick building ahead of me. I duck. Twist around corners. So close.

Pop. Pop. Pop. Pop.

I should fire back but I'm afraid that I might hit my mark. Then what? I'm a murderer, too. No.

Pop.

I need to keep going.

Pop.

There's more than one of them chasing me now.

Pop.

I need to move faster.

A guy comes out of a side alley. I don't see him at first. By the time I do, it's too late.

Pop. Pop.

I fall.

Time jumbles everything around me. Sirens and sounds. Shouts and echoes. Garbled noises like voices near me.

"Javier."

Someone else, opposite direction, says my name. My real name.

Crack. My eyes open. Just enough to see Monkey take aim. Shoot two MS-13 members. Dead.

That can't be right.

Silence falls and it feels like lights out. I glance at my stomach, dowsed, coated in blood.

"Javier."

Again, my name. From Monkey's mouth. How does he know?

"Stay awake," Monkey says.

"What's goin'—" Pause. Breathe. Pain. "On?"

Two lungs. Too many breaths. Not enough air.

"How did you know," cough, "that I ran here?"

My lungs burn like matches lit within.

"I traced your cell from the call you made," Monkey says.

"But I called *la policía.*" I cough up something wet. "How could you trace—"

I trail off.

No way, I think.

No puede ser.

"You're a cop," I say, understanding.

"And you're Diego's cousin," Monkey replies.

I try to stay awake. I try even harder to breathe. Each attempted breath rips my chest in two. My mouth tastes like blood.

"Stay awake," Monkey repeats.

Too hard. My world flips.

"Can't," I rasp, letting my eyes rest.

And I know it then, how serious my injuries are. I don't know how many times I've been hit. I don't know why I can't breathe. But I do know this:

I'm dying.

I feel it in my bones. I know it like I know the curves of Melissa's body. I know it like I know the pain of missing Diego.

"You need to stay awake," Monkey continues. "Because Diego isn't dead."

Suddenly what I understand, I don't actually understand. What I know is wrong.

Like this: Monkey is a cop.

Or this: I will soon be gone.

Or this: Diego isn't.

But those last words coming out of Monkey's mouth, the ones about Diego, I must be imagining them. Because they can't be true. But in all the agony of being shot, I see why I've heard the words.

Because they are the only good I can imagine in the face of so much pain.

47
melissa

B *ecause Diego isn't dead.*
I think about Faith's words. Decide she must be kidding. But I don't understand why she would joke about it.

"Come with me," Faith says.

I follow. Numbly. Move my limbs. Try to reason how Diego could possibly be alive.

Faith looks at me nervously. "Are you all right?"

No. "Sure."

"You're lying," she says.

Yep. "Nope."

"Stop lying to me."

"I should be saying the same thing to you," I reply.

Because she's been lying one way or another. Either Diego truly is alive, and she's lied about his death. Or he's dead and she's lying now.

Faith leads the way down a narrow trail. Branches and shade and prickly grass. We stop under a canopy of leaves. And I see truth with my own eyes.

Diego is here.

He's sitting on the ground. Eyes closed. Head resting against a tree. I can almost believe he's dead, he's so much like statue. But then Faith speaks, startling him.

"Hey."

Diego smiles at first, happy to see her. He blinks and reaches toward Faith. Real, real, real. He's real. He's *alive*. Faith steps aside. Reveals me standing behind her. Diego's face instantly changes. Angry. He stands abruptly.

"What have you done?" he asks Faith.

"I had to," she tells him.

Diego runs a hand down his face. Through his hair roughly. Paces, shaking his head in a silent *no*.

No one is speaking to me. I feel like I shouldn't be here.

"She needed to know," Faith tells Diego.

"You've put them all in danger," Diego says. "My whole family. We agreed to tell no one."

"You don't understand." Faith steps closer. Takes his hand. "They already are in danger."

Diego's head snaps up. "No."

Despair paints his face.

"Tell him," Faith says, this time to me.

"You're alive," I say. "Why would you let everyone think you're dead?"

Diego finally turns to me. "If I tell you everything, you gonna do the same?"

He needs to know why his family is in danger. I hold the answer. I think of Javier. How he's joined the gang. His need for revenge.

For nothing.

I look at Diego. I look at him because I still can't believe he's here. I look at him and trip over the fact that he's alive. I choke on questions that beg to be asked and words that press against my lips.

I push the heels of my hands to my eyes and wait. Because how, how, how can this be real?

Diego is still in front of me, wanting an answer.

I drop my hands. I'll give him his answer. And he'll give me mine.

"Yes."

Fear slithers up my spine. Uncertainty pinches the back of my throat.

Diego is alive.

I'm walking through an airport terminal. Suitcase in my hand. Our row is called over a loudspeaker. Our turn to board a plane back to the States. Now that I've told Diego about Javier, he wants to see him. He has to stop Javier from doing something stupid. Diego never wanted to endanger Javier; that's what he's explained. It's too late; that's what I've told him.

Because Javier has already joined the gang. Because danger greets him daily.

"Sorry 'bout earlier," Diego says, taking a seat next to me.

The plane is a tiny capsule that makes me feel claustrophobic. We've already flown hundreds of miles in a plane even smaller to carry us out of Nicaragua and into Miami. This trip will take us home.

One hour.

Sixty minutes.

Three thousand six hundred seconds until we touch down.

Even longer until I see Javier.

"Didn't mean to be rude," Diego continues. "Just didn't expect Faith to tell you 'bout me."

I've learned that Faith didn't always know that Diego was alive. That revelation came months after she left, explaining why Faith didn't answer many of my calls. She worried that I'd know something was up with her. She didn't want to lie about Diego. She'd never helped someone fake a death before. I don't blame Faith anymore.

I've also learned that Diego was working with the government. He didn't elaborate, other than to say that he told the government things they needed to know. They gave him freedom as a thank-you.

It's a pretty big gift.

That I'm now endangering.

It took several phone calls to the government, two flights, and one promise from me that I'd never tell a soul about Diego being alive to make this trip happen.

Diego will visit Javier today. Let loose secrets that will change his world.

"It's okay," I tell Diego.

Nervousness settles deep in my gut. Makes a home and refuses to leave.

"So," Diego says. "This thing with you and Javier . . ."

He's looking for an explanation. It's not only my story to tell.

"Yeah?" I ask, waiting for something more specific.

Diego grins. "I've never seen him with a *gringa*."

"Because of his mom?" I ask, curious.

Diego looks surprised. "You know 'bout that?"

The party. The uninvited stares. Not getting her approval.

"Yeah," I reply. "He brought me to his house. Refused to let me leave when his mom told me to go."

Diego smiles wider. "So it's like that?"

I shrug. "Like what?"

"Never mind," he says. "Never known Javier to bring a girl home."

This makes me smile.

Diego's phone rings just as the flight attendant asks everyone to buckle their seat belts. Faith exits the bathroom. Diego scoots over to let Faith sit next to me for the flight. One finger to his ear. Phone against the other. His face falls.

"No," he whispers.

Something's not right. Something is horribly, horribly wrong. It's the pain in Diego's expression that gets to me. It's the look Diego gives me.

"Okay," he says and slips the phone back in his pocket.

The fact that Diego is looking at me, and not Faith says it all.

"Don't tell me," I say.

I could fill the ocean with the amount of sadness in Diego's eyes.

"That was the government," Diego says. "Javier's in the hospital."

A knife to my heart.

No.

"We don't know the details," he says.

But I'm not listening anymore. He can't, he can't, Javier can't be there. Not there. No.

"Is he—" I can't finish. I need to finish. "Is he gone?"

"I don't know," Diego says.

And my world stills. The oceans stop and the sun freezes and my heart . . .

breaks.

I am floating, crashing, unraveling inside. I am pain and agony and so much more.

I am devastated.

"Is there a chance," I whisper, "that he will be okay?"

Please, please, please.
"Yes."
It is the only hope I have.

Four letters. One word. The smallest percentage of a chance.
Coma.
Javier is in a coma. Shot. Not breathing on his own. So many moments of uncertainty.
They don't know, they don't know, how can they not know if Javier will live?
I reach over. Bite my lip to keep it from trembling. Touch Javier's still hand with one finger. He's cold, so cold.
A tear slips. Lands soundlessly on his blanket. Tubes keep him alive. He's going to wake up, I tell myself. I have to believe that he will.
Javier's eyes are closed. His body's unmoving, save the rise and fall of his chest.
I know this isn't the best time, but I have to tell him how I feel. I just have to.
"Javier," I whisper. Hope for a response. Don't get one. "I love you."
One, two, three, four beats of his heart that I imagine say:
I.
Love.
You.
Too.

48
javier

I catch patched sentences. Distorted words that find me. I want to break each noise in half. I want to throw it far away and tell the sounds to just be quiet because this sleep is so peaceful. More peaceful than anything I've ever known.

Something squeezes me. A sharp pain lacerating my skin.

What is that?

I wince.

Beep, beep, beep.

Pressure, so much pressure.

I push at the spot that hurts. Hear a voice in my head.

"Just a blood pressure cuff," it says. "I need to take your vitals."

And I need sleep. I push harder.

"All done," the voice says, and the pressure leaves me.

I let my hand drop back to my side. The effort is painful beyond measure.

"Do you know where you are?" it asks.

I take a chance and crack open my eyes. Regret it almost instantly. Light fills my vision. Sleep ebbs away.

Do I know where I am?

A prick of pain in my left arm. I look down. A needle is piercing my skin. A lady—no, a nurse—is administering it. She's the voice I've been hearing.

"Yes," I answer. Because I do know where I am now. "Hospital," I rasp.

I think about how the sea goes out with the tide, exposing the ocean floor. All rocky and dry. That's how my throat feels now.

The sea creatures are left there, watching their home disappear farther and farther into the horizon. Their bodies exposed to the merciless sun. Dying slowly. That's how I feel now.

"That's right," the nurse says. "You've been here two days."

Which means that I'm alive. Which also means that I didn't imagine the conversation I had with Monkey when I was bleeding out. Or did I?

"You need to take it very slowly," the nurse says as I try to lift my head. "You were shot through the lung."

She pauses. Lets that sink in.

"And you lived," are her next words.

"Happen often?" I ask, swallowing to try and wet my throat. I have nothing to ease the ache.

"Not so much," she admits.

The nurse's dark skin matches the brown of her scrubs. She writes something on paper. Picks up a small Styrofoam cup.

"You can have ice chips only," she says. It sounds like an order. "You were also shot in the hip but the bullet didn't hit bone. That one was fixed easily. Your lung will need longer to heal."

I think about where I am. In a hospital. Hearing the fate of my life from a woman I don't even know. It makes me think of *mi familia*. I wonder where they are. No, on second thought, I don't want to know. I am in no hurry to see *mi mamá*. Her angry face. There's no rush to tell *tío* Adolfo that I failed to bring justice to Diego's name.

Unless I didn't fail. Unless Wink *was* caught.

Suddenly, I need to see Monkey.

"Is anyone here?" I ask the nurse, as she tilts the cup of ice chips toward my mouth. I relish how it cools my tongue. "Family? Friends?"

My chest feels like it's wrapped no less than one hundred times. Breathing is almost as painful as the moment MS-13 shot me.

She nods. "People have stopped by. A few are still here, in the family waiting room."

"I need you to find out if someone named Monkey is there. Can you bring him here if he is?" I request.

The nurse presses a series of buttons on a machine to my right. I think about who else might be in the waiting room.

"But don't let my family back yet, if they're out there," I amend.

Her eyes narrow. Suspicion in her stare. "One guy said you might ask for him. He's the cop, right?"

God, Monkey *is* a cop, then.

"Yep."

"Be right back," she says.

I think back to the moments right after I was shot. Monkey turned against his own gang. It was his gang as much as it was mine, it seems. Meaning that it was never either of ours.

I'm lost in thought. Until the door opens.

Monkey fills the room. Reminding me of the lie I swallowed too easily. He stops a couple feet from my bed. He looks the same.

How deceiving.

I never would have imagined that Monkey was anything but an MS-13 member, tatted up, marked by them, quick on his toes. He waits for me to speak.

"You're a cop," I say.

Unbelievable.

"And you're a liar," he fires back.

Truth.

"So how long you been workin' against MS-13?" I wonder aloud.

He answers my question, but not with his usual easiness. "Since Diego died."

His words tell me that I *did* imagine the last part of our conversation. The part where Monkey told me that Diego hadn't died. The weight of that realization is stifling.

"I don't understand," I admit. "Have you always known who I am? And how did you know my cousin?"

"That," says Monkey, "is a long story."

"I've got time," I say, glancing around at my hospital room, the sheets that cover me. The place that will be my home until my lung heals.

"Diego knew the interworking of the cartel he used to belong to," Monkey explains. "We needed inside info. Where the cartel meets, who leads what, when the shipments go out, who they supply to, what they expect of members, and so much more."

This version of Monkey doesn't sound like the MS-13

member I thought he was. Face serious. Talking business. No more laziness in his posture. And then I catch the slight bounce of his leg. I almost smile. Some things don't change, after all.

"Explain better," I say because it still doesn't make sense.

"We also wanted to see what kind of connections MS-13 had to the cartel," Monkey continues. "To see MS-13 and a Cuban cartel working together to find one member seemed strange. Unless they already had a connection to each other."

Never thought about it like that. I wonder if the connection started because of Diego.

"Diego, one escaped member, doesn't seem like enough to bring leaders of a cartel all the way from Cuba. Unless," Monkey says, "they were already planning on coming to the US and decided to take out Diego while they were here."

Pieces click.

"They were working together," I say.

Maybe the cartel helps supply MS-13. With who knows what. Drugs? Weapons? Buyers? It all seems possible. Highly likely. I wonder why I didn't connect the two earlier.

"*Sí,*" Monkey confirms.

"And what happened after I got shot?" I ask. I remember Monkey killing two gang members, but what about the others? "Did you bust the rest of the gang?"

"We got some of them," he says. "We couldn't get them all, though."

Moment of truth.

"What about Wink? Was he one of the ones you got?"

Monkey stares at me, holding the answer I need the most.

Was it worth it, every second spent hunting Wink?

"Yes."

I sigh, wincing at the pain in my lung. It's done. It's finally done. Wink has been caught.

And this time *revenge* is replaced with *justice*.

I still have so many questions. Like:

Did you know who I was when I joined? Did MS-13 know from the start that Diego belonged to the cartel? Did they care? Why didn't MS-13 turn him right over? Why offer him a position in their gang?

Monkey answers with things like:

No, I didn't realize who you were until it was too late. Yeah, they knew about Diego. They offered him the position because they knew he'd be good for it. If he chose MS-13, they wouldn't have turned him over, but they would have had something to hold over Diego's head to make him do their bidding, their dirty work. They would have kept him out of the cartel negotiations. Made him do work in MS-13. But Diego didn't join, so they handed him over. Retribution.

"You're going to have more questions," Monkey says.

Of course I do. I have enough questions to fill the space between us.

"I'm not the one who can answer," he says.

He's the perfect person to answer.

"But," Monkey says, checking his phone. "Someone else can."

The door opens. In walks a guy. I think. I can't see a face. Only a huge black sweatshirt, hood up over the head and falling down over the eyes. Baggy jeans.

But somehow I know.

I know who it is, even though I have to be wrong.

It's only once the door shuts that he finally looks at me.

From.

The.

Dead.

I've never known anyone to come back from the dead.

When I was younger, my older brothers used to tell me stories about monsters and legends to scare me before bed-time. The undead walking. The *bruja* who stole children from forests. People who turned into mythical creatures. I never told my brothers, but I liked the stories. They helped me forget about the scary things happening all around me in Cuba. The stories were never real.

But this?

This is real, even though it can't be.

"Hola, primo," he says.

Diego.

Same as before. Same face as in the pictures at his wake, which consisted of *familia* meeting in our yard to say a few words about him. *Tío* Adolfo didn't want to watch his son get lowered into the ground. It was enough to know he was buried; he didn't want to watch it happen. I couldn't have agreed more. Now I wonder if he lied. Maybe *tío* Adolfo knows that Diego is alive. But how could he sit through us saying words about how much we missed Diego, and know the whole time that he wasn't gone?

Maybe he didn't know.

Maybe Diego hid from everyone who used to matter to him.

"You fucking asshole!" I finally say, wincing at the pain yelling causes. My lungs work to bring oxygen in.

I took a bullet for him.

Three, actually.

Diego let me think that he was gone. No, not gone. Dead.

If I could get up from this bed, I would. This whole time—every minute of grief, every drop of vengeance—all for nothing.

"I swear on *la vida de mi mamá*—"

"I know," Diego says. "Got a lot to tell you."

"Start," I say, angry, happy. Both at once. "With why you let me think you were dead. Actually, no. Start with how you *came back* from the dead."

Hands in his pockets, face half hidden, he explains everything. How they resuscitated him in the ambulance. How he worked with the US government. How Monkey was assigned to infiltrate the gang and find Wink. Diego suspected that the cartel and MS-13 were working together, he says. He told the government everything he knew about the cartel, he admits. And yeah, that makes him a nark, he says. But it's worth it to have Faith again, to turn over the people who stabbed him in the back, and murdered his *mamá*.

"They would've killed you, *primo*. If they suspected that you knew anything 'bout me, if they suspected that I was alive, they would've taken out the whole *familia*." His voice cracks then. "I couldn't risk it. I didn't call 'cause I wanted to protect you," Diego says. "Lot of good that did. You found trouble anyway."

The hood drops from his face and I see remorse in his stare.

"I just wanted to protect you," he repeats.

You would have done the same thing, I mentally admit. *You would have done whatever it took to protect family.*

"I'm not gonna pretend that I'm not pissed at how this all went down," I say. "But I'm glad you're back."

Like the tide, I think.

Coming home to cover the broken pieces it left behind.

melissa 49

I hate that I can't go straight to the hospital to see Javier. Especially since I know that he's woken up. He's going to make it. I haven't wanted to admit to myself that there was a good chance he wouldn't. I take one look at life and know that this time, with Javier, it has been good to me.

I should be with him, but instead I'm here. White walls and endless turmoil. I'm waiting to see the doctor. I'm closed in a room with no windows. I need to see something besides these plain walls that have no character. I wonder what will happen to my character if the doctor delivers bad news.

I twist a ring on my pinky finger. Think back to when I got it.

"Wait for me!" Faith shouts, running up the boardwalk.

I'm yards ahead of her, weaving through the crowd.

"Hurry up, slowpoke!" I'm not sure if she's heard me over the constant boardwalk noise, the whooshing of waves, the chattering of people drifting everywhere on the beach.

Our parents have given us twenty bucks each, and one hour of free time before we have to meet them for dinner at a restaurant down the strip.

There are signs restricting kids my age from being alone.

DO NOT LEAVE CHILDREN UNDER 14 UNATTENDED.

I don't know why fourteen is the cutoff. It never made sense to me. Either way, I still have two years before I can technically walk this strip without my parents. Faith and I already agreed that if anyone asks our age, we'll lie. Say we're fourteen. They'll never know the difference.

"Let's go in here!" Faith says, catching up to me. She points at a jewelry shop that sells natural stones like onyx and moonstone and jade.

A bell jangles loudly as we open the door and step inside. It smells like lavender. A lady behind the counter asks if we're looking for anything in particular. We say no. But once we begin looking, we find it. Two matching rings with three tiny stones. Orange, yellow, and green amber. We have just enough money.

"To friendship," I say, smiling.

"Forever," Faith agrees.

I still have the ring, though it no longer fits the same finger.

"Everything is going to be fine," Faith says, disrupting my thoughts.

My lab results have already been determined. Whatever news the doctor plans to give me is already reality. Like it or not.

I never expected to hear news that could end my life while sitting next to Faith, but life is funny like that. Life gives you things you never asked for and takes away things you always dreamed of. I wonder where life gets the nerve.

Faith wanted to come today. She figured I'd need support. I wonder if Javier needs support, too. I don't like to think about it, how Diego will change Javier's world today. Maybe he already has. Maybe he's showed up at the hospital and delivered the news that he lied. Hid his survival. I wonder what Javier is going through. How he's going to take the news. I should be there with him.

I'm thinking about leaving. Calling the doctor later and asking for the results over the phone, even though that's not the normal protocol. But I don't get the chance because the doctor walks in. Smile on his face.

Just like last time.

I don't know if that's good or bad. Maybe he smiles no matter what.

"Hello, Melissa," he says. "How have you been?"

Horrible. Awful. Worried. "Fine."

"Any discomfort from the surgery sites?"

"No."

Just say it already.

"Do you mind if I take a look?"

I freeze. Yes, actually, I do mind. Because even though you put the scars there, Doctor, I haven't showed anyone besides May. That shouldn't change now.

I look at Faith. "I'm not sure."

Her eyes narrow. The doctor tries a different avenue.

"Maybe your friend could step outside?" He's politely asking Faith to give us privacy.

"It's just that I haven't showed anyone besides May," I explain to Faith.

"Remember when you dared me to take chances at the restaurant?" she asks.

I think back to it, a time when we were in high school and Faith still lived here. I pushed Faith to admit whether or not she thought Diego was hot. What I was really pushing her toward was stepping out of her shell. I have a feeling that she's about to do the same to me.

"You wanted me to be free. You wanted me to kill fear," she says.

Faith makes no move to leave.

"It's your turn," she challenges, her voice soft.

It's a gentle challenge. One I think she'll back down from if I insist. But I won't. Because she's Faith. And because she's right.

I lie down on the table. Lift my shirt above my belly button and push my jeans down slightly, enough to reveal my scars.

Cold fingers prod my belly. I wait for it to be over. Eventually, I will have to face that this is permanent. That I'm scarred. That cancer bit off pieces of me. Inside and out.

I stare blankly at my stomach. One long pink line digs into my abdomen. Two small ones hide inside my belly button. I can't look away.

"Would you like to know the results of your blood work?" the doctor asks. Quits poking me.

I fix my clothes. Faith takes my hand and squeezes, her way of telling me that she's here for me.

"Yes," I reply numbly.

No moment has ever mattered more.

"Your cancer," says the doctor, "is gone."

Time

just

stops.

I'm struggling to believe his words. They're the same words I've been wanting to hear for six months. They're all I've dreamed of. And here, now, I've got them. They're mine.

"Completely gone?" I double-check.

"Completely gone," the doctor echoes.

"Forever?"

"We hope," he says. "You'll have checkups, but everything looks good, Melissa. Congratulations."

I glance up. Find Faith's watery eyes. Fear doesn't have any place here.

"Thank you," are the words out of my lips.

To Faith. To the doctor. To life.

Because sometimes, people get second chances. For the first time.

I look back down to where my scars hide under my clothes. They're hard to accept. But one day, if I try hard enough, hopefully I'll see them not as ugly reminders, but as beautiful souvenirs.

They are what I've taken home from my battle with cancer.

One day, maybe, I can even wear them proudly.

EPILOGUE

Javier

She is beautiful, so beautiful. A thousand million thank-yous that all whisper her name. Over and over again I wish I could tell Melissa how grateful I am.

She saved me.

I don't blame her for ratting me out to Faith.

It brought Diego back.

I think of what she said on the day of my release from the hospital.

I'm in the passenger seat, staring at Melissa's beautiful face.

"I have something to tell you," she whispers as she pulls up to my house. She cuts the engine. Her eyes land on my hospital bag, then on my bandaged body.

I worry that me being in the hospital has reminded Melissa of her time there—her surgeries—and I want nothing more than to take the pain from her. But when she looks back up at me, there's a smile on her lips.

"My cancer is gone."

My eyes widen. I'm hearing the best news possible.

"I'm officially in remission."

I want to congratulate her. Ask how she feels. I don't want to push too far. I settle on: "I'm proud of you."

Because I am. Melissa is the strongest person I know. She battled a deadly monster, and won. She held hope tightly in her hand and promised to never let it go.

I look at Melissa now, cancer free, and I get this feeling like I never want to let her go.

"*Mami,*" I whisper into her ear.

Her breath catches. Her eyes switch direction. She stops looking at Faith and Diego—sitting in her living room across from us—and starts looking at me.

"Yeah?" she asks, so close to my face.

I pretend not to notice the way my cousin grins. I don't even care that I'm transparent. Yeah, I care about a *gringa.*

He does, too.

And yeah, it goes against everything I've been taught, everything I've ever known.

She's worth it.

"*Bésame.*" My demand is quiet. Only Melissa can hear me.

When her eyes drop to my lips, I forget that we're in her house, saying good-bye to Faith and Diego, who have been in town since I got shot, staying at Faith's old place. I forget they might be watching us. I don't know one single thing except for her lips, the way she presses them against mine. The power in her touch.

A throat clears. I don't welcome interruptions.

"Damn, man," Diego says, grinning. "We only got a few minutes."

The car will be here soon to pick up Diego and Faith. Take them back to the airport. For now, Nicaragua is their home. There's still more work to do there, Diego says. They're changing people's lives, Faith mentions. I wonder if Faith and Diego's lives are being changed, too. From the way my cousin smiles more, from the way he seems at peace, I think they are.

I'm happy for him.

Melissa and I will be leaving soon, too. We've talked about it the last couple weeks since my release from the hospital. There's a community college in a small Georgia town, a place Melissa once visited and loved. It's a college she always wanted to attend, but couldn't because of her cancer. Well, now she can. And as it turns out, my grades aren't an issue. They accept anyone who is willing to pay for classes. As long as I work, we can afford an apartment near campus, too.

It's still hard to believe. In a couple weeks, Melissa and I will move. Next semester, I'll be going to college. Melissa has her life back. We'll be together, in our own place. No more MS-13 and looking over my shoulder. No more wondering if they'll send members to find me, because I'll be gone.

A life, free.

"Two minutes, to be exact," Diego says.

"So?" I reply jokingly, glancing at *mi primo*. Way I see it—his arms wrapped around Faith, his fingers stroking the underside of her knee—Diego knows exactly how I feel.

I lean in for another kiss from Melissa. She shies away. Smiles mischievously. God, I love her smile. I want to memorize Melissa's face with my lips. I want to touch every part of her. And as much as I don't want my cousin to leave, I need time alone with Melissa.

"So, can't you wait two minutes?" Diego jokes.

"I don't know, man," I reply. "I can try."

It feels good to joke with *mi primo*. Like the deepest

breath of fresh air when all I've been breathing is toxic revenge.

Now I don't have to.

Diego gets that I've fallen hard for Melissa, but not all my family understands. I tried to tell *mi mamá* that Melissa saved me. I tried to explain that moving away to college with Melissa is a really good thing. But without being able to tell her about the gang, or Diego, she doesn't understand why I was shot, though she has her suspicions, or why I need to move to such a small town far away. And though she's happy that I want to attend college, she isn't happy that I'll be there with Melissa. I can only hope that *mi mamá* will accept Melissa one day. There's a chance she never will. There's a chance that some people will always look at me and Melissa together and wonder:

Why?

I may never be able to convince the universe, people like *mi mamá*. Because some people don't want change. But I'd like to think that with each chance taken, each kiss and touch and show of passion, we get one step closer.

"Will you guys be able to visit us at college?" Melissa asks, eyeing Faith.

I think their friendship is similar to mine and Diego's. It's the kind of bond that doesn't die. Not with distance. Not with tragedies.

"Maybe," Faith replies. "And maybe you can visit us, too."

It feels good to know that we don't have to worry about MS-13 anymore. They're still out there, free, some of them. But Wink isn't. He's behind bars for life—where he belongs—charged with too many crimes to name. And thanks to the US government sting, the cartel has returned to Cuba. Receding back onto Cuba's mainland like prey being hunted. Hopefully, they'll stay there. I wonder if one day, they'll be completely destroyed.

It's hard to imagine my homeland being safe. It's a long shot, but possible.

"You should visit on your college breaks," Diego says. *"Tómate unas vacaciones."*

"Sometime," I agree.

"You know how to reach me," Diego says.

An open invitation. A number in my phone and a life not finished.

"We have to go," Faith says.

It's a good good-bye. One filled with next times and until thens and a future worth living.

"Do me a favor," Diego says on his way to the door. "Don't find trouble this time."

He smiles, but he's serious. I promise, and I mean it. Faith hugs Melissa good-bye. My fist bumps Diego's. Our version.

I think maybe Melissa wants to cry, so I kiss her. Promise her that we'll see them soon.

"Take care of my girl," Faith says. Hops in the car.

From the doorway, I say, "Always."

I don't have to ask Faith to take care of Diego. I know she will.

I watch the car pull out of the driveway, then face the girl who changed everything for me.

"The house is ours until morning," she says.

My lips twitch, a grin forming. "Oh, yeah?"

I run fingers through her silky hair. Watch her mouth turn up in the smallest smile. She places a hand on my stomach, careful not to press near my lung. It's not quite healed.

"I have something for you," I tell her.

Wide eyes stare back. "You do?"

"It's on your bed." I put it there earlier when she thought I was using the bathroom.

"And how did you manage that?" she wonders.

I shrug. "Skills."

Melissa laughs and walks up the steps, leaving me to follow. I wait for Melissa to see it. A small square box on her pillow.

A memory for you.

"Open it," I say.

She does. First untying the red bow. Then cracking the lid. Her eyes land on the bracelet. She picks it up.

"From our date," she says, remembering.

It's the same shark's tooth I found at the sandbar, on a silver chain. Small, but hers. A part of us.

"I love it." She clasps the bracelet around her wrist. A token.

"And I love you," I say.

The words slip from my lips. I've known for a while.

Melissa stills. I want her to know I mean it.

"Te amo, mi princesa."

"I love you, too," she whispers.

It's happiness like I've never known.

It's all I need.

I gather Melissa in my arms. Taste the swell of her lips. She breathes like I'm made of air. She drinks me in with every inhale.

"There's something, one last thing, I need to do," Melissa says.

She takes one step back. Two deep breaths.

"You asked about—" Pause. Shaky breath. "About my . . ." Torturous look. "Scars."

The last word is a whisper. Barely there.

"You wanted to know about my scars," she continues,

trying to steel her voice. "They're horrible. But if you want me, they come, too."

Of course, they do. I never thought otherwise. Her scars don't make me want her any less.

Actually, I want her even more.

"I love you, *mami*," I repeat. Wait for her to look me in the eyes. "Whether you have scars or not."

A tear slips down her face. Gut reaction, I kiss it away.

"You have no idea," I say, pulling her closer, "how beautiful you are. It will never matter that you have scars. I will never see you as anything less than brave, beautiful, mine."

A kiss.

"Mine."

My voice is rough. Needy. Emotion and love and this amazing girl.

"I need—" She waits. Steadies her shaking hands. Clasps them to her shirt. "I need for you to see them."

I see the horror in her eyes. The absolute terror she feels at asking me to look.

"I need you to be sure that you are okay with this before we go away to college," she says, hitching her shirt up just enough. Lowering her pants to a level just below her hip bones. She looks off at the wall, waiting for my reaction. Like she's scared of how I'll respond.

I see them clearly. Her scars. Nothing will change the way I feel about her.

Why can't you see?

You're perfect.

My hands grip her hips. She tenses. I wait for it to pass. Finally, Melissa looks at me. I lower her to the bed.

Will you be offended if I tell you they're beautiful?

"Does it hurt?" I settle next to Melissa.

"No," she replies.

I stroke her ribs, her arms, her neck.

"Can I touch you now?"

She hesitates. "My scars?"

"Yes," I answer. Serious. I won't if she doesn't want me to. But I really hope she lets me.

Her lips press together. A thin line.

She's not telling me no.

"I would never hurt you," I promise. "These," I say, fingers hovering over her scars, "won't change the way I feel 'bout you."

Melissa lets go of fear. Nods.

With her permission, I lower my fingers. Meet warm flesh. Skim the tender surface of her scars.

I still my fingers. Wait to see if Melissa's okay. She's not. She's anxious. I kiss around her stomach, try to loosen her up. Try to show her that I have no problem with her scars. Maybe one day she won't either.

Maybe I can help her see.

I kiss down her hips. Listen as her breathing deepens.

It's hard not to lose myself in Melissa. The rise and fall of her chest. The way she lets me touch her so freely.

"These," I say, lips just above her scars, "are beautiful."

Melissa makes a noise like a whimper. I move up to her face.

"Is it okay that I think they're beautiful?"

I don't want to upset her. But, turns out, she's not upset. She's the opposite of upset. Melissa kisses me hard. Doesn't stop kissing me.

I want to kiss her lips forever. I want to wake up every morning knowing that Melissa is mine. Despite the scars. Even though I made mistakes. Regardless of whether or not *mi mamá* approves. Some never will. Through cancer and gangs and almost dying, both of us, we're still together.

Love, I think, is to blame.

And I understand, for the first time, that life does offer more than violence and hunger and trying to survive. Sometimes, if you want it bad enough, life will even give you a chance to become something better.

Melissa breathes passion. She moves closer and whispers how much I mean to her. I refuse to let her go.

Does she see it in my face?

Can she tell that I'll move the world for her?

Before Melissa? Pain. Suffering. Destruction.

This is what change looks like.

I've found a life worth living. Love worth having.

This is the face of redemption.

"I love you," she says.

"*Yo también,*" I whisper.

A thousand, million, billion times: This.

I throw to the ground what's left of me. Shatter what once was. Pick up the pieces of my life to find that they make something different. They whisper one word. One amazing keep-holding-on word. One beautiful never-give-up word.

A forever, believe-in-second-chances word.

The word is:

Hope.

Have you read the first novel in Amber Hart's Before and After series?
It's available now in print and e-book.

BEFORE YOU

"Beautiful . . . will settle deep in your heart."
—Sophie Jordan, *New York Times* bestselling author

Some say love is deadly. Some say love is beautiful. I say it's both.
It will haunt me. It will claim me. It will shatter me. And I don't care.

Faith Watters has a picture-perfect life. She's captain of the dance team, popular, happy. She even spent her junior year traveling the world before returning to Oviedo High School for senior year. But she's living a lie.

Diego Alvarez hates his new life in the States, but staying in Cuba is not an option. Covered in tattoos and scars, Diego doesn't stand a chance of fitting in, and doesn't want to. His only concern is his secret past—a past, which if it were to surface, would cost him his life.

Everyone knows that Faith and Diego don't belong together. But fate has its own plan. All they want is to be free. What they get is something different entirely.

Love—it will ruin you . . . and save you.

"Amber Hart's beautiful writing style will hook and hold you."
—K.A. Tucker, author of *Ten Tiny Breaths*

1
faith

My closet is a place of secrets.

This is where I change into Her, the girl everybody knows as me. Searching through hanger after hanger of neatly pressed clothes, I find the outfit I'm looking for. A black knee-length pleated skirt, a loose-fitting white top, and two-inch wedge shoes. Looking good at school is a must. Not that I do it for me. It's more for my dad's reputation. I have to play the part.

I am stuffed into a borrowed frame. One that fits too tightly. One that couldn't possibly capture the real me.

"Faith," my stepmom calls. "Are you joining us for breakfast?"

There is no time. "No," I reply, my voice carrying downstairs.

I quickly dress for school, catching my reflection in the closet door mirror. Waking sun shines off my hair, highlighting a few strands brighter than the rest. Everybody has a favorite body part. Mine is my hair, which is the fiery-brown of autumn leaves. My best friend, Melissa, swears my eyes are my best asset. Ivy-green, deep-set, haunting. Like they go on forever.

Speaking of Melissa, her horn blares outside. *Beep,*

beep, pause, *beep*. That's our code. I race downstairs, passing my dad, stepmom, and little sister on the way out.

"Wait," Dad says.

I sigh. "Yes, Dad?"

He glances at my outfit, pausing at my shoes. If it were up to Dad, I would wear turtleneck shirts and dress pants with lace-up boots forever. The perfect ensemble, it seems. As it is, I dress conservatively to protect his image. I'm eighteen. You'd think he'd stop cringing every time he saw me in anything that showed the least bit of skin.

"Hug," he says, waving me over.

I hug him. Place a kiss on my five-year-old sister's jelly-covered cheek. Then, grab a napkin to wipe the sticky jelly from my lips.

"Bye, Gracie," I say to her. "See you after school."

She waves a small hand at me and smiles.

"Take this." Susan, my stepmom, hands me a bagel even though I already declined breakfast. It's poppy seed. I'm allergic to poppy seed.

As usual, I don't put up a fight. My frame feels especially uncomfortable at the moment. It's always the same thing. I learned early on that it's easier to go with the flow than to be different. Different is bad. Standing out attracts attention, something I try to avoid at all costs. Unfortunately, being the dance captain makes that more difficult.

"Have to go," I say, shoving the bagel in my bag.

The screen door swings shut behind me.

Melissa waits in my driveway. We live in a modest, yellow-paneled house in Oviedo, Florida. The majority of the people here are middle class. We fit in well.

"What's up?" Melissa smiles. "Took you long enough."

"Yeah, well, you try waking up late and still looking as good as I do," I joke.

Melissa whips her blond hair into a ponytail and puts her red Camaro in reverse, careful not to hit my Jeep on the way out. I have my own car, but since Melissa lives three doors down, we have a deal where we alternate driving to school. She takes the first month; I take the second, and so on. Saves gas.

"You look smokin'," Melissa says, lighting a cigarette.

I roll my eyes.

"Liar."

She's always hated the way I dress.

Melissa laughs. "Okay, true, the clothes need to go. But your hair and makeup are flawless. And no matter what you wear, you still look beautiful."

"Thanks. You, too," I say, eyeing her tight jeans and sequined top. Melissa is effortlessly beautiful with her sun-freckled face and athletic build.

"Prediction," Melissa begins. This is something we have done since ninth grade: predict three things that will happen during the year. "Tracy Ram will try to overthrow you as dance captain, once again, but you'll keep your spot, of course, 'cause you rock. You'll quit dressing like an eighty-year-old and finally wear what you want to wear instead of what society dictates is appropriate for a pastor's daughter. And you'll come to your senses and dump Jason Magg for a hot new boy."

Melissa always predicts that I'll dump Jason, has done so since Jason and I began dating freshman year. It's not that she doesn't like him. It's just that she thinks my life is too bland, like the taste of celery. What's the point? she figures.

"First of all, I do not dress like the elderly," I say. "And second, I don't know what you have against Jason. He treats me nicely. It's not like he's a jerk."

"It's not like he's exciting, either," Melissa says.

She's right. What I have with Jason is comfortable, nice even, but excitement left a long time ago.

"Prediction," I say, turning to Melissa. "You will not be able to quit bugging me about dumping Jason, even though last year you swore you would. Despite your doubts, you *will* pass senior calculus. And you're going to win homecoming."

Melissa shakes her head. "No way. Homecoming is all you, girl."

I groan. "But I don't want to win."

Melissa laughs. "Tracy Ram would have a heart attack if she ever heard you say that."

"Great," I say. "Let her win homecoming."

We grin. Melissa and I have been friends since kindergarten. Memories come to me suddenly. I'm in elementary school, and it's sleepover night at Melissa's. In my overnight bag, I carry a small stuffed bunny, my steadfast companion since forever. People would laugh if they knew, me carrying around a stuffed baby toy, but Melissa never tells. Fast-forward to middle school. The braces on Melissa's teeth are still so new that the silver catches the light from the fluorescent fixtures when she smiles. The headgear is huge, cumbersome, and no one lets her forget it. But I relentlessly defend my friend. She's so beautiful, can't they see? Sometimes I leave flowers stolen from a neighbor's rosebush at her locker when no one is looking. That way people will know that she is loved. High school. Melissa and me, same as always.

"What do you want to bet?" Melissa asks.

Whoever gets the most predictions right wins.

"Hmm," I say. "If I win, you have to quit smoking."

Melissa almost chokes. "Pulling out the big guns, are

we? Okay, then. If I win, you have to break up with Jason."

"Deal," I say, knowing that she won't win. She never does.

Melissa purses her lips and gives me the stink eye. She knows I have a better chance.

"Faith, I will find a way to break you out of your mold," she says.

I laugh, partially because of the determination in my friend's eyes, but mostly because of the absurdity of her statement. Everybody knows that girls like me never break free.

$\overset{2}{diego}$

"**D**iego, *vamonos*."
    I can't help the frustrated sigh that escapes my lips, hurled at *mi padre*, my dad, like a gust of wind that threatens to flatten our house of cards. It's my fault. I should have built something stronger with the cards I was dealt. But I didn't. I didn't know how.

"Go away," I say. "*Vete.*"

I'm not planning to attend school today.

In fact, I didn't plan to be in the States at all.

"*Vamonos.* Let's go," *mi padre* repeats in his heavily accented voice, yanking me off of the couch. "You will not miss senior year."

He has this new thing where we have to speak English as much as possible now that we live in the States. I almost wish I weren't fluent. Several summers in Florida, and I am.

With a grimace, I pass him, reluctantly moving toward my room. It feels like my feet are sinking, like I'm walking over sticky sand instead of thick, dirty carpet.

How did I get stuck in this place?

I open my dresser drawer and pull out faded jeans, a white T-shirt, and my Smith & Wesson.

"No," *mi padre* says, grabbing the gun.

I take a step toward him, challenging. He does not back down.

"This is why we left," he says.

Hypocrite. Under his bed is a similar gun, waiting. Just in case. But he's also the one who taught me how to fight. I'm bigger than he is, but he has more experience. And the scars to prove it.

Not that I haven't been in countless fights myself.

"Fine," I say through clenched teeth, and turn toward the bathroom.

The hot water heater goes out after five minutes. The tiny two-bedroom apartment—this hole we now call home—is the only thing *mi padre* could afford. It's not much, but it's inexpensive. That's all that matters. The plain white walls remind me of an asylum. Feels like I'm going crazy already.

Our jobs keep us afloat. They're our life vests, our only chance of survival in a sea of ravenous sharks. *Mi padre* found a job with a lawn crew a couple of weeks ago. Not many people would hire him with his scarred face and tattooed body. A restaurant offered me work part-time. Two shifts as a cook, one as a busboy. They promised a free meal every night that I worked. Couldn't pass that up.

"Don't be late for school or work," *mi padre* says as I step out of the house.

School's only ten minutes away. I walk, staring at the graffiti-covered sidewalk that stretches in front of me like a ribbed canvas. Latinos roam the block. It didn't take moving to the States for me to know that's how it is. The *gringos*, white people, live in nice houses and drive cars to school while the rest of the world waits for a piece of their leftovers. I'm trying not to think about how screwed up it all is when a Latina walks up to me.

"*Hola*," she says. "*¿Hablas inglés?*"

"Yeah, I speak English," I answer, though I'm not sure why she asks since both of us speak Spanish.

"I'm Lola." She smiles, sexy brown eyes big and wide. She reminds me of a girl I knew back home. Just the thought, the image of home, makes my guts clench.

"What's your name?" she purrs.

"Lola," a Latino calls from across the street. She ignores him. He calls again. When she doesn't come, he approaches us.

One look tells me he's angry. He has a cocky stance and a shaved head.

"Am I interrupting something?" he snaps.

What's this guy's problem?

"Yep," Lola says, turning her back on him. "My ex," she explains, brushing a strand of curly hair out of her face.

Perfecto. Just what I need. I didn't even do anything. Not that I'm going to explain.

"She's mine," the guy says, staring me down. "*¿Entiendes, amigo?*"

"I'm not your friend," I say, gritting my teeth. "And you do not want to mess with me."

Lola is smiling. I wonder if she enjoys the attention. Probably. I've met too many girls like her. She fits the type.

"You don't know who *you're* messing with," he says, stepping closer.

A few guys come out of nowhere, closing in on me. Blue and white bandannas hang from their pockets like a bad-luck charm. I know what the colors signify. Mara Salvatrucha 13 Gang, or MS-13.

I turn to Lola. Watch her smile.

This is all part of the game. What I can't figure out is if the guy really is her ex and she doesn't care that she could be getting me killed, or if he sent her to see how tough I am, to help decide whether he wants to recruit me.

I turn to walk away, but someone blocks my path.

"Going somewhere?" another gangbanger asks.

This whole time I wondered if I'd end up fighting at school. I hadn't thought about the fact that I might never make it there in the first place. I silently curse *mi padre* for hiding my gun. He wouldn't get rid of it completely, though.

"What do you want?" I ask.

The original guy laughs, looks me up and down. The number 67 is tattooed behind his right ear in bold black numbers. It only takes me a second to figure out the meaning. Six plus seven equals thirteen.

"What are those markings?" he asks, eyeing my tattoos.

"Nothing," I lie.

If they wanted to fight me, they would've done it already. This is a recruit.

"Where you from?" he asks.

I don't answer. Members of MS-13 stretch around the globe like fingers. They can easily check my past. I'm not gonna give them a head start.

"Swallow your tongue?" one of the guys asks.

I'm trying to figure out if I can win a fight against the five guys who surround me. I look for weak spots, scars, old injuries. I look for bulges that might be weapons. I'm a good fighter. I think I can take them. But at the same time, fighting will guarantee me a follow-up visit from MS-13.

Just then, someone speaks behind us. "Is there a problem?" a police officer asks from the safety of his car.

Everyone backs away from me.

"Nope," one of the gangbangers answers. "We were just leaving."

"See you around," 67 says, throwing an arm around Lola.

I turn my back and walk the last block to school. The police officer trails slowly behind, like a hungry dog sniffing for scraps. He leaves as I enter the double doors.

I think about what my dad said. *Moving here will give you a brighter future.*

His words sit heavily on my mind, like humidity on every pore of my skin. His intentions are good, but he's wrong. So far, moving here has done nothing but remind me of my past.

3
faith

"Hi, I'm Faith Watters."

Those are the first words I speak to the new Cuban guy in the front office. He grimaces. He'll be a tough one. I can handle it, though. He's not the first.

I can't help but notice that he looks a lot like a model from the neck up—eyes the color of oak, strong bone structure. Everywhere else, he looks a lot like a criminal. Chiseled, scarred body . . . I wonder for a second about the meaning behind the tattoos scratched into his arms.

One thing's clear. He's dangerous.

And he's beautiful.

"I'll show you to your classes," I announce.

I'm one of the peer helpers at our school. It's not my favorite thing to do, but it counts as a class. Basically I spend the first two days with new students, introducing them around and answering their questions. Some parents with kids new to the school voluntarily sign their kids up, but it's only mandatory for the international students, of which we have a lot. Mostly Latinos.

This Cuban guy towers over me. I'm five-six. Not tall. Not short. Just average. Average is good.

This guy's not average. Not even a little bit. He must be over six feet.

I glance up at him, kind of like I do when I'm searching for the moon in a sea of darkness.

"Looks like you have math first. I'll walk you there," I offer.

"No thanks, *chica*. I can handle it."

"It's no problem," I say, leading the way.

He tries to snatch his schedule from my hands, but I move too fast.

"Why don't we start with your name?" I suggest.

I already know his name. Plus some. Diego Alvarez. Eighteen years old. Moved from Cuba two weeks ago. Only child. No previous school records. I read it in his bio. I want to hear him say it.

"You got some kinda control issues or somethin'?" he asks harshly, voice slightly accented.

"You got some kind of social issues or somethin'?" I fire back, holding my stance. I won't let him intimidate me, though I'll admit, he's hot. Too bad he has a nasty attitude.

The side of his lip twitches. "No. I just don't mix with your type," he answers.

"My type?"

"That's what I said."

"You don't even know my type." No one does. Well, except Melissa.

He chuckles humorlessly. "Sure I do. Head cheerleader? Date the football player? Daddy's little girl who gets everything she wants?" He leans closer to whisper. "Probably a virgin."

My cheeks burn hot. "I'm not a cheerleader," I say through clamped teeth.

"Whatever," he says. "Are you gonna give me my schedule or not?"

"Not," I answer. "But you can feel free to follow me to your first class."

He steps in front of me, intimately close. "Listen, *chica*, nobody tells me what to do."

I shrug. "Fine, suit yourself. It's your life. But if you want to attend this school, it's mandatory for me to show you to your classes for two days."

His eyes narrow. "Who says I want to attend this school?"

I take the last step toward him, closing the gap between us. When we were little, Melissa and I used to collect glass bottles. Whenever we accumulated twenty, we'd break them on the concrete. When the glass shattered, the slivered pieces made a breathtaking prism of light.

I cut myself on the glass by accident once. It was painful, but worth it. The beauty was worth it. It's funny how the bottle was never as beautiful as when it was broken.

You will not shatter me, I silently tell Diego. *Somebody already did.*

"If you don't want to be here, then don't come back," I say.

A taunting smile spreads across his face. My first thought is that he has nice teeth, but then I scold myself for thinking about him like that.

"My name is Diego," he says, like he's letting me in on some kind of secret.

"Well, Diego," I say, "better hurry. Class starts in two minutes." I step around him to lead the way.

While we walk to math, I feel Diego's eyes on me. I don't know what it is about him. All the other confident students had nothing on me, and I swear I've heard it all, but he seems different. He shines. In a dark way. When he looks at me, I get a tingly sensation, like I'm being zapped by electricity.

It doesn't matter. He's rude. And besides, I have a wonderful boyfriend. Jason. Think about Jason.

"Quit staring at me," I say, glancing at him.

He laughs, and strands of black hair fall into his eyes. I imagine it's a little like looking at the world through charred silk.

"Why? Does it make you uncomfortable?"

He's messing with me to get under my skin, like a pesky little splinter.

It's working.

"Yes," I answer.

In his white shirt, Diego's skin is dark. Perpetually tanned by heritage.

I keep Diego's schedule out of his reach. He inches closer, no doubt to grab it and run. I try to concentrate on the newly painted beige walls and tiled floors. Every few feet hangs a plaque about achievement or school clubs or tutoring programs.

When we come to the door, Diego rests an arm on the wall and leans toward me.

"I have a proposition for you," he says in a sultry voice.

It's hard to seem unaffected.

"I don't do propositions," I say dismissively.

He grins, his mouth arching up like the curl of a wave.

"But you haven't even heard me out," he says.

"Don't need to."

He ignores my comment. "What do you say we forget about this thing where I follow you around like a little dog? And when the guidance counselor asks, I will say you were superlative."

"Big word," I mumble. This guy did not do well on his entry exams, but he says things like *superlative*? What's with that?

He glares at me; I sigh.

"You know, it wouldn't kill you to drop the tough-guy act for two days. You'll be rid of me soon."

I turn to leave but Diego grabs my arm gently. My breath catches.

"It's not an act," he says, jaw hard.

I wave him away nonchalantly, like his touch didn't just do all kinds of crazy things to my body—things that make me want to forget about the warning blaring in my mind.

I need to stay away from him.

I need to forget him.

Will you touch me again please?

I walk away. He watches me go.

"By the way," I say as I flick a look over my shoulder at his hardened face, "I see right through you."

Don't miss the next novel in Amber Hart's Before and After series.
Maybe Me will be available this fall!

1
Maria

Night wraps around my body, sticky and hot, though it's nearly midnight.

"Maria!" my brother Javier yells to me, catching me on my way down the driveway. "Where you goin'?"

Spanish music thumps, bass shaking my veins, coming from inside our house.

"Fresh air," I lie.

What I'm actually doing is leaving. Thought I could handle it, Javier visiting from college to celebrate getting his Associate's degree, bringing his girlfriend who isn't Latina. Breaking all our rules of tradition.

"You promised," my brother says, eyes narrow.

I did. I promised to try. I made a deal that I wouldn't ruin the party—which is also for my older brothers Eduardo and Pedro, who recently graduated college. I promised to give Javier's girlfriend a shot. They've been together for years, it's about time I accept her, he says. It's not that she's horrible, it's just that she's not Latina. And in our family, that's a serious crime.

"Do you still have a problem with Melissa?" he asks.

Yes. "No." It's easier to lie.

Javier's lips press into a frown. "You sure?"

"Yes." I smile, but it's fake.

"Then why does it seem like you're avoidin' her all night?"

"I'm not. Just . . . *dame un minuto por favor*," I say in Spanish.

One minute, that's all I need, is what I say. *I can't stand another second of this*, is what I think.

Javier relents. Kisses me on the top of my head.

"*Cuidado*, okay," he warns, eyes taking in our surroundings.

He's been jumpy ever since he arrived yesterday, watching his back. I wonder what his deal is. I glance at the neighborhood. Nothing out of the ordinary. Just a jumble of small houses. Gray mist drifts, tangling around tree branches that are still ripe with leaves even though it's autumn. The Florida night is calm, heat lightning in the distance. Patches ignite the sky like a fireworks show. The concrete is littered: cigarette butts, an empty beer bottle, graffiti art. It's nice, especially compared to what we came from.

"Keep your eyes open," my brother says.

"Okay," I reply, though I don't see any danger. I'm only standing in the driveway, after all.

Living with overprotective brothers has taught me to put on a pretty smile and promise to be good. Not that I'm lying or anything. I do want to be good. Don't want to repeat their past mistakes of getting in with the wrong crowds, gangs, cartels, weapons, violence.

"Just a minute, then come back in," Javier says.

"Of course," I say. My voice is laced with sincerity.

If I admit that I want to leave, Javier will have an excuse

to make me stay. So I've done what I always do. Taken the safe route. Agreed to join him in a minute.

Javier walks inside. I count to twenty before taking off. No one's there to stop me.

Because I'm always good.

Because no one expects me to break the rules.

My heels click on the concrete sidewalk. *Clock, clock, clock.* Loudly penetrating the silence of the night. A puncture hole large enough to announce my presence if anyone was around to hear. They're not. The streets are empty.

My long, wavy hair sticks to my skin, wet and slightly curling. I pull it off my back. Moonlight drips over my shoulders, highlighting beads of sweat. I walk quickly.

A few moments alone, away from a house full of family, that's what I need. A short walk. Then I'll go back.

It doesn't take long for me to realize that I've walked farther than I intended. I stare at my surroundings. The block is mostly tiny apartments and condos. Some small houses squeeze between. I marvel at the difference a few blocks can make. Our tiny piece of Orlando has so many faces. Down by the water, it's huge mansion styled houses. A little closer inland, there's the middle class. Next comes lower class, where we live. Poor, but making it. Much better than the life we knew in Cuba. And then there's this neighborhood, the one I'm walking through, so run down that I wonder how people live here at all. It's made up of crumbling buildings. Concrete instead of lawns. I stop to stare at a dog chained up outside, linked to a fence, barking furiously at me.

I decide to turn back. I don't know this neighborhood, and I've gone far enough. Maybe by the time I get home, I can think up a reason to lock myself in my room and forget that tradition is falling through our fingers.

But I don't make it home.

The dog stops barking. Three guys step out of the shadows, quiet as the night. My heart lurches and slams into my throat. It's their look that worries me. They say nothing, creeping closer.

I glance down at my outfit. Realize how I must look to them. A yellow dress, skintight. Black heels. Makeup.

Think fast.

I try to see a way out of what's happening. Three guys closing in on me. I should have listened to Javier. Or maybe I should have listened to my gut and never agreed to the party in the first place.

Should haves broken by a sliver of a second, a mistake now made.

I try to run. It's the only way. And maybe I would actually stand a chance of getting away if it weren't for the heels I'm wearing. I try to ditch them. Too late.

My back slams into a wall, shoved by one of the guys chasing me. My head cracks against brick, aching immediately.

"In such a hurry," the guy says, and laughs darkly.

The smell of alcohol radiates from him. The other two catch up. All tattooed. One is small—maybe I could overpower him—but with the other two, I don't stand a chance.

"I like the chase, *mamacita*," one slurs.

I whimper.

What have I done?

I push against the guy holding me to the wall but it's no use. He's too strong. I think of Javier's warning. He would kill these guys if he were here. I look around for help. Flickering lamp posts and empty streets are all that look back.

"*Dejame ir*," I say, shoving the one holding me again.

But somehow I know he's not going to let go willingly. I bring a heel down on his foot. His hand slips a little. Enough for me to push past.

Rip. He catches my dress. Tears it at the shoulder, revealing a glimpse of my yellow lace bra.

Run faster, I tell myself.

But the smaller guy catches up. Snatches me by the arm and doesn't let go.

Of all the things to happen to me.

I scream as loud as I can. A large hand covers my mouth and part of my nose, making it hard to breathe.

And then, suddenly, his hand is gone and I'm screaming again. Someone throws my attacker to the ground. Punches him once in the face. Twice. Three times. He hits the second guy, then the third. I catch a glimpse of the guy saving me, hoping it's my brother or someone I know.

It's not.

What I see is an unfamiliar boy. Eyes an ashy gray like smoke. Hair as black as the sky.

"Back off," he says, eyes hard.

But he's not talking to me.

"You don't tell us what to do, *puto*," one of the other guys spits.

"Back off," he repeats, revealing a switchblade tucked in his palm.

He stands between me and my attackers. I let my scream die away. Hope builds. While they're distracted, I make a run for it.

"Damn it," I hear my protector curse.

He runs after me. And I wonder if maybe I was wrong. Maybe he's after me too. Maybe he's just as bad as they are.

I take a turn down a dark street. Another turn after that. I'm getting lost now, but I don't care as long as I get away.

Someone catches me. Shoves me into an alley. Up a few stairs into a front entrance alcove.

"Quiet," my protector warns.

Then I spot them, the guys who attacked me, running by. Not seeing us in the darkness that disguises our hiding spot.

He waits a moment. Makes sure the coast is clear.

"You need to come with me," he whispers. "Don't run again."

"I'm not going anywhere with you," I fire back. Not a chance.

He pockets the knife. Captures my stare.

"Those guys you ran into? They belong to a bigger gang. There are more out here. And they'll definitely be looking for you." Pause. "And me."

I notice the way he stays close, but leans away. As if to tell me he means me no harm.

"You're welcome to take your chances," he says. "I won't force you to come with me."

I bite my lip. Consider it. "Where do you think we should go?"

He catches his breath. Runs a hand roughly through his hair.

"I know a safe place, just down the way. You need to get off these streets." His stare slips down my body. "Especially in that."

I'm reminded that my bra is showing, that my dress is ripped.

"Okay," I agree, seeing no other option. "But give me your knife."

"What?" He talks quietly, careful to not give away our spot, voice low and deep. "I'm not giving you my knife."

"Yes, you are," I say. No backing down.

And then he does the strangest thing. He smiles, displaying a row of white teeth that overlap just the slightest bit. Dimples poke through both cheeks.

"Fine," he says, withdrawing the knife from his pocket.

He hands it to me. It's warm from his touch.

"Let's go," are his last words as we take off to maybe, possibly, save my life.

READER QUESTIONS

1. From the beginning, we learn that Melissa and Javier have complicated lives. Melissa's pain stems from childhood abandonment, from her scars, and from missing her best friend. Javier's comes from memories of his homeland, and from losing members of his family. What do you think about their decision to hold the pain inside?

2. Javier is obsessed with justice. Do you agree with his decision to take matters into his own hands, outside of the law? Is retribution ever the answer? Have you had to make decisions outside of what you were told was the "right way"?

3. Melissa is harboring the truth about what caused her scars, though she doesn't want to tell Javier at first. Have you ever loved someone who is sick? Do you think Melissa handled it well, knowing that her life could be cut short?

4. With her mom always working, sisters away at college, and her best friend living in another country, Melissa *feels* alone a lot. Is there a difference between feeling alone and actually being alone? Can you be alone but feel content? What about being around a lot of people but feeling alone? Has either of these situations happened to you?

5. Javier's home, Cuba, is a violent, desolate place that reminds him of his demons, of why he had to learn

how to fight. What do you think of Javier's tendency toward violence with the ones who harmed his cousin? Does a person's upbringing determine his or her behavior, or is it something ingrained from birth? What traits are valuable to you?

6. Javier's mom does not want him dating outside of his culture. What do you think about interracial, mixed culture relationships? What does diversity mean to you?

7. Both Melissa and Javier have strong family bonds, despite the differences in where they come from. How important is family? What's your definition of family? Can family be linked by more than blood?

8. Even when Melissa learns of Javier's involvement with the gang, she still loves him. Do you think love is a choice? Should love be unconditional, or should it have boundaries?

9. In the end, Melissa helps Javier believe in himself and in a brighter future, one where he can go to college and make his own choices freely. Likewise, Javier helps Melissa learn how to let go of fear by telling her that her scars are beautiful, and by loving her no matter what. What is your greatest fear? What, exactly, does freedom mean to you? And perhaps even more importantly, what is hope?

PLAYLIST

"Corazón Sin Cara" by Prince Royce
Reminds me of Javier, of how I hope he sees me.

"Blown Away" by Carrie Underwood
Why did Dad have to create these storms?

"Still into You" by Paramore
I can't erase the memory of Javier's lips.

"Swing Life Away" by Rise Against
Your scars for mine.

"I Want Crazy" by Hunter Hayes
Who knows how much time I have left? I want this feeling, this kind of love.

"22" by Taylor Swift
We end up dreaming instead of sleeping.

♥~ Melissa